TOLEMAC

A NOVEL

H.J. CRUZ

PublishAmerica
Baltimore

This is a work of fiction. Names, characters, corporations, institutions, organizations, events or locales in this novel are either the product of the author's imagination or, if real, used fictitiously. Any resemblance to actual persons (living or dead) is entirely coincidental.

First printing

At the specific preference of the author, PublishAmerica allowed this work to remain exactly as the author intended, verbatim, without editorial input.

ISBN: 1-4241-4281-4
PUBLISHED BY PUBLISHAMERICA, LLLP
www.publishamerica.com
Baltimore

Printed in the United States of America

TOLEMAC

A NOVEL

H.J. CRUZ

Introduction

Is the future of humanity woven like a patchwork quilt by past and present deeds, thoughts and beliefs, or is it liquid like a river etching its way through creation before returning to the sea from which it was born?

Tolemac (Camelot spelled backwards) is an inspirational writing that first came to me in 1996 in a crude and latent form but got shelved for many years before the urge rekindled. It is an unusual book in the sense that it's a love story without romance; its protagonist would be humanity itself while the antagonist mother nature.

An epic adventure about mans survival on a fed up and hostile planet combined with a story of the spiritual transcendence of human consciousness. We all can hypothesize about the future and we can all be reasonably certain that an escalating population can only aggravate things and that we currently are taking a heavy ecological toll on all our natural resources, yet business as usual continues for the most part with only a token effort made to minimize the hazards we create. I don't know if we are spiritually ready for a place like Tolemac due to the overwhelming amount of fear and control in our society but I know there are many who will love the idea of it yet still remain fence sitters awaiting a stiff wind. I understand that material madness is an obsessive compulsive disorder on a colossal, cultural scale and that Tolemac could be considered Utopian at this stage of the game. However the demographics of our planet are not the only things changing these days, we are clearly inching our way to higher consciousness and I'm not just talking about the explosion of psychics, there's the quickened pace of intellectual pursuits in all sciences, the rewriting of history through more and more recent discoveries and mans newfound ability to think outside the box. It's true that these don't necessarily represent spiritual progress but spirit and consciousness are inextricably linked when one expands it eventually overlaps into another discipline as well as the universality of consciousness itself. The paradox being that even the most ardent scientist, physicist, mathematician, geometer, astronomer, musician, philosopher, biologist, farmer etc. will inevitably be led back to God within their individual pursuits where they will have a so called religious experience when the perfection within the chaos is discovered.

I can say first hand that writing Tolemac has changed me but I can't be certain if it will change you, we all taste gruel differently. I often wonder if it was written by me or in spite of me. Perhaps that's just the artist finding God, yet I still feel as if it were the other way around.

1
THE RETURN

I could now see a small and frail Earth in the window of the shuttle as we approached. A tiny blue ball in a sea of blackness; a precious gem suspended in animation. My pulse sped up as adrenalin shot through my veins without provocation. Was it apprehension driven by fear of the unknown, or just pent up anxiety from being cooped up in a shuttle for six long years.

As the planet grew bigger so did the questions—would there be human life? Was this the earth of the past or future? Was it even earth? No one really knew with certainty where we would end up after passing through a wormhole. It was all hypothesized, nothing more than an educated guess. A scientist once told me, "It's like trying to figure out where an object might land after it is sucked up into a category five tornado, you can narrow it down mathematically to a general area of about a square mile but since natures reality and theory don't always collaborate the object could be found twenty miles away, or possibly never found."

I kept checking the instrument panel over and over as we neared the outer atmosphere. I could now see the outline of continents and something seemed out of place. Landmasses seemed greener and larger; perhaps I wasn't seeing clearly, the window had fogged up as the dense atmosphere rapidly approached and began smashing into the

---

hull of the ship causing the temperature to soar and the inner hull to vibrate uncontrollably. The heat of re-entry penetrated the hull causing moisture to pool on the once cool instrument panel; sparks flew causing the autopilot to malfunction.

My sweaty hands grappled with the manual controls as I fought to regain control of the tumbling shuttle. My training in the simulator never prepared me for this. The spin of the ship had me in a panic, my hands frozen with fear as I fought the shuttering controls. *If I could just get the nose up and add thrust I might regain her*, I thought. The controls wouldn't budge as I struggled against enormous pressure to free them as the altimeter raced backward and warning lights flashed. I reached for the thrust lever; my arm straining against the weight of the freefall now seemed to be in slow motion as every muscle began to burn with resistance. The lever was now firmly in my hand as I pulled it to full throttle—I felt nothing.

"My God was this how it was all to end after all those years in space, was this some sort of cruel joke," I thought as my heart sank. Then I felt the ships engine fire and the speed increase as the spin slowed enough for the controls to function. I turned hard left out of the dive. *"My God she leveled out."* I cut back the thrust and threw the lever for the landing gear to slow her down further; there was no response just a flashing light to tell me what I already knew.

I saw what appeared to be a shoreline and parallel her as I descended rapidly upon the ever changing landscape. I tried hard to ensure that I would clear the forested terrain; to land in the shallow water. Now within a mile of impact I slowly brought the nose up and soon began to feel the hard shutter of the waves as they sliced into the tail section forcing the nose back down. I hit the reverse thrusters and the emergency chutes simultaneously just as the nose slammed into the wake with a jolt that slammed me forward, then back again as she now planed out and skidded through the surf at two hundred plus miles an hour. There was a blur of water, then sand, then water again, suddenly darkness approached as we hurled into a forest. There was a deafening roar of underbrush being crushed by the ship as the fire extinguishers filled the air. The ship snared with a tremendous impact, squeezing the air from my lungs as the cabin filled with debris thrust forward from the rear of the ship. I was now facing the ground as the tail still in flight recoiled around the buried nose before crashing back down with a large wallop, followed by a loud groaning coming from the metal hull as it released its tensile stresses. An erie silence prevailed, but was soon overcome by the sound of pressure releasing. I ripped off my helmet and grasped for air, only to be overcome by darkness.

2
A REFUGE FOR REFUGEES

I stared into the fire, a pastime that I had come to prefer over any other; here I could lose myself in a meditative state for hours, void of all desire, all passion and all memories. It took what seemed to be an eternity to get to this mental paradise, for I was deeply wrought with emotion. I knew that if I was to be any aid at all to my young and eager associates I would have to rid myself of this cloak of calluses.

It had been over two years since we crash landed on this Earth clone. It was nothing short of a miracle that we survived the landing—if we were a meteor, we would have been reduced to fragments and dust. It cannot be logically explained but then again nothing had seemed logical since we left the Earth we called home as it was being reduced to smoke, ash and rubble.

We had a great ship, a ship that was recycled from a previous crash landing and retrofitted for the new mission. The shuttle's hull was designed well and suffered minor damage externally, however the internal damage was severe. The autonomous onboard computer was completely dead, no energy and no memory. The fuel cell that generated the hydrogen propulsion was mangled beyond repair. Re-entry ruptured the skin causing a major melt down to several internal components.

The speed and angle of entry were all wrong. If not for the ingeniously constructed hull, we would have been incinerated, and landing in a peat filled swamp undoubtedly helped. My calculations, from the last log entry backed by the size of the children told me it had been approximately eight years since we left Tolemac—Eight long years. The first three spent traveling through interplanetary space to the edge of the wormhole and three to return. The last two were spent trying to establish ourselves in our new home.

My beard was now long and gray and the hair on most of the children was down to their waist. Luckily, they recuperated rather quickly from the long period in the isolation chambers. Learning to walk and to speak seemed to be their biggest challenges, but you wouldn't know it now for they are just as healthy, sharp, and normal as any children aged eight to ten. We were very lucky to have lost so few passengers; poor little things, they never knew what hit them. The casualties were the result of gasket failures within their individual compression chambers, leaking the precious gases that preserved their tiny bodies. They were the ones near the fuel cell when the intense heat caused the rich nitrogen, oxygen and helium to somehow ignite charring them beyond recognition.

We're probably somewhere near the equator since we have yet to see a cold winter, but as far as when; God only knows. Calendars have yet to be introduced here, or perhaps I should say reintroduced. We are without want of food, as the forest and sea are ever abundant with a wide variety. There are large beasts; however we have yet to see signs of aggression. Although the sun, moon and evening stars have no apparent differences, something tells me that this seemingly innocent planet contains a natural order that is too precise to be mere coincidence.

I have yet to hold a conversation with the locals, they seem despondent, whenever I come too close they turn and run. I believe it to be my eyes. They probably have never seen so bright a color. Then there's the ship that they constantly visit, brooding about like apes, touching the hull then jerking there hand back and looking at it inquisitively; I guess they never experienced static electricity before. They are no doubt primitive but seem harmless enough.

We have remained upon the seashore since the crash landing in several small huts we built from reeds and thatch, furnished with straw mats. Now that the oldest children have reached the age of ten, they hold me to my promise and will not budge until I tell the story, "the whole story," of their home—Tolemac. I have delayed the tale for as long as possible. I could no more talk about it than I could think about it, for when I did at any length I became somber and withdrawn. Then there were the technical aspects of the story which young children may fail to grasp, but I was sure this would not be the last time their ears would be bent with such a tale. I would no doubt have to repeat it like some annual holiday event until every word was etched in their hearts and minds.

So now without further delay the children gather before me in the shade of a giant eucalyptus tree as I compose myself upon the remaining seat from the shuttle and dig my feet into the cool sand reflecting on the once great past civilization known as Tolemac and how I had came to be the one they called the Messenger. I pause to look over the eager shining faces, so innocent and full of promise. All eyes gleaming in anticipation. Aries sits in the front row, with disheveled hair, his bright eyes a mirrors reflection of my own, his grandmother's signature dimple and trademark chin tug gently on my overplayed heart strings.

The first few attempts to speak are stifled with emotion, but after several minutes I managed to speak the first words through trembling lips, despite teary eyes.

3
THE BEGINNING OF THE END

I, Meno Olikai, was born to a small tribe on the seventh hour of the seventh day of the seventh month of the year 2036, on a small island that was part of the Aleutian chain in the time before the great floods. We fled in our vessel during the night for the angered sea had risen up that very night and consumed the land we called home. I was no older than many of you at the time and we were the only known survivors.

My father was a seaman and hunter and knew the waters well. He had stored a small sailing vessel on the ridge with a week's provisions after grandfather prophesized of such an event prior to his death, but during those times modern ways replaced the old ones and no one cared about the ramblings of an old man. Their new sciences had a reason if not a cure for everything including the dead seas; or so they thought.

The evening prior to the disaster father awaited the receding waves to search for stranded fish, clams and mussels and not only had the tide gone out but it had exposed a large portion of the seabed. His attempt to warn other villagers fell on deaf ears.

We quickly prepared the boat—nothing more than a seal-skin skiff with a makeshift sail made from sea lion intestines. The colossal wave caught the entire village asleep. Without a vessel near they quickly drowned in the frigid water.

We were fortunate to have been at sea, but now it was our hearts which were being swept away, we wept uncontrollably for those less fortunate and for all that had been lost. Not just our people but our way of life and all we ever knew.

We were a simple people who had lived as our ancestors had done for hundreds of years. My father was a stubbornly independent man who would rather die living the old ways then become spoiled and soft from the modern lifestyle. He believed in what my Grandfather taught; that all is provided for and we need only to open our eyes to see the bounty in the most desolate and bleak environment. But living the old ways was becoming more and more difficult. The seas were dying, slowly forcing us to find other means of survival. Mother had insisted that I be schooled in Unalaska, the main island where Father went to trade. They sent me there to be with my cousins, returning each summer to help Mother and Father with daily chores.

It was in Unalaska that I learned to speak English and to use letters and numbers. I never cared much for school; the other children always teased me, calling me white eye or dog eye. My grandfather also had been called white eye, a character trait handed down from a time centuries past when Russian fur traders had raided the camps, killing and raping all they saw.

I wanted to hunt whale, sea lion and the white bear as my father had, but my father would always say, "The Great Spirit has other plans for you my son," then smile with a toothless grin as if he was not telling the whole story.

Now what was left of our little family was at the mercy of the great seas. We had sailed with the prevailing winds for days and the food supply dwindled. When we came upon open seas where Unalaska had once been and found only debris floating for miles, among these debris were floating bodies, grotesque, bloated and pale. Mother put her head in my fathers lap and wept as never before knowing that some of these were loved ones. After a few days the wind became still. Only a southeast current propelled the small vessel, but we knew not where. After eight days at sea, Father's fishing yielded nothing. I wondered if the fish too were displaced. The sun was faint through the continually misty skies.

On day ten, my parents forced me to drink the last cup of water. We hadn't eaten in four days since the last of the supplies ran out, the only item left was a small jar of wild-flower honey which they gave to me. By day twelve my mother was delirious and dying from drinking sea water and my father too weak to do anything other than watch in pain as her body convulsed.

The next morning I awoke to my father grunting with a large tuna in his arms. We tore at the fish with our bare hands and teeth until all that remained was the tail and bones. Mother, now almost twenty hours gone, stared skyward void of all expression. Her arms now curled in as she lay motionless on the floor of the boat humbled forevermore yet cheated out of her prime, her tiny hands now curled as if to grip an unknown beckoning compensation. Father and I tossed her over after a brief ceremony, while we still had the strength to do so. It was a difficult but necessary act and a piece of us went to the bottom of the sea that day as well. The next afternoon we spotted a small outcropping of land and made port to search for food and water. After being cramped in the small vessel for so long, every step felt as if my leg muscles were being stabbed with red hot pokers. I quickly sat back down on a boulder and feverishly rubbed them.

We spotted a few albatross flying over some rocks on the other side of a windswept rocky knoll and went to investigate. We found small rock puddles carefully guarded by these birds; they quickly became our staple for the next few days. Father noticed that the water level was continually rising on our small island, so we made plans to disembark. We smoked some albatross and a couple of salmon that were sand-trapped, and with four flasks of boiled water we set out with a early morning breeze filling our sail. We sailed southeast for four days before spotting mountains, we camped near a dry riverbed at the base of a mountain on the shoreline and rested.

Game was plentiful and supplies were exhausted, so the next morning we set out with the only weapons we had: grandfather's bow and quiver which contained twelve whalebone tipped arrows, one old cane fishing pole, and father's skinning knife and harpoon. Father was an old hand with a bow and could drop a caribou at fifty yards, he preferred the bow & arrow to the rifle because he never needed ammunition and it didn't scare away other game. We built a shelter out of saplings, bark and moist earth and began preparing for the coming winter in the case we weren't rescued, for winter came quick in those parts of the Northwest.

My father was not one to waste any part of the animal. Each skin was scraped, treated with moist ashes, and buried then unearthed a few weeks later to be scraped again to remove any unwanted hair. Within a few months time, we had new skin and fur clothing along with backpacks, moccasins, and bedding of fox and rabbit. The winter was long and cold. I stayed huddled around the fire most evenings, sewing skins in the dim firelight. During the day I would collect firewood and carry water or help father clean and cut fresh kills. We anxiously awaited spring and the journey inland over the mountains. At times my father was gone for two or three days before dragging back a litter of fresh quarry already cleaned, beheaded, and field sewn.

When the weather was mild, my father taught me how to use the bow and spear and how to cut, clean, and prepare the skins and meats to last. When the weather was foul I heard all the great legends handed down from our ancestors just as he had decade's prior, tales of giant whales that refused to die and bears that stood ten feet tall and took ten men to bring down. I became a great help to my to my father as time went by and with each new kill I realized my wish of becoming a great hunter like my father was becoming a reality after all.

The spring came early that year and we prepared to travel southeast upon seeing the opening of the first tree buds. I helped my father bring the boat to higher ground because of the continually rising water level. We tore down the shelter and used it to camouflage the boat, packed our bedding and tools and headed toward a road we had seen during a hunt.

We were hopefull of finding other people and possibly a market to buy things. The mountainous terrain made for difficult travel; we scarcely covered twenty miles the first day, always being mindful of game and edible herbs and berries to restore our vitality after the long winter. Smaller game was preferred, because it could be dressed and cooked quickly over an open flame limiting time and energy after a full day of travel.

After three days of travel we came across a town void of people or any signs of life. Many doors lay open on businesses and homes alike, but nothing stirred not even a crow. The old market's shelves were bare. A small post office was also vacant, bins still over-flowed with mail. While my father rummaged through the packages for anything useful I practiced reading English on the notices in the front lobby; I learned that the town was called Plain, in the state of Washington, elevation 6018, the population read zero after someone had purposely crossed out the actual numbers and wrote in the pun underneath.

A small map showed that the road we were on continued south to a larger town called Leavenworth, in the Cascade Mountains. I began reading a large warning about the disease that was sweeping across the entire state, something about tainted water causing cattle to become too toxic for consumption. Before I finished Father yelled for me.

I hurried to the musty, dimly lit backroom. He was holding up a bag of hard candy in one hand and a bottle of pills in the other. I rushed for the lemon drop candy which soon overwhelmed my glands with more sweet and sour than I had for as long as I could remember. Father tried to read the label on the bottle of pills then shook his head and handed them to me. I could only make out a few words, something about disease and one tablet every other hour for twenty-four hours. I thought that would be nearly impossible.

I began to throw the bottle out, but my father grabbed my arm, saying, "Save them for now. They might be useful." I shoved them, the candy, some matches, and an old canvas tarp that my father took from a closet into my pack and we headed out again. Judging by the map, the town Leavenworth was within a couple days walk, so we started in its direction. We made it to an old campsite where there was a pump well and a fire pit. I gathered wood in the dying light while father fished in a small lake. I came across some berries, still not ripe, and picked a hatful in hopes that they would ripen more once off the bush. Once again we feasted on seasoned trout as we gazed upon the brightly lit canopy of stars. That night, the woods were filled with animal noises; we heard coyotes and screech owls along with the sound of cracking twigs in the dense forest to remind us that we were not alone.

In Leavenworth, again we found everything ominously still, stores were empty; a large motel at the edge of town was also abandoned, its vacancy sign swung by one corner while the small pool in the courtyard lay choked with algae. Father entered the front office littered with papers and checked the register; it had received its last entry over eighteen months ago. We nosed around, looking for clues. He then tried to open a door marked "Private," but something was blocking it. We both put our backs into it and shoved it open. A heavily decomposed corpse lay face down on the floor. The smell was so foul I almost vomited as we both ran for the door.

A small ranch house in the distance seemed like a safe haven, but a rancid, maggot infested dog carcass, with all four legs sticking straight up, greeted us. The smell once again began to make me gag. The front door of the cabin was torn completely off its hinges and lie on the floor in pieces as if a wrecking ball had smashed it. The kitchen cabinets were a mass of splintered wood and canned provisions lie strewn about the floor mingled with flour and pasta. Father started handing me cans of fruit, beans, and soups that were still sealed, I packed them away until he stopped suddenly and arose with his knife in hand. I followed his eyes to a very large bear footprint imprinted in the flour. Father slowly put the knife back and said, "Ahh—It's at least a month old, don't worry about it."

I moved to the bedrooms while Father searched the rest of the property, upon entering the first room and let out a scream which sent my father running back with knife in hand to be greeted by the most hideous corpse yet; she was sitting up in her bed, two deep wells where her eyes had once been with a silent scream of horror through her open jaw. The long silver hair covered the shoulders of her pink night gown. He grabbed me by the shirt and once again we ran, this time until our heels could no longer carry us. We skipped dinner and camped in the open that night, neither of us eager to sleep or eat the food we had. My father's face was contorted as he slowly scrapped the surface of a large rock with an old hand ax he had found in the shed of the ranch.

He said nothing all night but finally stopped dragging the ax over that stone after hours. I wondered if he was more worried about the dead bodies than the large bear. I wondered what those people had died from and did it have anything to do with the warning bulletin back in Plain? If not what—And where were all the people that once had lived here?

More days and more small towns revealed little more than the last, one difference being the number of graves bearing the same year of death. We found some old bicycles in a machine shed and headed for the large town called Monitor. The road was mostly down hill so we coasted effortlessly. Upon entering the town we were greeted by a pack of wild dogs that began to chase us, barking and curling their lips as we passed. There were at least five, all of whom looked rabid; their ribs were hard pressed against their mangy coats. They snapped at our feet as we peddled by, causing us to flee in a panic.

A large dog was trying to grab hold of my ankle as it spun like a top. Father kept yelling, "Pedal faster! Pedal faster!" I never knew a bike could go so fast! We did not stop until the town was far distant. We collapsed on the side of the road in the tall grass until we could once again speak. Then Father pointed at me and started laughing. I joined in, not knowing why.

"Meno, you passed me on that bike like a scared rabbit with that skinny old dog nipping at your heels."

I forgot how good it felt to laugh so hard my sides began to ache; it was liberating. We started out again to put more miles between us and that dog infested town before sundown and pedaled until the road ended into a large reservoir with no bridge in sight.

The thought that we would have to pedal uphill through the town of bloodthirsty dogs was more than I could take and I began to sob and within moments my entire body was limp and quivering. The hard week of travel finally caught up with me and seemed more than I could bear. My father put his arm on my shoulder.

"I know it's hard, son. We will camp here tonight."

That night he told me that he too was saddened by all that he had seen, but that he still had plenty of hope. There were still many mountains to travel through, with many towns which should eventually show signs of life.

We warmed cans of beans over a small fire and discussed our options. Father wanted to head back north to find a way around the lake, but I told him there were more towns on the map if we continued south. My father knew the Rocky Mountain chain could be eventually found to the northeast but was not sure of a southern route so we headed north the next day.

After three days of traveling north we found a trail along the crest of the mountains. There were plenty of large horned rams, but their meat was tough and foul. Occasionally we encountered geese near small lakes and ponds. These were much tastier but not so easy to sneak up on in the open. With the rock and sling, I was able to surprise one bird at close range and stuffed it in my pack. Father was proud of me but still wouldn't take a chance on me losing any more arrows, so only he hunted with the bow.

We slowly descended to lower areas with more trees and lakes, and stopped by a scenic mountain lake and refilled our bladder lined skins and checked the trout supply. Father grabbed the cane pole and told me to search for berries and herbs and a suitable campsite. I went into a grove of scrub oak in search of anything I could find. As I came around a large boulder, I startled a bear foraging there—I froze in shock. The bear stood up on its hind legs and let out a large moan, then the enormous animal came crashing down into a run towards me. My feet finally unstuck themselves and I ran toward my father yelling his name, my pack slowed me down and I was no match for the swift bear. He swiped at my legs causing me to dive face first into a large bush. I tried to crawl through the bush, but he clawed at the side of my leg, tearing into my calf. I screamed in pain while kicking wildly at the bear with my other leg. As soon as my leg was released, I rolled through the bush only to hear him coming around the side before I could get up to run. I crawled out from the underbrush to find the animal standing over me on his hind legs growling and preparing to pounce.

Just as I was sure I had no chance an arrow struck him in the center of his chest. He let out an awful groan and I took advantage of the moment to roll off to the side. My father came yelling, "Meno!" out of the bushes with knife in hand. He slammed into the bear with such force that the beast lost its balance and fell backward with father on top. Father jammed the long knife into the snarling predator's heart. The bear let out a loud yell and swiped my father's head with a hard blow that sent him flying.

I got to my feet and limped to my father's side. He lay motionless next to the large bear. The bears claws had torn into the side of his face and neck and blood now flowed heavily soaking his clothes. I put my hand tightly against his neck to slow the blood and called to him several times. My only response was the bear's final sigh when all the air had been stolen from its large lungs. I jumped back and tried to drag my father away from it with little success.

I grabbed the water bottle and shook it over his face for a response. Father turned his head involuntarily and began swatting at me. I grabbed his hands and yelled his name until he calmed down enough for me to apply pressure to his neck wound. Slowly he came to. He explored the wounds with his hand and then told me their was nothing I could do that he had little time. Fear and pain welled up within me as I trembled and cried uncontrollably. Father grabbed my arm and tried to speak my name as loud as he could but it came out like a whine from his swollen throat. He called my name again and looked into my eyes.

"Meno, listen close my son; you have made me a proud father but now I see you as a man—a man who can and will survive! You are here for a very important reason; you must carry a very important message to the children of tomorrow to insure there will be a tomorrow." He lay back gasping for air as blood filled his throat and caused him to cough.

"Your grandfather gave me a message for you; you must find the jewel of the rainbow. Be strong, my son for your journey will be long and hard."

He put his hand to his neck and fell back to silently await the final moment. I felt his grip slowly ease from my hand and his head rolled to the side.

"FATHER!"

4
TESHA

That night I built a fire, cauterized my wound with a hot knife and then dug my father's grave with that same knife. I had just begun to dig when I heard them—my father had warned me that they were present from the increasing presence of tracks. They must have been downwind, now attracted to the campsite by the smell of blood. Still, the growling took me by surprise. I whirled around to see four of them surrounding my father's body. Three of the wolves began to tear at my father, and my yelling did not seem to faze them. The fourth one stood by and curled his upper lip. He slowly came towards me, growling and barking as if to warn me away. I could see that this one was not all wolf but of mixed blood, for he was shorter with the ears of a hound. I grabbed my pack and grandfather's bow and quiver, knowing that I stood no chance in fighting them, I rushed off exhausted and bitter.

I don't remember how far I limped. The sound of the wolves tearing into my father pushed me as fast as I could go until I dropped. The next morning, I awoke shivering and wincing in pain. I was in a meadow of gold grass that towered over me and swayed to a gentle breeze. I sat up for a better look, "Ahyeee!" The pain caused me to grab my leg. The wound was much worse this morning than it was the night before; it throbbed and burned. I grabbed the last can of fruit and thrust the knife into the top and bent it open just enough to slide a peach half into my hand. I placed the cool fruit upon my leg for a few moments of comfort before devouring it.

I realized that my survival for the first time was left in my own hands. No longer could I depend upon father's skill as a hunter. My heart sank. I was no hunter. I tossed the empty can and wept. When my sobs subsided I began to hear Father's words in my head: "*You must now become the man… You must survive to become a messenger to the children of tomorrow and find the jewel of the rainbow.*" I was not sure what all this meant, but it gave me the strength to stand up. Yet the thought of never seeing my parents again brought trembling hands and tears to my eyes once again. A sobering thought; those wolves may have finished their meal and would be in search of their next one soon. I grabbed my pack and set off, hoping to keep a distance between the pack and myself.

I traveled east for a few days, with the aid of a stick I had fashioned into a crutch and without any trouble from wild animals. I was heading into the morning sun which streamed over the mountain ridges. I was weak from lack of food and needed fresh water to refill my skins. The last of the canned food was now long gone and I lost a precious arrow when I missed a shot at a deer which bolted as I struggled with the bow. It wasn't until I spotted some prairie dogs that hope returned. I grabbed for my sling and crept up slowly on my belly from the lower terrain and surprised one, knocking it cold with one shot to the head. It rolled from its mound lifeless and still. As I stared at the innocent face I felt strange; I had never killed such a cute little animal before and remorse began to creep in but was subdued quickly by pangs of hunger.

I headed downhill looking for a suitable place to make camp and saw a small lake in the distance. At the lake's edge, I cleaned the animal, being mindful to wash the blood into the lake and avoid unwanted predators. Although I was starving I began to wretch after a few bites of the raw meat as if my stomach was sealed shut. I chewed the raw flesh until I was once again able to swallow just enough to give me the energy to build a fire. I dozed off for several hours by the fire, then awoke in the dark after hearing a strange noise coming from the other side of the lake, a terrible hacking sound. It sounded more like a cough of a person rather than that of an animal. I grabbed my bow and quiver and cautiously approached to investigate.

Slowly I drew closer. I could see my fire now reflecting off the lake in the distance. Perhaps the noise was a person calling to me upon seeing the fire. I called out hello in English a couple times, but all remained silent. I edged cautiously forward and saw the silhouette of a body face down at the water's edge. I ran forward and turned the body over—a young woman barely conscious with white foam around her mouth. I shook her and said, "Hello! Hello!"

Her eyes opened a crack and for a moment I thought she would speak, but no words emerged from her, not even a sound. I dragged her over to my camp by her arms and tried to get her to drink, but she coughed it all up. I was not sure what to do with her but I didn't want her to die, I didn't think I could handle another death even if it was with a total stranger. Then I remembered the pills we had found. I was not sure if they would work but figured she had nothing to lose. I ground one up with two rocks and mixed it with a little water to make a paste and dabbed it on her tongue. I repeated this every other hour through the night. I splashed myself with cold water to avoid falling asleep more than once as the night wore on.

She was still unconscious at dawn, but she was alive and not coughing. Her forehead was flushed and sweating so I soaked my chamois and wiped her face with cold water. She began talking a strange language. All I could guess from her coloring was that she was a native-American. She was beautiful—more so than anyone I had ever known. I wondered how much older she was; at least ten years I thought.

I fished near her and kept an eye on her. I couldn't help but stare at her. She looked so peaceful, with her long black hair and a dress made from tanned deerskin with colorful beads along the fringe, pieces of antler and abalone adorned the breastwork. It was as if she had walked right out of one of my history books from Unalaska. Even her tall-laced moccasins were hand-made and decorated with beadwork. Her high cheekbones and well-sculpted nose gave her a magnificence that her soft slender lips tried to steal away but she was thin—much too thin. A tug on my pole brought me crashing back to the task at hand—it was a good, hard bite and I almost fell in as it caused me to lose my balance. I reeled in the biggest brown trout I'd ever seen. Once cleaned and put on the fire it slowly it browned over the hot coals filling the air with a familiar aroma that made me think of home.

In my flash of success I'd lost track of time. Had it been two hours? Just in case I prepared another pill. As I put some more paste on the strange woman's tongue, she opened her eyes and shouted; "wah-nee-chee!" I jumped back in shock. She spit the paste out and again shouted, "wah-nee-chee!"

"My God, she's alive!" was all I could think.

She tried to sit up but collapsed. Slowly she reached over and grabbed the bottle of pills. After staring at the label, she shook one pill out. With it grasped firmly in her hand, she crawled to the water's edge, swallowed it, then cupped handful after handful of water from the lake to her mouth. She crawled back to the fire and turned to me. She said something I didn't understand, then, "Thank you."

"You're wa-wa-welcome," I replied with a bit of hesitation. Hearing my own voice felt a bit uncomfortable.

She lay back down with a wisp of a smile across her lips and nodded off. I walked tall that morning, not only did I save a woman's life but I also caught a great fish and made my first friend. Perhaps there were many more as well, I no longer felt so alone and helpless.

The small lake lay in a secluded valley with aspen covered hills on each side. I listened carefully but heard no threatening sounds and the cover gave me a sense of protection. I knew I had to stay off my leg for a while anyway, even though the pain had begun to subside, and I was sure that the young woman would need someone to watch out for her while she recovered. It was time to make camp.

I made a temporary shelter out of saplings and bark to keep the sun and rain off of us while my new friend recuperated. It wasn't until the next day that she was able to speak. She told me her name was Tesha Tooniqua and that she had been poisoned from bad meat her grandfather had gotten from butchering a stray cow. Her grandfather had died two nights before and like him she was awaiting the same fate when she saw my fire in the distance and crawled in its direction.

She told me how she and her grandfather had been traveling by canoe for weeks after the people of her town had all died out or left for greener pastures. She said, "Grandfather knew that the cow may have been infected but we were so hungry. Grandfather was not much of a hunter. He had been a skilled carpenter in his early days before the revolution, but that was almost thirty years ago. We were surviving on anything that swam, flew, or crawled, hunger had become a way of life for us since my father died five years ago. When we saw the cow it showed no signs of illness. We were too hungry to let it go; what a costly mistake."

"I'm Nez Perce, or what's left of my people. After the revolution ten years ago, what was left of our people came back to this area to try to live the old ways and start new lives and families. Life was a constant struggle. For many the old ways were forgotten and getting supplies with little or no money or with bartering when trade goods were available was not enough. Hunting and farming worked for some, but many died over the first few winters from the flu and malnutrition. There was no medicine available for most of us. Small bands of well armed post revolutionaries would take whatever they wanted without asking, so sticking together in large groups was more of a necessity than an option."

"Our family chose isolation far out of the reach of travelers after my mother was killed by robbers for the bread she was baking. We had a small ranch with chickens, goats, and rabbits, and we grew plenty of root vegetables. Father usually found at least one Deer or Elk each month, while grandfather fished the mountain lakes. That which we could not raise we traded for like corn, wheat, and honey. We did pretty good before father's death. That was the beginning of the end. Many people died similar deaths, or just left in hopes of finding something more. I watched close friends die off from strange sicknesses and we had nothing other than wild herbs to try to fight them. Some claimed the disease was bacterial, others said it was viral, but we knew that a great deal of it came from contaminated meats and waters."

I asked her how the water and meat got poisoned, but Tesha was too tired to continue. Tomorrow she would tell me more. We ate some smoked trout before she fell silent and closed her eyes. I thought about all Tesha had said as I stared into the fire. She had been through far worse than I and I now understood why those towns were deserted. It had come down to survival of the fittest, and even the fittest were dead or dying.

The next morning I went hunting for small game. I managed to wound a wild turkey with an arrow and then finish it off with a rock. I also came across some large though tart berries. When I got back to camp, Tesha was standing with the aid of my stick, slowly walking around with a slight wobble. She smiled at me and said something in her native tongue that I did not understand but took for hello.

She saw the turkey and smiled. But more remarkable was that she came over to me, hugged me and thanked me for saving her life. I silently went by the lake to pluck feathers hoping she wouldn't notice my shade of red, leaving the berries by the fire.

"These are wild plums!" she exclaimed, grabbing them and washing them in the water. Before I finished plucking, Tesha had eaten almost all the wild plums. She smiled all the while like a child lost in a game, unmindful about her surroundings.

When I finished cleaning the bird I sat in the lean-to with Tesha and tried a plum. After one taste my mouth puckered up so bad I could not bear another.

Tesha smiled; "when I was a little girl my mother would pick these plums and use them for baking and making jam. I would always sneak a few to suck on. I like the way they overwhelm my senses." She paused and looked at me intently. "Who are you? Where did you come from? And where did you get those wild eyes?"

I told her my own story of my small village being inundated by high tides, sailing across miles of seas and losing my parents. I grew quite fond of Tesha and trusted her like a family member. I couldn't help blurting out that I had no clue about where I was going.

Tesha stared at me for what seemed like an eternity before finally saying, "I know where you're going."

"Where?" I replied.

"With me to Tolemac."

"Tolemac? What's a Tolemac?"

"It's where my grandfather was taking me. I've never been there but Grandfather said he'd been there when he was a young man and that there would be people left there that cared. Grandfather lived there before the revolution. He said they'd built public works projects for natural energy and agriculture like none ever seen before."

"My grandfather knew that if there was still civilization anywhere Tolemac would be the place to start. The people there all seemed to have high ideals and caring natures. He said that no matter how big a mistake he made he could do no wrong. It was almost spooky the way they controlled their emotions, at least to Grandfather."

"He said he left because he was tired of being cooped up and well behaved, but would always find himself falling back on Tolemac's teachings and how blessed he was to have worked there."

I could see that Tesha now had her head in her lap, silently weeping. I got up and walked over by the edge of the water feeling a bit uncomfortable.

"Oh my god, his body is still by the side of the road. I cannot leave him that way. Will you help me?"

"I think so, as long as we can get there before the wolves do! Are you strong enough to show me where he is?"

"I'll have to be" she said and got up quickly only to fall backwards. I helped her up and told her to put her arm over my shoulder. Together we walked off to find her grandfather.

It took over an hour to find the body and over another hour to dig in the rocky ground with my knife and her bare hands. The grave was shallow but there were plenty of rocks to deter the predators. After we dragged the body into the ditch I saw something around his neck and removed it to give to Tesha before covering him up. It was a small medallion, very worn but solid gold with the letters T and F. I handed it to Tesha and told her I was sure that he would want her to keep this.

She grabbed it and held it to her chest savoring it. We headed back to camp trying to beat the setting sun. Tesha spoke few words all evening. The shock of seeing her grandfather's lifeless body somehow changed her. I felt helpless not knowing what to say or do. I no longer felt the sorrow of my own losses. I just wanted to somehow ease her pain. I sat close to her and put my arm around her. She cried and said, "Oh, Meno, what's happening to our world?"

We held onto each other and gazed into the fire for answers; but none came.

5
THE QUEST FOR TOLEMAC

The river was flowing swiftly and when we disembarked I lost my balance and was flung to the rear of the canoe and nearly into the cold current. I quickly grabbed the paddle and started in to disguise my embarrassment but Tesha yelled;

"Just help me steer and let the current do the work.!"

The swollen river was full of boulders and log jambs that could flip a canoe on contact, our utmost attention was required and Tesha could navigate well, barking out an occasional order for a turn or hazard ahead. We had spent two days resting and preparing for the trip and were now heading south down the Snake River, just as Tesha and her grandfather had started a month ago. Tesha knew that the journey would be rough without her grandfather, who knew the river well as a young man. He had been a skilled kayaker who favored the Snake over all the other rivers and knew every boulder, turn, and rapid. The fiberglass canoe would be light enough to carry if rough spots and rapids were encountered—that is if we identified them before it was too late!

I liked being in a boat again it made me feel safe—out of reach of predators. The river had created a sanctuary by artistically carving its way around huge boulders and rocky cliffs, through golden meadows and fertile forests; I was overwhelmed. We silently let the river work its magical therapy on us.

I asked Tesha to tell me more about Tolemac. She said she didn't know all that much, but would tell me what she could.

"Tolemac is located in the high country of Colorado in a large valley east of the Sawatch mountain range and on the East of the divide watershed. The valley is a very fertile area because the South Platte River winds its way through it. The mountain and plains native peoples in the old days made it a winter refuge because of the plentiful game there long before the Spaniards and white miners came.

"Construction on Tolemac began there at the beginning of the century after a visionary by the name of John Olandis inherited twenty thousand acres from a wealthy cattle rancher. The rancher had fallen in love with John's idea of the ultimate Utopian civilization and bequeathed all his land to him in his will. It started out small, just a few like-minded families looking for a new way of life, a way of life that they could develop with their own hands unencumbered by the present cultural ideologies and infrastructures.

"The village was to be totally self sufficient, no waste going out and no outside energy coming in. As time went by, Tolemac grew in population, and more revolutionary structures were built. Grandfather said that there was even a huge pyramid of glass, similar to the one in Las Vegas; they called it the center."

"The center of what?" I asked.

Tesha just shrugged her shoulders. "Eventually they required very little outside resources including food which they grew a great deal of. Tolemac even had its own schools and places to work. Tolemac had become a large independent civilization with its own rules, laws, and beliefs, including its own teaching systems and culture. A culture that was revolutionary or a cultural revolution whichever you prefer."

I was not sure what all this meant, but I could listen to her talk all day. We stopped for a late breakfast and ate the last of the turkey with some wild onions Tesha spotted on the riverbank. While she napped under a pine tree I went scouting downriver. I walked for a short while until I heard the roar of a waterfall. I followed the sound to an area where the river narrowed and made a sharp turn before thundering through a tight rocky ravine. There's no way the canoe would make it without crashing into the boulders along the bottom. A chill ran up the back of my spine at the thought of our narrow escape. I scouted a path around it and headed back. Tesha's need for a break was well timed!

When Tesha awoke, we dragged the canoe along the rocky edge of the river to the path I scouted earlier and unloaded its contents to make it easier to carry. Soon we were once again floating down the river.

"Meno I think you just saved our butts." Tesha said as she hunkered down in the front of the canoe grabbing her paddle. I was quick to remind her that it was she who needed a rest, which caused us both to laugh.

She stopped and turned towards me with a grin on her face. "Just who the heck is this guy anyway?"

"Meno Olikai," I said with my chest thrust out. "Great Tlingit hunter."

She again burst out laughing, but I grimaced, failing to find humor in my words.

Tesha said, "You are adorable! I have been blessed by the Great Spirit to make your acquaintance Mr. Olikai!"

Now it was my turn to laugh.

We settled that evening in a small clearing by the river. We had no food, just the campfire to keep us company; I tried to catch some fish while Tesha gathered wood but had no luck. The current was too swift in this area, and the bait kept washing ashore. Tesha boiled water for tea with an herb called chamomile. She said she always picked and dried this little flower to rinse her hair with.

I thought it tasted pretty good for hair tonic and said so.

She told me, "Grandmother was a healer and knew many things about the earth's plants and about its people as well. She would listen to a person's symptom and wait until she got a message from the Great Spirit before searching for the cure. Sometimes it came in a dream and other times the plants would somehow let her know. Her success rate was probably as good as any trained physician, as far as I could tell. She would always say that we caused our own problems directly or indirectly and that she was just adding a little T.L.C."

That night it got very cold. I awoke to find Tesha snuggled against me for warmth, at first it felt comforting but I soon found it awkward. I quickly rekindled the fire while shivering in the morning frost. I grabbed my bow and sling and crept away for a morning hunt. I figured with the frost, minimal wind, and the dawn light, I might have the edge we needed to catch any wandering game with my last three arrows. I climbed a gently sloping hill with an arrow half-cocked, waiting for the slightest movement or tracks in the frosty tundra. The hill was big and steeper than it looked and after several minutes of uphill walking I was huffing and puffing and a bit humbled. The sun would soon rise over the frosty hill and lessen my chances for game.

As I put my head in my hands, I heard something stir behind me. I grabbed my bow and turned. I saw nothing as I crept over to where the sound came from. Again I heard it—a faint scratching and grunting noise. I jumped over a small hedge to get a better look and surprised a small black and white animal. I raised the arrow for the shot and was suddenly overcome by a noxious gas that gagged me and brought tears to my eyes.

With my vision blurred I ran for the river in a panic, gasping for air, tripping and rolling several times before reaching the river's edge. I plunged my head in the ice-cold water to stop the fire that seemed to be raging on my face and burning my eyes. The cold water caused my head to turn painfully numb but at least the fire subsided in my eyes. I lay there in the mud for several minutes, applying water to my face until I could open my eyes without tears. I got up slowly and stumbled back toward camp.

I wasn't even fifteen yards from camp when Tesha jumped up, looked around quickly and yelled at me; "Stop right there you stinking Skunk! What in the world have you been hunting?"

"I tried to get a small black animal, but it got me before I got him."

"You actually tried to hunt Skunk? You stinking fool!"

"What is Skunk?"

She began to laugh but stopped abruptly when I took a few steps closer. "Do *not* come any closer to the camp. Do you have any other clothes?"

"Yes there's one more pair of skins in my bag."

"Good. Go in the water, take all your clothes off and let the river take them. And don't come out until I tell you to!"

When I told her these were the only shoes I had, she just said, "Not anymore."

Reluctantly, I undressed and crouched in the freezing water. Tesha made a slurry of mud on the bank, going on and on in her native tongue. She told me to get into the mud and bathe in it, getting it all over my body and then working it into my hair. I was cold and embarrassed and could not stand to be in that cold water another minute so I ran into the mud. I covered every inch of my body, hoping to get warmer. Tesha stood over by the warm fire with my clothes in hand yelling for me to rub it in better, over and over; "More mud, more rub!"

I shivered in the mud and waited for further instructions. The sun finally began to crest and shine upon me. I absorbed it like a sponge. When I was finally warm, Tesha was already yelling at me again to get back into the cold river to rinse off.

I trudged in again, looking forward to sitting by the fire after I was clean. When I came back out and Tesha came a little closer—but only to tell me to get back in the mud and take another bath. This time as I sat with cold mud drying in the sun, she brought me a hot cup of tea and put my clothes on a nearby rock. I was numb from the cold and the hunger, but the humiliation seemed to me far worse. After just a minute, it seemed, Tesha yelled for me to get cleaned up and dressed before I turned blue. I warmed myself by the fire while she loaded the canoe. When we took off, she told me to stay in the furthest back point of the canoe for the rest of the day. I staggered into the rear and covered myself with my fur bedding.

Tesha went herb hunting after several hours on the river while I started a fire and cut up the trout we caught that afternoon. The sun's heat was intense. I took refuge in the shade of a large pine tree in the thick soft carpet of pine needles while the fire burned down some coals. My head soon felt as heavy as a river boulder that my neck could no longer support. I slowly drifted off, falling into a deep sleep. I soon began to hear the distant voice of my father calling my name over and over as if I were lost. I called back but he couldn't hear me. I was surrounded by a dense fog and ran towards my father's voice but my feet felt as if they were shrouded in lead. Suddenly the fog began to clear and I could see him in the distance and as I ran to him with a heart full of joy he changed into the killer bear, I began to scream as the bear pounced over me and commenced to finish what it started.

I awoke to Tesha yelling my name and blocking my onslaught of frantic swipes as she lay over me trying to subdue my hysteria.

"It's O.K., it's O.K.; you're just having a bad dream." She said as she held my now sobbing face to her chest with words of reassurance.

She did not probe the tender wounds, only asking if I was hungry when she felt the trembling slowly subside. I did not answer but stayed a moment longer in her embrace. Her aroma was awash in tanned deerskin bathed in her bodily oil with remnants of various wild herbs, which soon gave way to the wonderful smell of trout cooking—along with a spicy aroma that I was unfamiliar with. Tesha had added something she called wild basil. She had also found some wild mint for tea. The smell of the trout was making my mouth water. We could no longer wait and began to pick the cooked parts off the fish as the rest browned. Within minutes there were only bones in the pan.

"That was probably the best tasting trout I ever had. Good job, Meno! Even though you are still a bit stinky, you're much easier to tolerate on a full stomach."

I felt a bit confused and sniffed at my skins.

"Now grab your bow and follow me. I want to investigate a cabin I saw over the hill. If it's abandoned there may be supplies we can use."

"What cabin, where?" I said as I made my way toward the canoe to grab the bow, Tesha just pointed and started off in that direction. We approached the cabin from the rear. Nothing was moving. There was an old hand-pump well, so we helped ourselves to a drink and looked for containers to fill with water. An old shed out back that looked as though a stiff wind would blow it down had some auto parts and antifreeze containers, which we rinsed out and filled to bring back to the canoe.

The weathered log cabin looked like it had been built before the birth of lumber mills; half the shingles were blown off the roof exposing the old roofing and planking. There were no other structures for as far as the eye could see, just rolling hills with the occasional clump of trees. The door on the back of the house would not open, so we went around to the front. Tesha let out a scream which made me jump and awoke a skinny old man sitting in a rocking chair on the front porch.

The old man opened his eyes and shouted, "Whose thay'a?"

His eyes were frightful, set back in there dark sockets, one stared upward and was mostly covered while the other was barely visible under a milky film with a nervous twitch.

. "Whose thay'a?"

Tesha answered, "Were sorry to disturb you, sir. Please forgive us we will be on our way!"

"Wait—pla'ease wait! Who are ya, and whay'a did ya come from?"

"I'M Tesha and this is Meno we come from up north and are just traveling through on the river."

The old man said, "Meno...Meno...who...how old is Meno?"

"I am nine years old," I said.

"Are ye from Alaska boy?"

"I'm from Aleutia."

"Of course Aleutia. Where the water rose up up in the night."

"Yes, but how did you know?" I said surprised.

"I've been a waitin on ya, Mr. Olikai. I have a messige fer the messenger."

Tesha and I looked at each other with blank stares and eyes bulging. The old man invited us in. We hesitated for a moment before entering the small cabin. We sat down at his small table while he grabbed some cups and a jug of water and put them on the cluttered table saying,

"Pla-ease help yur'self to a drink."

The old man sat down with us and said his name was Harold Wiggan and that he had been living there alone for over six months waiting for us. He had outlived his sister who had taken care of him all his life.

"Sis passed on, and I buried her out back, next to her old yeller dog that she loved more than life itself. She stockpiled a couple of ye'as rations during the plague that swept cross the country a couple ye'as back. We were the only ones left in the whole damn county, all the others havin died or run off. Pardon me while I open dis winder. The smell of skunk is a bit po-tent in he'ya.

Tesha momentarily looked over at me and winked as if to ease my pain. "I am glad you's came when ya did. I have only enough ratshuns fer another month er so. Now gettin back to the subject at haynd. I'm a bit more sens'tive dan most folk. Maybe cuz I'z born widout good eyeballs, maybe not. I'm bout eighty five year ol, and all through my life thar's been accasions wheya I know's somthin bad was a'gonna happen, use'ly by feelin bad or depressed for no cleya reasin. Sometimes I jus get a terrible feelin right in the solar plexiz, as if somethin was suckin out my enagy. Otha times it would be a depresshun that put me in teyas fer owuz. The strenth of the bad feelins use'ly coincided with the size of the event. I have also been warned in dreams of catastrophe or a comin deyath."

"There's been times when those neya me have caught me havin talks wit invisible folks, leavin us both equally surprised. Please unerstan that I'm not tryin to scare ya wit all this. It's just a way of preparin ya fer what I'm bout to tell ya. Ya see, I have a unique abil'ty to act as an instrument of communication, sort of like a tel'phone—that is, with me actin the part of the racee'va, ya see. Now I don know how or why that is, or how it works; it juz been known to turn is'self on at will while I nod off, not rememberin much bout the convasayshun."

"Some calls me a speaka of sorts, others a channa but I'm not the fir's one to posses such abil'ties nor will I be the las. The Bible is full of such folk as I. They'a called profits, but everone of em is as unique as his words and it's been done dis way fer a long, long time. Now bout nine mun'ts ago I wuz in a reyal bad way, suff'rin from many of the syn'toms most of the plague victims had. My sister did ever'thin she could to keep me as comf'table as possible knowin my fate was neya."

"I was dehydrated and had a bad feva that made stayin awake fer more than a few minutes at a time diff'cult and very uncomf'table. I passed way that night and left this old body with its visu'l lim-tations behind. All my pain was gone and I was overcome by white light. Smiling figures from the past made theya way towa'ds me. I rec'nized em all instantly—all that is cept one. He just stood there smilin at me, an old native man with glowin eye's in a sealskin robe holdin some sort of carved staff and weayin a large bear tooth necklace with a small wood carving of a bear on it."

I shouted out, "Grandfather!"

The old blind man looked my way and said, "Yes, your granfather, Keno Olikai. He introduced hisself and asked me if I would do him a gran fayva."

"Now when Keno spoke I sum how knew tha meanin of them words but God nows how. He spoke of the comin of nature's wrath upon the Earth, leavin human'ty in a bad, bad way—so bad that if his message didn't get through to his granson, Meno, civ'lizashun as we nowz it might cease to exist fer a millyin or mowa ye'uz, draggin our race back ta'da primor'jal soup!"

"The thought of goin back to my ailin body after all I had seen saddened me greatly. It was as if Keno read my mind. He said, 'Y'ur body has no more ailments, but the eyesight is un-restorable. The return stay will be but of the lifespan of one hummin bee. Everathin ya see heya will be waitin fer ya and much, much mowa. I also promise that the moment ya have fafilled y'ur obligashun, ya will be back heya immejitly, with no sufferin in the transishun whatsoeva.'

"So as ya both kin see, I sac'ficed myse'f to be heya with ya now and afta I prepaya ya both a nice meyal of rice and beans, we will discuss dis messige."

Tesha and I did, not say a word for several minutes. *Me a messenger? I'm just a kid*, I thought. *What sort of message could I hope to carry?*

Harold asked if we would stay the night, and we agreed, although we had to get some things from the canoe. On the way there, Tesha said, "I knew there was something special about you Meno; I can't wait to here what the old man has to tell us."

"Me too!" I replied. But in a way I felt a large burden bearing down upon me. All I could think was, *God, why me?*

6
HELL'S CANYON

Harold was a pretty good cook for a blind man. After dinner I gathered some wood and made a fire in the small woodburning stove to take the evening chill—and the skunk smell—out of the air.

The house reminded me of a museum; everything in the rooms was from the mid twentieth century, including the old maroon couch which absorbed one until you were peering over your knees. There was an old painting on the wall of a man clad in a brass buttoned uniform with a sword on his side and a hat that looked like something George Washington might wear. The face on the portrait was hard to make out beyond the cracked paint but the bushy eyebrows and angular forehead did bare a slight resemblance to old Harold. Harold sat down in his rocker and said, "Let's get dis done fer times a waistin. Please come e'r, for my voice don't carry far no mowa."

In the setting sun his face seemed skeleton-like with its deep-set eye sockets, hollowed jaws and bald head.

"Now, Meno ya may be wonderin bout why all this fuss is over little ol you. Let me tell ya, you're special for many reasins, an one is cuz ya'ar still a youngin and will outlive most others. The other reasins is cuz ya'ar the las of a now extinct tribe of hunters who kept ther skills of sarviva long afta all otha's wuz mod'nized and ya also have talent for rememberin small details no matt'a how trivial they appe'ya at furst and there is something mowa but they be keep'n it secret fer some reasin."

"Keno knows all bout ya, and he is very proud of ye, an alldow it wuz he who give me dis message the message itself didn't riginate wit him, he wuz simply a messenj'a just as I myself have become. They knew you'd trust the words of yer granddaddy fore anyone else and this is why they enlisted his support."

I looked at Tesha and could see that she too was just as confused by this statement. I asked; "They who?"

But the old man raised his hand and said, "I'z jus gettin to that. Please be patient my boy. All will be revealed in due time!"

"Now dis may sound a bit odd, but neverda'less it's all true. The message was sent from someone on Earth from a place called Tol'mac, from a group of people called the star del'gation by way of yer granddaddy, or ratha the spirit of yo' granddaddy. This body of people called the star del'gation is in charge of the welfaya of dis great city. They aid in the establishen of the rules fer just livin an truth teachin. The del'gation is made up of five peoples that all have unique qual'ties. They are what's called transitionals—people's who's very avolved spirit'aly while residin in a phys'cal body. They call them transitionals cuz they are believed to be the first folk's of the future of human'ty, or the future brain chillin of human'ty, an cuz they is heya for the great transishun. Ther not bound by ego, self-expressin or motional traumas. They have no need for educatin, religion, or careeyas. They reqwar min'mal sustenance fer sarviva and spen most of ther lives in a semi-conscious state. They know thin's on the horiz'n that we could nev'a dream fer they trava astrally throughout the heavens while their body remain he'ya."

"Now I know much of this may be a bit hod fer ya to digest at this point but ya will come to find out all bout these thin's in due time. Now the main thin for ya to know is that the del'gation wants ya to come to Tol'mac more than ya could possibly know and are very concerned for you're welfaya, they believe you're some sorta angelic messinj'a. You must una'stan that there are dark forces at work presently that would like to see ya fail just as well and they will come in all kinda forms, like human or animal or nature's wrath an won't stop ya unner'stan boy neva! But we a step ahead of e'm…use'ly—hopefully. So wit dis in mine I'll now give ya specific instrucshuns ta folla, so ye don't fall prey to the beasts who manip'late time an space."

Harold sat back and took a few deep breaths. I wasn't sure but It looked like his face became distorted somehow, or maybe it was the dim light playing with my eyes. Harold began to speak, but it was not his voice. It was the voice of Grandfather using our native tongue:

"Meno. It is I Keno I am sorry I cannot be there with you. I can only send you my words and my love. Your mother and father are doing fine in their new home and also send you their love. Listen closely Meno your life will depend on it!"

"The first thing is that you must not make human contact. This is absolutely the most important rule your adversaries will use every trick possible to trap you or harm you. You must also stay clear of main roads they are full of ambushers eagerly awaiting anyone that comes their way. Towns, cities, and homes must be avoided as well. I know this sounds dreadful, but if you follow these simple instructions you will be just fine."

"Stay your course down river for two days and avoid the rapids at the end of the first day, port where the river narrows. On the second day travel as far as the canyon entrance, but do not proceed through the canyon of the devil. The evening of the second day cook meat as long as it's not beef and await a new transport. The third day will be needed for recuperation and provision stocking. On day four follow along the river, this same night you must watch for the comet just after dusk. On the fifth day proceed in the direction of the comet. On day six, head south keeping the morning sun on your left. Day seven, head east into the morning sun. The eighth day you must climb the nearest mountain and camp at the summit. Look for a large lake and travel to it on the ninth day. On day ten, find the old ranger station at the lake of the Bear, make camp and wait there for however long it takes for your escort to arrive. Unkar will be your escort, he is of Mongolian descent and rides a large black charger with a red saddle and silver trimmings. He is to protect you and the woman from harm for she now plays an important role in all of this as well. I will be waiting for you when your work here is done. The Great Spirit is watching over you my grandson. Be brave and strong we are all counting on you so make us proud and when your job is done at Tolemac the jewel of the rainbow will be yours for eternity."

Harold reverted to his usual raspy voice and asked, "Any q'estuns, boy?"

I was overcome by sadness at the sound of Harold's voice and took a moment to refocus. Then asked if there was anything that I could use to write all this information down on. Tesha went in search of the pencil and paper as well as a candle to light the now pitch-dark house. When she returned I translated the message to her as she wrote. Then I asked him about the new transport. Harold said he was not sure what I would find there but believed the message was vague for good reason; "ta keep em guessin boy."

"I'll leave the res fer ya ta figya out good night and may God go with ye." Harold said as he slowly got up with his head and shoulders being dragged down from an eventful day and he retired to the bedroom while we went over the list carefully. Tesha did not know what to think— strange voices, chasing comets and waiting for Mongol escorts—it all sounded like something out of a science-fiction novel. She said, "I want to believe it, but its all so fantastic. But how else could Harold have known your grandfather and what does he mean about me playing a role in all of this?" "I think it will be very interesting to see if any of these prophecies hold up, besides Tolemac was still the destination regardless of the trail."

The next morning I awoke to Tesha screaming. I ran into the bedroom to find her holding her hand over her mouth. It appeared that the old man had died during the night for rigor mortis had begun contorting his limbs forcing his upper torso to curl off the bed. His mouth was wide open. Only his right index finger looked as if it had any purpose left in it, pointing to the closet door. I walked over and opened it and shoved past all the old shoes and clothes. Something shimmered in the back corner. I pulled hard, fighting the clothes that enshrouded it and came away with a sword in its scabbard. It was beautiful even though the years had taken away the luster of the metal one could still make out the elaborate artwork. When I pulled the blade from the sheath it was still shiny. I lightly touched the blade to see if it was still sharp. "Ouch!" It split my thumb open. I dropped it and ran to the well pump.

Tesha came out to say that Harold deserved a proper burial. She found a bandage for me while I hunted up a shovel then we buried Harold beside his sister and the dog she loved more than life. Before we left we helped ourselves to all the leftover provisions, including one very sharp sword, the instructions for the trip, and a pair of oversized boots. We loaded the canoe and headed down river once again letting nature sooth us with its magic. After about an hour, the river quickened and we worked feverishly to negotiate the turns and boulders. Wherever we were headed we were getting there in a hurry.

That evening we camped on a sandy knoll over looking the river and watched the busy swallows burrowing into the sandy cliffs across the way, tending to their nests. Too tired to hunt for food, we settled on reheated rice and beans. In the campfire light Tesha studied the sword. With its jeweled handle and elaborate scabbard, she said the workmanship was beautiful and thought that it may have been Japanese. She pulled out the blade just enough to see an inscription near the handle; she brought it closer to the flame to read it.

"Look at this. This sword was a gift to one of Harold's ancestors, given to him by a shogun. In 1801. Wow!"

I came over to read the inscription: To Captain Wiggan from your good friend Mysiato, Shogun 1801.

"What's a shogun?"

"They were military leaders and rulers and more often than not, Samurai," Tesha answered.

"What's a Samurai?" I asked, even more confused.

She said, "An ancient Japanese warrior bound by honor and very good with a sword just like this one."

I thought to myself that maybe one day I could learn to use it, with that sharp of a blade I could split bears in half and skin them in one flick of the wrist.

That night as I gazed at the starry heavens, thoughts of Harold's corpse and sword yielding Samurai occupied my mind. I could not sleep. Too many things were going through my head and the coyotes would not let up. I rekindled the fire and watched Tesha sleep, it was one time that I could without her giving me the eye. I was so fortunate to have found her and she was so smart not to mention beautiful. Sometimes she would catch me staring at her and she would give a curt little smirk and nod, sort of a trademark with her. Sometimes I wished I were not so young.

We hit the river hard the next morning until lunchtime. I saw some trapped ponds off the side of the river and with a makeshift spear of my knife and a stick, spear fished two good sized salmon. As they cooked the smell reminded me of my village and home. Salmon was a staple and I could eat it night and day the way my mother made it but when we ate the first fish I was sure that it was the best thing I had ever tasted.

That afternoon the speed of the river picked up as well as the number of turns, rocks and boulders. We smashed the canoe into rocks and took on some water in a few tight spots but we couldn't stop because the water's pace was too swift. Fortunately there was no real damage done. The sun was setting so we began searching for the place to port just before the canyon began.

Tesha started shouting something in her native tongue, which sounded like, "Sal-wah, Sal-wah!"

"What?"

I bit my lip when I heard the thundering water; I quickly understood why they called this place Hell's Canyon, we were headed into the mouth of a raging rapid with no clear way out. Quickly I jumped into the water and was surprised to find it too deep to get a foothold. Tesha too jumped in when she saw it was too deep for me. I grabbed the towline and began swimming to the shore which was nothing more than a heap of large boulders, Tesha was now at the back end of the canoe in a frenzy trying to push us out.

The current now dragging us downstream in a furry seemed to become stronger, I was kicking my feet as hard as I could but moved very little we were now a few feet from the rocky edge. I grabbed hold of a willow branch and to my surprise it held us. I could hear the water crashing down the other side of the rocks and sound made my pulse race. Tesha worked her way around me and was able to scale the rocky terrain. She positioned herself atop a large boulder and stretched down over the edge to grab my hand. The shore was too steep to dock the canoe, so I gave the towline to her and yelled for her to tie it to the base of the willow. I handed her up everything and she piled it onto the boulder.

I began to make my escape with her help when the towline came loose. Tesha clenched my hand as the canoe was swept out from under me and quickly crashed into the rocky ravine. I struggled to get a foothold; I knew she couldn't hold me for long and then heard her scream my name just before I hit the water. I floated to the surface disoriented and swam for the wrong side. The current attacked me and I plunged through a steep and narrow chute and found myself trapped by an eddy on the other side, I couldn't escape the thundering water. I grabbed furiously for anything within my reach as the water washed over me with tremendous force, trapping me at the bottom like a sliver of metal to a large magnet.

I gathered my wits and dove to the bottom to find another way out. Immediately I was sucked downward through a hole in the rocks and quickly shot up to the outside surface with a large gasp. The current still yanked me downstream but I no longer feared death as I had a moment before. I pushed off oncoming boulders with my feet missing one which slammed into my side. After a short while the river's current became weaker and I was able to swim out. I sat for a while rubbing my side and catching my breath as pieces of the canoe drifted by. I looked around, there was nothing but the towering walls of the canyon and it was beginning to get dark.

I began to shiver uncontrollably. I removed my shirt in hopes that my drying skin would add warmth and frantically searched the canyon walls for a way out. Behind a small group of shrubs there lay a separation in the wall just wide enough to walk through.

I walked into the crevice but immediately lost hope, it was a lost cause. The crevice went straight up about fifty feet to the top and it was only a few feet wide. I crouched down and hugged my knees trying to gather warmth while trying to figure out what to do, then I heard Tesha calling my name, I whistled as loud as I could. Within a few minutes I could see her face at the top of the opening but she still couldn't see me so I yelled her name and waved my shirt until she spotted me. After determining that I could still walk and climb she told me to listen carefully and that she was going to teach me how to walk these walls out.

"Put your back against one side and prop the heal of your right foot under your butt, then extend your other leg forward against the opposite wall. Just use your hands at your sides to slide your but up as your forward leg keeps you pinned to the wall you just need to skip it upward and switch feet when it tires."

I placed my bare back against one side of the cold rock with one bare foot forward just as she said. The rock was anything but smooth and began to dig its way into my skin. My side began to ache causing me to wince every time I moved my leg, I slowly worked my body to the top of the crevice with Tesha coaching me the entire way. When I made it to the top, I froze.

"Now spring forward onto the front shelf using the power of your back leg!" She said

I was so weak, cold, and scared that I couldn't do it. She grabbed my hands as she stood over me and said, "Okay then, spring upwards as hard as you can on the count of three. One... two... THREE!"

Up and over I went, falling on top of her. I could now smell the wild sage growing next to me. Tesha rolled me over and said, "Great. Now I'm soaked again too. Let's get back and make a fire to dry these clothes."

The sound of a warm fire in its self brought warmth but after walking a short distance I wasn't sure if I would have enough strength to build it; I felt every tender step. We made a large fire to dry our clothes and warm the salmon. Wrapped in our blankets and eating the wonderful fish, I felt strangely secure after a day of so much uncertainty and bewilderment, just the sight of Tesha wrapped in a blanket with her long black hair draped over the top and struggling to free her arms enough to feed herself gave me comfort.

"When I saw you go under I thought that was the end of you, but then I figured that if any boy your age could make it through that canyon it would be you!" She said as she began to shred the Salmon.

"Thanks for helping me out of the big canyon I was beginning to worry about how I was to get out of there."

"It was the least I could do since I was the one who put you there in the first place." She said before tearing off a large chunk of Salmon and biting into it.

"I thought it was the river that put me down there, Sal-Wah."

She just looked back with a big grin full of fish trying hard to keep from laughing. I lay back against a stump as Tesha got the pot ready to make tea. My hip now thawed by the fire throbbed. Just then we simultaneously turned our heads toward a stirring in the trees behind us. I grabbed my bow, and Tesha grabbed the sword and a stick from the fire. We crept bravely toward the trees to investigate. Perhaps the smell of fish attracted a bear, or even wolves. It was so dark that we couldn't see a thing, but then we heard the crunching of underbrush I knew whatever it was— it was close. A gust of wind blew the flame on the stick out. When our eyes adjusted to the dark, we could see a large ominous figure heading in our direction. We both whirled around and ran back to the safety of the firelight. Back at the fire we stared into the trees waiting to see enough of the foe to defend against. My heart was racing and my mouth became bone dry as I tried to catch my breath and ready my aim. Tesha raised the sword high. Out from the trees ambled a mule with a pack on its back. It honked and raised its ears in approval, as if it too was terrified by the incident. I lowered my bow with a sigh as Tesha began to laugh in relief.

"My god, that homely Donkey had me scared stiff." She said as she dropped her guard.

We composed ourselves and then rummaged through the mule's pack, coughing from the dust that came loose. We poured through the contents and I made a mental inventory of what it contained:

One canteen / Two pair of socks/ One coil of rope/ One pouch full of jerky / One pouch of rock hard biscuits (this we gave to the mule) /

One hammer/ A tin of nails/ One bedroll/ A flint and a striker/ One bottle of wine / One bottle of what smelled like rubbing alcohol/ One deck of cards/ One survival guide / Two metal cups with matching plates, metal forks, knives, and spoons / One pair of overalls / One pot and skillet / One can of some sort of lubricant/ Two towels / Some old papers/ One bar of soap / A compass / And lastly a pouch of coffee.

We unloaded the mule and tied her to a tree. Tesha brought the bundle of papers by the fire while I took a gander at the book. *The Only Survival Guide You'll Ever Need*, by William Bosshart. Inside the cover was the owner's name; Bill Elliot of Kansas City.

She had found a map in the papers along with a supplies list, an address book and a pouch of papers that composed some sort of loose diary.

"Is tonight the night that we were supposed to be getting our new source of transportation?" she asked.

"Yes, that's right." I replied.

"Then this must be it, good o'l fashioned four hoofed transportation!"

She poured herself a cup of wine and went through the diary by firelight, reading to me as she went. The writer was a lonely wanderer, who was good at describing what he witnessed in his travels, including plenty of death. First he talked about the drought that lasted for many years and created food scarcity and water rationing. Then the wild fires that burnt up the prairies and what little forests that were left. He spoke of twisters that were larger and stronger than anything witnessed before that would come in groups of twelve or more wiping out entire cities and towns as if they were programmed for maximum destruction. Then there came a rebellion that put neighbor against neighbor until cities and towns were battlegrounds and eventually wastelands of stinking corpses, rabid dogs and outlaws who raped and pillaged as they went. Much of the diary spoke of the struggles to find food and shelter on a daily basis. Many nights were spent eating dog under bridges in awkward and absolute silence. The wheels of the industrial world were no longer spinning.

His last days were spent as a hunted man after helping a family defend itself against outlaws. We guessed that these outlaws had finally caught up with him. The tale was depressing to say the least. *Is this what our world has come to?* I thought. *It would be better if the tide washed the slate clean if this was all that's left of civilization!*

7

RIDING THE TAIL OF A COMET

We awoke the next morning to the strange sound of the mule honking like a broken tuba. I needed to sleep more but decided to try and find some breakfast instead. Getting up proved to be a painful experience; my left arm would not bend easily due to a swollen elbow and I walked with a marked limp. There would be no hunting today but I could try to catch another salmon, a fish I could eat morning, noon and night. Tesha saw me hobbling toward the clothes and said; "Try fishing off the large rock where you fell in yesterday, maybe it owes us a favor."

The makeshift clothesline of twigs and branches had worked like a charm and I quickly got into my dry skins and headed towards the river with grandfather's old cane pole. I scrounged around in the dirt until I found a big fat worm. I dangled my worm directly in front of a nice sized trout and it wouldn't budge, finally the sun came over the ridge and reflectected on the bait, the fish finely lunged at it. I laughed at the thought that he had been snoozing.

I caught many fish that day while Tesha went on a wild herb safari. That evening she cooked up some trout, simmered in wild onions and mushrooms along with rice and beans; we feasted. After dinner she showed me how to play a card game called Rummy, which she won all the hands.

I finally gave up my losing streak and Tesha read me more of Mr. Elliot's diary while sipping wine with a tin cup. The diary pulled me into the terrible drought that lasted for years, turning farmland across the country into deserts and into the revolution that started during the mid-twenties due to food scarcity and civil unrest. Mr. Elliot wrote about people getting fed up with the government and large corporations because of dwindling aid to the farmers and ranchers and all the environmental damage being caused globally. Many blamed the drought on government supported super corporations called the untouchables due to their deep pockets and it was rumored that congress was becoming more of a corporation itself with the majority of the shares being owned by the super corporations, who often threatened massive layoffs that would cripple an already faltering economy. Mr. Elliot made his views clear: the minimal aid and rationing being provided was just a token handout, the billions of inhabitants of the country was a number that needed to be tamed and the drought was better than any virus that they could have hoped for. The financial aid was the first to go and then health care tanked just as the social security did years earlier.

Millions were forced out of work in the farm belt and millions more had their own county and state level wars over the misuse of the rivers, streams and precious resources. The forests were constantly ablaze, scorching acres from coast to coast. Businesses throughout the heartlands had closed up, towns were dangerous if not deserted, and the lack of local taxes made local government agencies dry up. On top of all this congress had approved the sale of nuclear submarines to a third world country with a history of violent terrorism in hopes of some sort of financial bail out.

This was the straw that broke Uncle Sam's back, already weakened by oversized government and an exploding immigrant population that was fuming over governmental regulations, lack of opportunity and free enterprise.

It all started like any other protest, but this one seemed to gather strength like no other. After years of colossal protests and angry slandering an assembly of local militias executed the destruction of several large energy companies for price gouging, then targeted other environmentally degrading manufacturing companies. They called themselves mockingly; The Green Berets. They were quite willing to die for what they believed was killing their way of life and the planet itself.

A foiled attempt to blow up a large oil refinery led to a bloody gun battle with government agents. Some how a passing school bus got peppered with machine gun fire killing some the children inside. This ignited a full scale riot, fought with weapons of all types, which led to more casualties as well as more anti-government sentiment.

The guard was called in for a crackdown and many cities and towns were put under martial law, but this made matters worse. Snipers started shooting any military personnel as well as any authority figures. Soon police and military ignored orders and left their posts by the thousands to protest the violence against their brethren who were shot down in the streets. The underground movement against the government and big business grew exponentially; it was not a civil war like the one fought between the North and South. This was more like guerilla warfare within the largest of cities and towns.

The revolution lasted for years, crippling the economy, which in turn added to the looting and rioting that was rampant. Many left everything behind to search for a new life, away from large towns and cities. Bill Elliot was one of those refugees. In one of his last writings he wrote, "Our America the beautiful has now become America the dreadful."

The revolution put an end to the slow economic decline and pushed it to the point of no return. The drought raged on, food and grain supplies were depleted in a few short years, imports could not keep up with demand and farms across the country were abandoned. Scrawny pigs, cows and other livestock roamed the countryside in search of food and water. Their rotting corpses contributed to a rash of pestilence—plagues resurfaced, some immune to modern medicines, if one were lucky enough to find any. The country slipped into chaos and confusion. Normal law abiding citizens panicked and murdered their neighbors in cold blood for stored supplies. Merchants were killed for the meager rations on their shelves. The winters killed off the weak since many of the local energy companies had ceased production. Tap water was no longer safe to drink and garbage piled up in the streets.

The same reasons cities and towns were built for now worked against their inhabitants. The streets in all major cities and towns were reduced to war zones, it became a game of survival of the fittest and the old and young became the first victims.

Thunder and wind put an end to Tesha's reading by firelight and soon it began to rain hard. I slept terribly as the dampness crept into my already sore bones. The next morning I awoke to the smell of coffee, a smell that took me back to my home on our small island in Aleutia and to my mother cooking breakfast and calling for me to come eat.

I silently wept knowing I would no longer feel the warmth and comfort of her arms. I was suddenly distracted by a humming sound coming from the riverbank. I sat up to see Tesha bathing at the river's edge with our newfound bar of soap. She was totally nude but did not seem to mind the morning cold, nor the cold river water for that matter. I was transfixed on her, never had I—?

"Meno!" she yelled with a look of contempt.

I quickly turned and covered my head. The smoke from the damp wood began burning my eyes as I tried to get close enough to shake the morning chill. In the pot was a sock full of coffee. I wondered if she had washed it first, but I didn't refuse the hot cup she offered. The coffee tasted like old socks while the tin cup burned my fingers, but I kept it to myself and sipped it becoming transfixed on watching her comb her long black wet hair. She noted my gaze and smirked shaking her head then telling me to roll up the bed rolls.

We loaded up the mule and headed down along the river, riding the rocky ridge until the landscape once again flattened out. The mule was able to carry all our supplies and equipment, which enabled us to travel about thirty miles before making our next camp near what once was an old dam. The dam had collapsed, or had possibly been purposely destroyed sometime ago and the river poured forcefully through the large opening. I figured the edges would be good places to fish but I wanted some real game instead of the same old trout. My throbbing feet told a different story though. The oversized boots that Tesha had tried to shrink by pounding a bunch of nails through the toes and bending them over were very heavy, ill fitting, and uncomfortable and my feet were beginning to burning with blisters.

I decided to sit back against a boulder and overlook the small valley with my bow at the ready while Tesha set up camp. The view was breathtaking, but I was tired and closed my eyes for a moment but soon I was jolted awake by the sounds of crows wailing at the setting sun. I had dozed off longer than I thought. I wondered if these crows had been assuming that I was carrion. I thought I could get close enough for a lucky shot but before I moved a muscle a large crow landed on a scrub oak about ten feet from me. It crowed loudly as if to intimidate me. I slowly pulled back the arrow keeping him in my sight and shot as the startled crow took flight. The arrow struck clear through a wing spread for takeoff. The crow now circled down flapping and squawking and causing quite a ruckus.

I grabbed a stone and threw it but missed. I tried and missed again. I ran after the panicked bird and reached for its tail feathers, the crow was quick and fleeting and out maneuvered me. Frustration turned into anger and I dove on him, grabbing his broken wing. He bit me hard, but I grabbed his head and gave him a quick twist putting an end the battle.

Tesha's face was contorted with concern. "Where have you been for so long?" Her expression quickly changed to a smile at the sight of the big black bird. She grabbed it and said that she would clean it for dinner. That evening we feasted on one mean old crow, and then stargazed waiting for the comet. I was so tired that I could hardly hold my burning eyes open. The night sky was littered with millions of bright stars. We saw a couple of shooting stars but no comet. I could not hold my eyes open a minute longer; I fell fast asleep.

The next morning I was startled awake by the sound of crows once again, greeting the light of day, for a moment I thought that they might have been seeking revenge. My mind flew from them when I realized that I had fallen asleep without seeing the comet. I yelled to Tesha who was still asleep to see if she had seen the comet.

She mumbled, "Yes, but it came very late. I need more sleep."

The next few days and nights we traveled a great distance finally making it to the top of the highest windswept hill late on the eighth day and dry camped there, both too exhausted to cook the prairie dog we caught that day or to even think of making a fire. It was a cold and windy night on that mountain making sleep for more than an hour at a time difficult. The next morning we sighted two large lakes—one north and one south. Tesha chose the southern lake, since this was the closer of the two.

We decided to wait for the prairie dog breakfast until we reached the first river where we could clean it and get fresh water for us and the mule. My feet had become so blistered that I winced with every step. When we got to the river Tesha cleaned the animal quickly and skillfully while I made a fire. After the meat was on the fire, she ripped bark off a tree and cooked it in water for the tannic acid. She stretched out the hide on stakes, scraped it, and then tanned the hide with the acid. Tesha claimed that it would make good foot wear after it dried, so I would be able to continue the long hike. She then picked some weeds called Yarrow and cooked up a paste to dress the blisters on my feet which had began to bleed. "If you wear those boots another day you will be unable to walk for weeks." She said as she dabbed the paste on cooling my burning sores.

"Thank you, they feel much better." I said, propping them up with a bedroll.

The lake looked close, but it was still a long journey. We made its banks as night fell and went directly to sleep out of sheer exhaustion. The next day we hunted for the ranger station, but Tesha believed that we were on the wrong side of the lake. We found footsteps on the shore that did not look very old as well as a well used fire pit——We were not alone.

We circled the majority of the lake keeping our eye's peeled and then made camp when we felt the coast was clear. Tesha said she got an uneasy feeling there, but she wasn't sure if it was the openness of the lake or if someone else was watching us.

We camped back from the shoreline in a pine grove where we would be difficult to spot in the undulating terrain. The ranger station could not be to far off we thought as we made tea and planned our next day's search with the pungent smell of the pine forest lulling us as the setting sun filtered golden rays through the short conifers. Although we wondered that the escort may have already arrived at the rendezvous point, we had to be patient until we could find out the truth. We were both too tired from all the traveling and lack of steady food to be overly concerned. I made plans to rise early to catch some fish while preparing my bed. Traveling another day on a cup of tea was something I would just as soon avoid.

Tesha never complained about being hungry, although I wasn't sure if she thought that it would do no good anyhow or if she was trying to keep the subject in check for my sake. She was a mystery sometimes. She could go for the entire day saying only a few words. I often wondered what she was thinking; her big brown eyes would peer deeply over the landscape with a concerned but confident demeanor. The only times I had ever seen her facial expression change dramatically were when I got skunked and the day she was helpless to save me from the raging river.

I believe that the incident at the river brought us much closer together, although she did not say it; I think she was happy to be with me. There was something about her eyes that night by the fire, perhaps a glimpse of frailty or softness that told me her confidence was beginning to wane. Whatever it was she seemed spooked. Perhaps it was woman's intuition, for I felt nothing but fatigue.

If there had been a better place to be that night, I couldn't imagine it. With all the stars shining through the pines and Tesha curled up in a fur lined robe gazing into the fire as if it held all the answers, I truly felt at home.

The next morning I fished in the calm waters of the lake with the rising sun at my back. Never had I seen so many fish so eager to hook themselves on the line. I had a half-dozen large fish in just as many minutes; what a wonderful lake!

Tesha had also found plenty of edible berries and herbs, not to mention three duck eggs. Our breakfast was fit for kings!

The ranger station could not be far, so we packed in the hot morning sun and set out along the lakeshore in search of it. An hour later the silence was broken by the screaming of a woman and the wailing of a child. Tesha told me to stay with the mule and scrambled off in the direction of the screams. Within moments she came running back.

"Keep quiet," she ordered. "Follow me now!"

"What was it?"

"Not now!" she whispered harshly.

We ran for what seemed to be a mile, finally resting at the mouth of an old trail for a few minutes. My feet were throbbing again but Tesha was anxious to keep moving. We took the trail, but after a few miles it circled back toward the lake. An old service road was off to one side with the roof of a building of some sort just visible above the trees. That seemed better than the other option, so we headed down the service road.

"This is the place!" Tesha said, pointing to an old rusted "Ranger Station" sign partially buried by underbrush. The station wasn't much better—an old log cabin with a large front porch rotting into the ground and covered in brush. It may have overlooked the lake at one time but years of neglect had given the forest free reign. The windows and doors were all boarded up and I could see where squirrels had made a nest in the peak of the roof. I went around back while Tesha tried to get a peek inside though the gaps in the boards.

The back door was well boarded up as well. I looked in the storage shed out back and found plenty of cut firewood, some old fishing tackle, and plenty of odds and ends. When I came back around the front Tesha had the hammer from our packs and was using the claw end to pry off the boards from the front door. Inside there was a thick layer of dust on the table and the floor had so much dirt on it that it was indistinguishable from the ground outside. The musty smell was so strong that it was hard to breathe.

At least the place had some furnishings—an old couch that predated Harold's; an old trunk that was used as a coffee table, some lamps that Tesha said were kerosene and a big wood-burning stove that was for both heating and cooking. Another room revealed a closet that contained a fold-up bed. The wallpaper in the room was peeling exposing cracked dingy plaster walls and the flooring was rutted at the doorways from years of use and groaned when stepped across. The kitchen had a few empty cupboards; whatever was there the mice had carried away years ago.

The old cabin had no indoor plumbing and no electricity, but there was a small hand-pump over the wash basin, which Tesha said probably connected to an old cistern. In the back was a privy that had only half a door and a roof that allowed in plenty of light. Tesha told me to unload the mule while she cleaned the place out. We spent the remainder of the day removing boards from windows and sweeping floors. By nightfall we had our new home in a somewhat hospitable condition, there was even kerosene for the lamps and wood for the fire to cook the remaining fish.

We played cards that evening and joked around like we didn't have a care in the world. It was cozy and quiet and I got the first good night's sleep I had had in a long time.

8

UNKAR THE MONGOL

Eager to fish the lake, I awoke early the next morning anxious to leave the musty old cabin and smell the morning air. After stoking the wood burner, I rummaged through the old fishing gear in the dilapidated woodshed. There were plenty of hooks, fishing line, rubber worms and lures of many shapes and sizes. I beamed with anticipation as I headed to the shore of the large lake.

The mule honked at me as I passed. I glanced at the door making sure the braying hadn't woken Tesha and then hobbled the mule's legs together so she could graze but not go far.

The shoreline was a bit shallow so I went out on a short peninsula. With my back against a large boulder I waited for a nibble. The sun would be up in about an hour to take away the morning chill. It had suddenly occurred to me that Tesha never did tell me what all the commotion was about on the other side of the ridge yesterday, but grave concern was written all over her face. She kept me so busy cleaning that I had forgotten all about the incident. I was sure she planned it that way!

I got my first bite, a small one. I threw it back in hopes that his daddy would be along. Did fish have daddies? They must, I thought. Another bite—and yes, this must have been the daddy. An identical ringer to junior and what a fuss he was making;

I slowly reeled him in when he wasn't tugging so hard, so as not to lose him then swung him over towards me while he squirmed in a frenzy. I stepped on him and made a quick slash up the middle with my knife, which took the fight right out of him. Not bad for a morning's work, more than one meal here.

Something plopped in the water near me. I turned and looked down the shoreline. A small boy was throwing rocks in my direction. I waved to him, motioning for him to come over but he ran away. I figured him to be no more than five and thought it strange to see such a young boy alone so early in the morning.

When I returned to the cabin, Tesha was sipping tea on the old couch.

"What has my great hunter brought for breakfast?" she asked.

"One great fish," I replied, holding up my quarry.

She smiled. "That is one great fish, isn't it?"

As she followed me—and my fish—to the kitchen, I told her that I had a visitor.

"Who?" She said as she whirled toward me with as surprised look.

"A small boy throwing rocks at me before running away."

She looked relieved. This prompted me to ask her about what she had seen over the ridge the day before.

"After breakfast I'll tell you about what I saw if you promise to take a bath in that old steel tub in the shed."

I reluctantly agreed, but only after she promised to warm the water on the stove. She poured some more tea for both of us and said, "I wasn't going to tell you what I saw, for fear that you might be bothered by it, but I think that you're mature enough to handle it. The screaming coming from the woods was a woman being raped by several armed men. Another man was on the ground bleeding and possibly dead and there was a small boy screaming while being held by one of the men, forced to witness his mother's attack." She fell silent, searching my eyes for a response. I wondered if I could have done anything; that poor boy!

"Do you think the boy I saw this morning was the same one?"

"It probably was, he probably managed to run off during the commotion and he may be in some sort of denial or shock."

"Should we go back to see if there were any survivors and search for the boy?" I said.

"It's too soon. Those men could be anywhere!" Tesha's eyes were wide and full of alarm.

"Remember the message your grandfather told you: Steer clear of all and any people!"

I suddenly wished our escort were here. My mouth ran dry and I swallowed hard at the thought of those murdering rapists out there and most of the lakefront was in the open—easy to spot a bird let alone a person!

Tesha must have sensed my discomfort because she quickly stood up and asked, "Meno I need your help getting a door open on an old root cellar I found out back."

I eagerly said, "There's tools in the shed that we may be able to use." Then bolted out the door without another word.

On our way to the root cellar she pointed out a web that was host to a very large and hairy spider and said, "My grandmother used to say that you could forecast weather by the size and pattern of a spider's web. This one says that the next two weeks will be very mild. I still remember her rhyme: don't plan your trip when webs are small and thick."

We both began prying on the padlocked clasp with a long bar that I had found in the shed. The clasp screeched as the rusty nails resisted. Finally, with a loud crack the clasp popped off and the lock fell to the ground with a thud. We opened up the heavy old door and found some rotted steps leading to a ton of spider webs.

"EEWWW!" Tesha cried. "There's no way I am going in there, but I'll get you a lantern."

"Some spider lover you are," I called after her as she ran to the cabin. I got an old broom from the shed to remove the webs. The walls came alive as hordes of spiders scurried away as I snagged the webs with the broom. Must have been their breeding grounds, I thought. Tesha came back with the lantern and I started down the rotten staircase, being careful to miss the rotten centers. The walls were stone and mortar and lined with shelves. A thick layer of dust obscured old jars full of unknown substances. On the bottom shelves there were several crates. I grabbed a crate and handed it up to Tesha as well as a few of the dusty jars. Tesha opened the crate to find it full of cans of beans. She blew the dust off a label on the jar. There was a date, 10/20/99.

"These were saved before the millennium change. Must have been all the frightening predictions of gloom and doom to make them go through all that trouble." She said.

"But I'm sure glad they did!" I answered as my stomach grumbled its agreement.

After washing the jars off, we could see some sort of preserves. Tesha opened one of the jars and it popped—"the sign of a good seal" she said peering into the jar. I could smell the fruit and volunteered to try some, but she wanted to examine it closer to see if there were any signs of spoilage. We emptied the peaches into a kitchen pot. Tesha probed them with a knife and smelled them, tasted them with a small nibble. Her eyes lit up.

"I can't believe that after all the years in storage that they still taste sweet and fresh."

We both dug in. The sweet taste of the fruit made me salivate like a scared snake. We both fell silent as we gorged; brandishing dripping wet chins without the least bit of concern; the taste was utterly fantastic! There were only a few jars out of the bunch that stood the test of time and they were all peaches for some reason. The canned food was all still good as far as we knew. We stocked the empty cupboard with beans, peas and carrots, corn, soup, and the jars of peaches.

That afternoon I decided to see if I could hunt something to go along with the veggies. I grabbed my bow and the last arrow and headed into the dense woods. It was over an hour before I heard the garbled sounds of a turkey, a sound that had me puzzled at first.

I followed the sounds until I spotted the fat, feathered rump in a clearing. I let the arrow fly. For the first time I was confident and precise; the arrow hit dead center, dropping the bird without a sound.

I strode back to the cabin with my trophy; Tesha would be pleased! My reverie was broken by the sound of distant voices.

I froze, then carefully crept closer to the trail. I could see at least four men; one had a long black beard and well-worn cowboy hat and was pointing to something on the ground as the others followed. One of the followers had a long grey beard and a deep scar under one eye and carried a rifle. A short red haired man with a coon skin hat stood a few feet back talking with a skinny black man that looked no older than Tesha and carried a spear of some sort. In the distance was a man who could not be recognized other than by the yellow slicker he wore with the hood up.

I figured that these were the men Tesha had seen over the ridge. They must have seen the hoof prints of the mule and if they find her they'll find Tesha! Avoiding the trail, I ran back as fast as my aching feet would carry me; I had to warn her before it was too late.

Sweating, huffing and puffing I reached the cabin——She was gone! "Great! Just great!" I said to myself. She was probably out herb hunting. "What now?"

After I packed up the mule for a quick getaway, I grabbed a branch and tried to cover her tracks. There were too many, so I concentrated on the ones near the road. I took the mule through the pine forest, far enough away from the cabin that she would be safe while I hunted Tesha. For the next hour I searched everywhere with no sight of her. When a chilling thought crossed my mind, *"what if the bandits have already caught her*; I decided to risk running back to the cabin. Upon my arrival I saw no sign's of danger and quietly crept into the cabin; she popped up from the couch. Startled, I grabbed my chest and let out a silent scream.

"What a great bird," she said, holding the partially plucked turkey by the legs as a heap of feathers fell to the floor. "But where is all our stuff?"

The lack of oxygen from running compiled by the rush of fear laced adrenalin had me gasping for words as I tried to tell her about the men, but she never gave me a second look and bent over to light a fire in the wood-burner. The smoke would be a signal too obvious to hide. I jumped over her to close the flue.

"Meno, what are you doing?" she yelled.

I screamed back finding my stricken voice, "The bad men!"

63

Tesha's eyes got big. "Where's our stuff?"

"I packed the mule and hid her in the woods before coming back for you. I must have forgotten the bird."

"How close are they?"

"I'm not sure, but I think they were tracking the mule."

"Let's go—*now!*" she said, heading for the door.

I grabbed the bird and we ran towards the mule. The sun was hanging low through the trees and would soon be igniting all of creation so we didn't have much time to gain a lead. We headed for the lake since the trail lay in the opposite direction. As we approached the shoreline Tesha told me to stay back while she checked it out. From the cover of the trees I watched her fade into the distance and then I spotted two figures heading right for her on the shoreline. She was facing the other direction, oblivious to their approach. I called to her in a low voice but she was too far to hear me.

I went to grab my bow but realized the last arrow's tip had broken off in the bird. "What good's a bow without arrows," I mumbled. Then I heard her scream "No!" As the two men began running in her direction. Oh no they spotted her! A cold chill ran down my spine; I was temporarily paralyzed by fear. Then as if on impulse, I ripped the pack from the mule. As the pack hit the ground I saw the answer I had been looking for roll to my feet with a thunk. "Harold's old sword!" I pulled it from the scabbard and jumped on the mule's back. With reins in hand, I kicked my heels into her underbelly causing her to honk and jolt forward as we made a mad dash for the shoreline.

The wind whistled in my ears. My face got stung by a low branches and I struggled to stay up as we darted to the beach. Once clear of the trees, I pulled back on the reins and could see the men frantically pursuing Tesha. I raced down the shoreline hoping to surprise them from behind—until I saw more figures emerge in front of them. The rest of the bad men; they must have circled around on the trail.

Tesha ran for the trees but the big one with a long black beard and the cowboy hat tackled her, slamming her hard into the rocky shore. As she screamed, my blood boiled. The skinny black man turned at the sound of the mule's galloping hooves, but he was too late. I was upon him before he could defend himself and slashed him across the middle as his arms rose up in defense. The man's eyes rolled back in his head and his knees buckled as his limp body slammed into the shore face first. I charged the other man but Blackbeard was too swift, he ducked and rolled, grabbing the spear that lay on the ground. I circled and made another charge. I could hear Tesha scream, "Meno—No!" as the black bearded foe heaved the lance toward me striking the mule in the throat. She balked as if she hit a wall catapulting me forward like a rag doll; I slammed hard on my back losing the sword. Disoriented, I struggled to regain my breath and I staggered up. They now surrounded us. Graybeard dragged Tesha by the hair as she screamed in pain. I tried rushing to her aid but the man in the yellow slicker backhanded me so hard I saw stars as I hit the ground.

Lying motionless with my ear pressed to the rocky sand and tasting the warm, salty blood streaming from my nose I began to hear the thunder of many hooves and rolled over to see four horsemen charging up the shoreline in the distance. The front charger was black as coal, and the rider was large, dark, and fierce, wielding a saber and wailing like a madman. Tesha must have seen them because she let out a loud scream for help in their direction. The man holding her slapped her hard and she fell backward.

The men turned toward the charging horses. Graybeard aimed his rifle at the black mount as Blackbeard retrieved his lance from the dead mule as the two others drew swords, showing no sign of fear. The black mount rushed forward as a shot rang out; the rider momentarily winced and jerked his shoulder back, yet onward he came. Graybeard reloaded to fire again. As he took aim I kicked the side of his knee. He struggled to take aim again, but the black charger and its fierce rider raced past striking him with a sword across his chest with such force that graybeard was knocked off his feet.

I saw the red saddle with silver trimmings as our savior rode past. "It's the Mongol!" I yelled.

The second rider caught a lance in the side from the large blackbearded attacker and went down hard. As two more chargers raced in Blackbeard grabbed for the rifle from the dead man's hands.

He stood to take aim but never got the chance. The saber from the third horseman severed his head in one swift blow. His lifeless corpse crumpled next to me showering me with blood. His head landing at the feet of the remaining men was expressing a morbid surprise as the eyelids twitched from nerve impulses now running amok and the mouth chattered in silent horror with out the necessary vocal chords to make sound.

They both turned and fled in terror. The last horsemen thrust his lance with great precision and such force into the back of the red head that the point came out the fleeing man's chest as one last moan escaped his mouth before he slammed face first onto the rocky soil. The Mongol kicked his horse into action and detoured the last man into the lake, where he was surrounded by the three horsemen and hacked down shredding his yellow slicker into crimson swirl before crashing into the lake. The water ran red as the riders dismounted to confirm their dead.

Tesha was already at the side of the badly wounded rider. The man lay upon sand that failed to absorb his precious red fluid. His eyes, void of thought, stared out upon the lake. He was young, not much older than her. The Mongol dismounted to look at the wound.

"I'm so sorry, there is nothing I can do for him the cut is much too deep." Tesha said without looking up.

She glanced up at the Mongol's hulking frame and his bleeding shoulder, then called out.

"Meno go get our supplies!" The Mongol's head jerked up.

"Meno! Meno Olikai?" He said with one eye puckered and the other searching me. His voice was deep and gravelly, with an accent that his good English failed to hide.

"Yes, that's me." I said as I threw my shoulders back.

"I am Unkar of the Tolemac guard, sent here to escort you back with us!"

"Yes I know, thank you." I said not so sure how else to respond and ran toward the bag quickly returning with it.

The Mongol wrinkled his forehead at Tesha asking.

"And who are you?"

"We will talk later. Please remove your shirt so I can look at your wound."

"Are you some sort of medic?" he asked searching her small frame from head to toe with a look of uncertainty.

"I'm as close as you're gonna get today."

The Mongol smiled. "Fair enough," he said, then took off his shirt. His upper torso was littered with scars—a virtual battlefield in its own right. Tesha briefly turned away trying to compose herself.

"It's all right. They don't hurt anymore. Besides they're all for a good cause."

Tesha examined the massive blood soaked shoulder and exclaimed, "The bullet is still lodged in the muscle but not deep enough to have damaged the bone, if you come back to the cabin with me I should be able to remove it."

"And what about our friend there?" he asked, nodding in the direction of the wounded guard.

Tesha looked over at the body. The sun illuminated his pale lifeless face and icy stare. "There's a root storage where we can lay his body for burial," she said as she stooped over the water to rinse her hands.

The Mongol told the other riders, "Load him on his horse and follow the women to the cabin where we'll all stay the night."

I dragged the supplies back from where I had just come, but with no complaints. I was eager to leave this bloody field of death.

I must have been in a state of shock from all that happened because I was feeling an eerie sort of joy about the entire incident. Perhaps it was pride, for I looked death in the eye and stood my ground, yet this was soon replaced with a strange hollow feeling that made me feel numb and a bit guilty, but then the taking of another's life had begun to hit home and no matter how hard I tried to justify it deep down I knew how wrong it was and I now began to feel queasy. But the thought that Tesha was safe now and would never be bothered by those bad men again gave me solace. I suddenly remembered Harold's sword was still in the sand and ran back, grabbed it and wiped the bloody blade on the headless body before returning the sword to its scabbard.

The small cabin was cramped with all five of us and the odor from the men was a bit shocking in such a confined area. I finished plucking the turkey while Tesha operated on Unkar's shoulder. Unkar lay back on the couch with his large frame hanging over the edge and his long wavy black hair draped over the armrest. I never saw a man with such a build before. There was not one spot on his upper torso that didn't ripple with might. One of the guards assisted Tesha while the other built a fire to warm the room and to cook with.

Tesha sharpened a small pocket knife with a stone and heated it over the fire, she told the other men;

"Hold his arm as still as possible or the wound could get worse in a hurry." I was called over and held the lantern over the wound while she cut the bullet out. The Mongol yelled in agony as the knife made contact. Tesha pried his skin back with the knife while searching with her finger for the right hold. Smiling like a rookie surgeon, she slowly removed her fingers and the knife with the bloody fragment in her hand. She told me to get her bag of herbs and the remaining wine from the pack as she reheated the knife.

As I came back into the room with her bag and the bottle she was probing the red hot knife into Unkar's bloody shoulder to cauterize the wound, he jerked back as the men tried to restrain him. I covered my ears as he let out a wail causing the room to vibrate. She grabbed the wine and ordered, "Drink!"

Tesha made a poultice with her herbs and applied the pasty substance to the wound before wrapping it with a torn cloth. She made a sling and told the Mongol not to use the arm for a few days. I now had the turkey cleaned and ready to cook, but no pot was big enough. Tesha told me to cut it all into parts and pieces. She would cook it in the skillet, while I cooked beans in the small pot. We were all pretty tired from the eventful day and Unkar and his aides were asleep before Tesha and I had finished cutting the turkey. I ended up falling asleep as well. Tesha finished cooking all the food and stored it for the morning.

The next morning I woke up to the sounds of the guard through the crack where the old bedroom door wouldn't close. Tesha was sleeping on the old rollaway mattress with me, wrapped up in her fur-lined skin. I t was a comforting feeling when she snuggled up close to me.

Someone began stoking the fire and setting pots on the stove. I heard Unkar's low, deep growl, mentioning something about being sore and staying another day. One of the other men noted how good Tesha's wound dressing was and how it was a damn shame she couldn't come back with us." Another agreed. I thought for a moment about what I had just overheard. That and the smell of the warming beans brought me to my feet. Barefoot, I crept into the next room.

A floorboard squeaked and the guard called Troy spun around. After his initial look of surprise, he smiled at me as he accepted a tin of beans and some turkey from the guard called Michael. Unkar now sitting up on the old couch looked at me and said, "This could be the best meal I have had in quite a while."

My chest swelled as the others shook their heads in agreement.

"How did you get a turkey without a rifle?" Unkar asked.

"I used my last arrow."

"You're a better hunter than I." Troy said.

Unkar asked, "If you used your last arrow to kill the turkey, then who killed the first man on the beach?"

I stepped out back and grabbed the sword that lay beneath the pack. "With this!"

Unkar took a giant stride toward me. "Is that what I think it is?"

"No way man, that must be a replica." Troy mentioned.

Unkar asked if he could examine it and grabbed it from my hands without waiting for an answer. He pulled the blade from the scabbard.

"This is no replica." He transferred his gaze to my face and asked where I got such a magnificent weapon.

"From an old man named Harold who helped us get here just before his death."

Unkar examined the blade again, read the inscription.

"It is indeed an authentic Samurai sword. The steel on this sword has been folded a thousand times making the edge stronger and sharper than anything known to man." He balanced it in one hand and then said, "It's well balanced and heavier than it looks, but feels so natural in the hand as if it were part of me, and to think that such a blade should be christened by the hand of so young a man tells me that we are in the company of a king in the making."

He looked at me sternly and said, "I don't know why the Star

Delegation sent me so far out of our territory to gather you. Whatever the reason, I'm sure it's a good one. But if you ever feel like joining the guard in the future I would be honored to have you Meno. You have all the qualifications and would need very little training."

The others nodded there head in agreement as Unkar sheathed the blade and held it out to me on open palms with a bowed head saying, "my wish is your command." Followed by the hearty laughter of all three.

I grabbed the sword looking down in embarrassment.

Tesha came out of the other room rubbing her eyes and asking what all the commotion was about, then heading over to the stove to check the beans, I held back my question regarding her coming with us until a more suitable time. We all ate and discussed the lengthy trip back. We were to rendezvous with another guard at a place called Grand Junction when the moon was full, which gave us almost a week. I told them all that I was going to fish the lake and the two guards, troy and Michael expressed interest in going as well claiming that if no fish were caught that they could always eat the mule. I just stared in disgust. Luckily, we managed to gather enough equipment from the shed for one more and I let them go ahead saying that I would catch-up later.

Tesha examined Unkar's shoulder. Mentioning that the swelling and coloring were normal, and then said, "I will reapply a poultice in the evening to make sure no infection set's in."

"Thanks," Unkar growled.

"It's the least I can do after you risked your life for us, not to mention losing one of your men in the process." Tesha now turned to prepare coffee in the kitchen and then put the pot on the stove.

Unkar followed her as he replied. "Yes, the young one…always the young ones. We had just replaced another one of the same age before we left Tolemac. But it's our duty; it's what we are trained to do. If death is there to greet us, we welcome it with open arms, there is no fear involved. We are all well versed in the philosophies of Tolemac and will gladly give our lives for the protection of those philosophies as well as those who teach and live by them."

"How long have you been a Tolemac guard?" She asked.

"More than twenty years, I was brought to Tolemac from Mongolia when still a child with a dozen others after our lands was left in ruins by a series of earthquakes. A recruit for the Tolemac guard had come to Mongolia after hearing about the calamities, hoping to convince some local orphanages to relinquish some of their boys of a certain age and temperament. Most of us had never heard of Tolemac, let alone Colorado but we wanted to get the hell out of that awful place and would do anything or go anywhere to do so. The recruiter's timing was impeccable. Food and funding were scarce and there were few willing to stay behind to nurture the children. We had all begun a slow death of starvation. When we reached the ship—a long clipper named 'The Sea Goddess.' We encountered many other orphans from various countries, like Greenland, Norway, Ireland, and Russia. All of the children spoke of enduring great hardships in their native land. We set sail for America when all the bunks were full."

"How old were you when you became a guard?" she asked.

"I volunteered for the guard when I was nineteen, but no one is asked to join until he is twenty-one, and it is still a choice one is free to make, but not until he finishes school and completes training in the art of war. Some consider it boot camp, but it goes way beyond any military training."

"This must be why there are only four of you." Tesha said as she checked the coffee pot.

"Four is always enough for small skirmishes. You can cover more area that way and be harder to detect. The need for pooling the guard to face overwhelming odds happens very rarely and can never be won by just numbers but only by stealth, cunning and a superior attitude."

"Are there any women in your guard?"

"A woman would prove to be a major distraction since male guards are in the field for long periods of time. We return to the barracks for supplies and information once a month or so. It is critical that all guards be in total control of their emotional selves as well as their vanity."

Tesha nodded slowly and then asked, "If I can't be a guard, what else can I do at Tolemac?"

Unkar fell silent for a moment. "Is that coffee I smell?" He said trying to change the subject. Tesha nodded.

"Wow! I haven't had a cup of coffee since the trade routs disappeared." Unkar grabbed a metal cup and began to pour. He cleared his throat and when he spoke again his voice was softer than before. "I'm afraid you are not yet welcome at Tolemac. Only the boy was invited."

Tesha now was speechless looking down.

"I'm sorry, but Tolemac has been dealing with population problems as well as dwindling resources. The doors have been sealed to all outsiders for nearly twenty years, except family and special cases like Meno."

"Oh I see." She replied with her eyes searching the worn linoleum, then softly asked, "What do you consider family?"

"Someone who has immediate roots there, like a living relative or a founder. You must have close family ties too, a cousin would not do; it would have to be immediate family."

"I will not leave without her, there's no way I can leave her do you hear!" I yelled to Unkar with my arms crossed in a steadfast manner.

"Meno these men have come a long way for you and remember what Harold said; this is all about you and your safety, you must go and not concern yourself with me, I'm plenty capable of taking care of myself." Tesha said as she gazed at him through teary eyes.

Unkar now stood up and walked over to Meno, the light from the doorway was now blocked as Unkar towered over him with his intimidating presence. "I have orders to escort you to Tolemac and if that means bound and gagged so be it, but I'll be dammed if I'm leaving here empty handed after loosing one of my men to save your skin!" He said pointing a large finger at me before sitting back down.

I panicked and made a break for the door but he tripped me and I slapped the floor with a wallop! He reached down to grab me and Tesha pushed him back onto the couch by slamming into his wounded shoulder. Unkar yelled in pain but recovered quickly and stood fast.

"Don't you touch him you bastard!" she screamed shielding me with her body.

He grabbed her by the neck and tossed her aside but she bounced back with surprising speed, grabbing hold of his good arm and hanging on for dear life as he tried to shake her off as they tumbled back onto the couch where he tried to use his foot to pry her loose. Tesha now sunk her teeth into his arm and he let out a hair raising yell before yanking it back, but before he could make another move toward me he saw that I now had raised the sword in my defense.

"Wait! Wait! O.K. she can come if it means that much too you, but I can't guarantee that they will allow her in O.K. now please put that thing down." Unkar said, out of breath and checking his now bleeding forearm.

"Geez woman you got teeth like a crocodile, I hope this don't get infected we have a long way to go before antibiotics are available!"

"I'm Sorry; can I please have my pendant back now?" Tesha said as she held out her hand.

Unkar not realizing that within his clenched fist he had parts of a shell necklace and a broken gold chain with a pendant attached. He now gazed upon the pendant with excitement as Troy and Michael came rushing into the small cabin with a flushed look on their faces. They saw Meno with the sword in his hands and the blood dripping from Unkar's arm. Quickly Unkar interjected "It's alright, we just had a little misunderstanding." Turning towards Tesha and asking, "Where did you get this pendant?"

"It was my Grandfather's; Meno took it from his body before we buried him."

"This is a founders pendant, who the heck was your Grandfather and just how was he affiliated with Tolemac?"

"All I know is that he worked there for a number of years after the turn of the century as a carpenter or something. He died trying to take me there, saying that if there was civilization anywhere it would be at Tolemac."

"I don't know what the worn letters spell, but I've always thought the bottom one looked like the letter F." Tesha said.

Unkar began to laugh a deep hardy laugh that shook the whole room.

"Yes my child An F under a T. You not only opened the door but gave us good reason to celebrate. A Tolemac founder's granddaughter is considered royalty and although it seems that your Grandfather earned his keep during Tolemac's humble beginnings they will investigate your lineage but I think you will have no problem joining the family. I will not only escort you back, I will let you ride my own horse all the way while I ride the fallen guard's horse with our little friend here."

Tesha was now the one bellowing laughter. "You have no idea how terrible I felt when you said I couldn't come with you. My heart sank. Oh God—I'm so relieved!" In a rush, she threw her arms around him, squeezing him without any thought of his wounded shoulder.

"AAAGH! GEEEZUSSS, WOMAN!"

"Oops, sorry." Tesha cringed and flushed with embarrassment.

9
THE RENDEZVOUS

We traveled a fair distance over the next few days and learned many stories of the Tolemac guard by the light of the campfire. The soldiers spoke of epic battles and overcoming outrageous odds; they spoke of men so morally corrupt that death was their only salvation. They had seen the side of humanity that could only be dreamt up by writers of the most gruesome sort of horror. Tesha and I peppered their stories with questions. The Mongol would usually be the one to answer, unless he prompted one of the others to do so.

When Tesha asked why they refused to collect the dead man's rifle on the beach, Unkar nodded to the black bearded guard called Troy. Troy was slightly younger and shorter than Unkar but was built solidly with dark skin, a head full of small braids and an unfamiliar accent. His eyes had an intensity that held me in their grip as he spoke, with his broad low brow and straight, narrow eyebrows.

"Weapons are a very important commodity to the guard. We are trained in all manner of their use, the gun being no exception, but the gun cannot be considered an extension of one's body and therefore is not trustworthy. They also require maintenance and ammunition which is no longer commercially manufactured. Some gunmen refill old shells when powder is acquired, but they skimp on the powder so they can make more bullets. That's what happened with the one that struck our captain. If the bullet that hit his shoulder had been correctly made, it would have blown the bone apart, but instead the shot got the rifle bearer killed."

"Which was the guard's favorite weapon?" I asked.

Troy pondered the question and replied, "The mind. All else is just an extension of the body, which in itself is a dangerous weapon when well trained."

We traveled two more days to make the rendezvous point and made camp by a large river they called the Colorado. There we waited for the moon to become full and the other guards to arrive. During our stay one of the guards killed an antelope from a small herd and we feasted. Tesha once again stretched and scraped the skin to make leggings and moccasins. She would sing her old songs when she did this, bringing back memories of my home on the island. It made me feel happy at first but then I wondered if I would ever see any of my people again. Surely some had survived, but for how long and where? More and more unsettling questions plagued my mind when the guard called Michael saw the sadness in my eyes and came over to sit next to me. Michael put his hand on my shoulder. "Is everythin okay?" He asked with his had kind blue eyes, long sandy hair and a full set of white teeth—a rarity for a guard.

"Just thinking about home." As he often did when he looked at me, Michael smiled which was somehow reassuring.

"You may not understand this Maeno but you are at home. I lost my family when I was just a dad burn kid too, matter of fact ever guard I knew was just orphans. The guard found me and took me to Tolemac. Otherwise, I would have never survived." He said with his southern drawl.

I nodded, but without any conviction. I still didn't see how this made the middle of nowhere home. Michael continued.

"What I'm trying to say Maeno, is that yer now part of Tolemac's family. We are like a great big family with many sisters, brothers, mothers, and fathers, who all want nothing better than to see you become all that you can, while providin you any tool or technique to help you get yer loftiest goals accomplished. You'll see what I mean when we get back."

Unkar called Michael over before he could utter another word and whispered in his ear and Michael quickly mounted and rode off without a backward glance. About twenty minutes later Michael was back, but now he was whispering in the Mongol's ear. Unkar nodded his head in agreement. Both guards apparently satisfied with the whispered conference tore into the leftover meat, which hung near the fire.

Tesha came over and began the evening ritual of brewing herbal teas, asking the men if they cared to join her. Instead of answering, Michael began loading water and meat on the back onto his large gray mare in preparation to go somewhere.

Tesha looked at Unkar in alarm and asked, "Is everything all right?"

The Mongol replied, "There was someone scouting us out earlier, probably just a stray Navajo. Michael will just make sure there are no surprises tonight."

"Are the Navajo considered a threat?" She asked stirring her tea cup.

"Never to the guard, but they have been trying to re-establish themselves in these lands. They usually just use their numbers to scare off most, but they occasionally take horses and even a life to show they mean business. Unfortunately there's a chance that they may not have recognized us as guards so far from Tolemac, particularly with a boy and young woman. We cannot afford to take any chances of losing such a precious cargo—nor a single horse for that matter."

Tesha handed Unkar a cup of tea, and both fell silent staring into the fire. That night, I lay awake thinking about Michael out there all alone and hoped that the other guard members would soon arrive. I stared at the bright moon, but I wasn't sure if it was completely full, but full or not I could see the reflection upon the backs of trout as they flipped out of the river to catch flies. The next morning Tesha woke me up by dropping a bundle of branches in my lap. I was a bit confused.

"Willow shoots. They make good arrows. She said before walking back to the fire."

"Oh…thank you!"

Troy, who was squatting near the fire asked, "Have you ever made arrows before, Meno?"

"No, but I helped my father make whale harpoons."

Troy gave me an approving smile. "I'll show you as soon as you get the materials for points and tails."

I was eager to start and sprung out of my bedroll toward the fire to conquer the morning chill. Michael strode back in with a heavy head and red eyes.

He quietly talked to Unkar before lying down and throwing a blanket over his head while still struggling to get his boots off.

Unkar now told Troy to patrol the perimeter. My arrow making lesson would have to wait. Tesha brewed up the last of the coffee and Troy had a cup before saddling up and riding off. The sun now illuminated the crest of the mountains and the tall peaks began to gleam brilliant white. I gathered myself by the fire; once warmed I tore into the tough Antelope meat while I thought about scouting the riverbanks for flint rock to make arrow points.

Tesha was enjoying a morning cup with Unkar, who was trying to answer one of the many questions of Tolemac that she continually bombarded him with. This time Tesha had asked, "What do they grow inside Tolemac?"

Unkar replied softly and tactfully, which sometimes felt out of place for the thundering hulk.

"Tesha, my little curious cat, all your questions will be answered when we get there, but if you must know I will give you a general idea. The greenhouses within the perimeter of Tolemac are very large and have many workers during planting and harvesting times and only a handful during the growing season. Each residential pod has their own greenhouse and all work in them on a rotating schedule. It's all volunteer, there's no currency at Tolemac but there's always plenty of public projects going on. Eventually, after trying many different projects, you will likely feel more comfortable with one or two and devote most of your spare time to a labor of love. The colossal greenhouses grow produce and allow us to alternate menus and have variety in our diets, but most grains are grown in the fertile valleys outside the village. Working in the greenhouses is an education in itself." Unkar headed for his horse, but Tesha stopped him.

"Please, just one more question?"

"Right after these horses have been watered." Unkar kept walking. Several minutes later, he came back. He asked Tesha pointedly, but with a smile.

"What's your last question of the day?"

Tesha held a cup of coffee under chin, poised to drink. "What are the religious beliefs like at Tolemac?"

Unkar raised his eyebrows causing deep crevices to litter his forehead as his smile faded and said, "Awful early for these types of questions ain't it, besides this is not my area of expertise, but I suppose I could tell you Tolemac's position regarding religion. Tolemac does not subscribe to any one specific creed. There are no churches, mosques, or synagogues within the village and you won't find anyone openly on bent knees in prayer, that's not to say that some at Tolemac don't carry their own religious beliefs. Many do that grew up outside the village. You may learn about major religions as a history lesson and you may study the aspects of these if you wish, but the teaching of truth is all around you at Tolemac, woven into the very fabric of society's culture and consciousness. You will see soon enough."

Tesha now stared into the fire as if she was trying to visualize all of this in her head, then she got up and headed towards the river. The sun was peeking over the mountains and the warmth made her stop at the riverbank to bask in the light. She bent over to splash herself and snapped her head back up when she heard the sounds of a horse traveling fast and close. She could see a rider thundering straight at her along the river's edge. The rider was native, perhaps Navajo and as he approached she could see his lance held high. She screamed and ran for the camp.

The rider was bearing down upon her as she turned to run. Her legs were taught and heavy with fear. As she stumbled for the camp a figure emerged from the short hedges; another Navajo, this one with a knife came after her! Out of the corner of her eye she saw the lance fly overhead before tearing into the chest of the knife wielding Navajo, dropping him. Tesha screamed again continuing to run in a panic, ignoring the rider shouting for her to stop.

She finally slowed her pace when Unkar raced past her on his stallion. Unkar quickly greeted the other rider with the salute of arms over their chests calling him Lance. Tesha was now trying to hide her embarrassment seeing that she had been so afraid of a guard; she held her hand over her mouth as she abruptly sat down in the weeds to compose herself. The two riders dismounted to see if the victim had any last words. He was dead and definitely Navajo.

"When I spotted the girl at the river I noticed a figure in the growth behind her just before I saw the glimmer of a weapon, I think she got the wrong impression," He said, pulling his weapon from the Navajo's chest, then taking the knife from the dead man's hand.

"She'll get over it, but what the hell is this man doing waiting here in ambush?" Unkar said shaking his finger mockingly at the body. "Is the rest of the guard here yet?"

"They should be along any minute," The guard replied as he wiped the blood from the weapon with the dead man's shirt. Then walking over and offering Tesha a hand up. She wouldn't even bring her eye's to meet his, let alone take his hand.

Back at camp Troy was heading in with two other riders. Unkar peered west, combing the sparse grassland for the customary fourth guard, advancing from the fourth cardinal direction. "Aha! The shimmering helmet of Volsung," he cackled like a teenager as he rode out to greet his blond bearded brother. They both dismounted and embraced calling each other by their boy names; Shipmate.

Tesha and I were both confused with all the commotion. The guard named Lance came towards us and said to Tesha, "Please forgive me for giving you such a scare, I was only looking out for your best interest and had no chance to explain as you could surely see. I am Lance of the Tolemac guard at your service." He then prostrated himself before Tesha.

"May I ask your name?"

It seemed Tesha was not yet over the morning event, for she stared at the long haired man for a moment with a blank look on her face before quickly interjecting, "I'm Tesha Tooniqua of Washington."

"It is truly an honor, Tesha Tooniqua," Lance replied.

"Your name fits you well," she replied.

"Will you be accompanying us back to Tolemac?" he asked.

"Yes, all the way back. I am a founder's granddaughter," she said as she held out the pendant from her collar, with great
pride.

"Well, a founder's granddaughter. The wonders never cease to amaze!" Lance then turned toward me.

"And this must be our precious cargo, Meno Olikai." He shook my hand vigorously. "It's nice to see that everyone is in good health. Is that coffee I smell?"

Troy pulled up with two other bearded men, all dismounted to wait for the leaders, who were walking their horses and leisurely chatting. When Unkar got there he sent a sleepy Michael over to the body at the river to see if it was the same man he had seen the day before. Then Unkar introduced everyone.

I was taken by the size of the long bearded one they called Volsung, and that metal helmet he wore made him seem all the more prehistoric. He looked just like those Vikings I read about at school. All he needed was a long boat and an ax. The other two guards looked to be of Mexican descent. Volsung sent them both back out to watch the perimeter after he heard of the foiled attack, then sat down next to Unkar and began catching up on old times. It was interesting to see these two together, it seemed as though they tuned out the world around them until they had shared their secrets in full. There could be fifty crazed Navajos in the bush, but at that moment they couldn't care less.

Tesha was still shaken up by the morning's events. Her hand trembled as she poured Lance a cup of coffee. She told him, "Enjoy it while you can. That's the last pot."

Michael rode back in and went straight to Unkar. "The body at the river ain't the one I saw yesterday; his clothes are different."

Unkar just shook his head.

"Is an attack possible?" Volsung asked with a startled gaze.

"Now that we have killed one of their own it's just a matter of when and where. I can only guess at their current number, for no ones stealthier than the Din'e, but now there are more of us they will get reinforcements before they try anything." Unkar said, then shouted for everyone to get ready to move out in one hour, then sent the weary Michael back out to collect the other two guards. Lance followed suit.

"We can get to the high country in a couple days. The Navajo won't follow through the passes. Let's head for McClure pass and then through Cottonwood it should be melting by now." Volsung stated.

Within an hour, we were traveling over hills and through the canyons in the hot dry sun at a quick pace, watching for any signs of a potential ambush. Unkar insisted that we take the long, difficult trail around a ravine that was in his opinion the perfect place for an ambush. Getting to the top of the sandstone plateau was hard on the horses, which were in need of water.

That night we camped on the cold windswept plateau without the warmth of a campfire. Fortunately there was still antelope meat. Water was rationed to men and horses alike. It seemed no sooner did my shivering stop than I was being poked by a stick held by Troy, who along with the other guards, had already packed in the dim morning light. I rubbed my now burning eyes trying to understand why we were up before the birds and wanted so much to get back into those warm blankets.

We traveled till noon, stopping for a short while by a small seasonal creek to let the horses drink and refill our canteens. Lance had been riding alongside Tesha, talking and joking with her. I knew he was flirting when he asked Tesha how old she was.

"I turned nineteen this spring, and since were on the subject, how old are you?"

"I just turned twenty-one!"

"Liar! More like thirty-one!" She replied squinting at him as if she was half blind. Lance jokingly pointed to himself with an open mouth, tossing his long black hair backward with a jolt of the head in amusing defiance, making her laugh. These two were becoming close, which made me a little jealous. Lance was now holding out some jerky to Tesha for us both, knowing that we hadn't eaten all morning. My feelings about Lance changed rapidly at the taste of the meat. As we nibbled and rested under a large pine tree, Tesha asked Lance how he became a Tolemac guard.

"When I was a chubby little boy my family had a trading post outside the Ute reservation that did a lot of business with the traders that purchased for Tolemac. They were the mainstay of our business. As I got older my father took me along to their village to drop off large orders. My father was a good businessman and was able to get things through a network of reservations, including the Navajo. After the industrialized world as we knew it no longer existed, he was the first one to utilize the llama as the preferred pack animal. He built special carts that they could tow up and down steep grade. We began losing a lot of cargo en route to Tolemac from robberies due to the large migration of people fleeing the large cities and towns in search of something better, which they never found. The Tolemac guard was sent to escort us and police the area. Eventually the routes got so treacherous that even the guard could not offer certain protection. One day our trading post was ransacked, my father and his workers killed for what little they had. Soon afterward my sisters and I were escorted to Tolemac by Volsung; it was there I trained to become a guard."

Tesha looked at Lance now sporting a strange grin on his face. It was the kind of face one had when they were trying to hide the tender side of self.

"I'm sorry," she said.

Lance stood up. "Please don't be, death is not something so terrible. My father had a good life and died defending that way of life, we call that a good death."

"As do we," she said as she stared at his worn buckskin shirt nearly black from the fat of wild game, with one lone Eagle feather dangling from its center knot.

"What became of your mother?" Tesha asked, getting more personal with each question.

"Mother went back to live on the rez or what was left of it, She said Tolemac's culture was too radical for her. She was a stubborn woman."

I saw Volsung position his helmet onto his red-faced head full of graying-blonde hair, a sign for the guard to remount. Unkar told me to ride with Tesha on his charger in case we encountered any trouble. I was only too happy to oblige, however Tesha seemed less pleased, abruptly taking off as I was mounting with the aid of Michael, but since I accidentally grabbed her braided hair to catch myself, she immediately stopped and turned with her eyes and mouth shrieking in silence. I let go as soon as could but I could see she thought it was intentional.

We rode all afternoon, the hot sun making us weaker with each mile. The high country was visible in the distance with its fresh spring waters, cool mountain air and plentiful game. We were ascending a wide incline that leveled out onto a plateau full of scrubby little trees that clung to the rocks from the smallest of crevices. Near the high point, Unkar joined Volsung in the front, both of them talking too soft for us to hear. After a short conference Unkar turned to the other guards and gave a hand sign. The Tolemac men spread out in an inverted V. I tensed even though I couldn't see trouble, I felt sure it was coming. Suddenly I heard the clamor of many hoofs coming up the hillside from the rear and front all at once. We waited while they assembled around us. About thirty Navajo, they were dirty from riding hard and looked bitter and wild. As two of them came forward to speak Unkar and Volsung rode out to meet them.

"Turn the murderer over to us and we'll allow the rest of you to pass unharmed." A large Navajo without a shirt ordered.

"No murderer resides with us. What happened at the river was an act of defense for the woman who came under attack by one of your men." Unkar quickly replied without hesitation. The two leading Navajo talked quietly among themselves for a moment. The larger one turned back to Unkar.

"We shall determine the truth by our own means. Hand him over."

"I'M THE ONE YOU WANT—COME GET ME!" Volsung bellowed pulling his double edged sword.

"WAIT!" Unkar yelled raising his hands.

Several Navajos had trained their arrows on Volsung holding their bowstrings taught. Then a large cry sounded off behind me. I turned to see Lance holding up the dead Navajo's knife for all to see, sealing his fate. The two leading Navajos grimaced and quickly turned their ponies and sped down the hill with their entourage in tow.

Volsung raced over to Lance. "What have you done? You damn fool!" He slapped the knife out of Lance's hand. "There will be no heroes in my group today or any day. Heroes will be the death of us all!"

"There was no other way out!" Lance replied, chopping the air with his hands. "We must forget custom when our responsibility is greater than ourselves."

The pain was evident on Volsung's face as he turned his horse forward, slowly shaking his head. Unkar followed with the rest. In front of me Tesha still held her hand over her mouth. Finally she kicked the black charger so we could fall in line. I didn't blame her for the delay, though. I was so riveted with fear that Tesha had to slap my hands to keep my nails from digging into her sides. We found a small defensible hilltop near a creek to make camp but we still couldn't have a fire. We had nothing to cook anyway and it was a bit warmer than the night before. Lance handed Tesha and me the last of the jerky claiming that he already had some while smiling at Tesha, then he rode to a nearby bluff. Soon we could hear native wailing. Tesha began to cry as if she knew the true meaning of the native song coming from the bluff, while the sun set on an otherwise silent camp. Volsung sent Troy and Alvaro to stand watch until they were relieved at high moon. "Ask anyone to relieve you but Lance." He said as he re-secured his saddle of his horse rather than removing it as usual.

"Why didn't the Navajo attack us back there when they outnumbered us?" I asked Unkar. Michael quickly interjected; "That's neither their style nor their strength boy, they would rather crawl on their bellies for half a mile for a guaranteed kill than risk one dead in a face off."

The setting sun created a beautiful paintbrush lavender& gold sky and the chilly night air was upon us as the big yellow moon crested with an eerie glow that swept the hills and valleys. It seemed no one was eager to sleep, including myself. When I finally nodded off the coyotes screeched for almost an hour. At times, I could have sworn they sounded like the cries of a man. Later that night I was awakened by the shuffling feet and low voices of the returning guard, or what I thought was the returning guard. I opened my eyes to see Troy whispering something in Volsung's ear that made his eyes shoot wide open. Volsung jumped up, mounted his horse and galloped off with Troy while the others were still fast asleep.

After seeing that stone-cold look on Volsung's face I dared not sleep. I got up to relieve myself and accidentally kicked Tesha's tin cup with a loud clanging noise, rousing everyone in the camp. Unkar jumped to his feet and grabbed his sword razing it at me in defense before his eyes had a chance to focus.

"I'm sorry!" I yelled ducking for cover.

In the dim morning light he saw that Lance and Volsung were not in their bedrolls. Then we heard it—wailing echoing through the canyon. Unkar told Michael to stay at the camp while he and Manuel grabbed weapons and ran on foot toward the sounds.

Tesha soon let out after Unkar left with the others, ignoring Michael's plea's to stay put. He then mounted in hot pursuit leaving me alone at the camp. I ran like the wind after them finally reaching the dark ravine. As I got closer I could see Volsung bent over someone and Troy dragging the body of another out of the creek. Several other bodies dotted the hillside as well.

Volsung was clinging to Lance's lifeless corpse and wailing. He held his head like a distressed mother oblivious to the carnage of his disemboweled body. Unkar could now see that the Navajos had gagged Lance, which meant they had cut him open while he was still conscious and hoping the coyotes would smell the fresh blood before we got there.

Troy knelt over Alvaro's body. Three fingers on his right hand were missing, which told Unkar that the Navajos had used him to sucker in Lance for an ambush before cutting his throat. The three dead Navajo meant that the Tolemac guards had both put up a fight before being overpowered—but it also meant the raiding party was still close by without yet having a chance to remove their dead.

Unkar had never seen Volsung so upset at the loss of a brother guard, but Lance had always been his favorite. Volsung had sort of adopted him after his father died. Unkar did not know what it felt like to lose a son, but was sure that this was the kind of pain his brother now felt. Tesha screamed at the sight of Lance's shredded body. Unkar tried to keep her away, but she pushed him aside and knelt beside him. "No! No! No!" She cried.

Suddenly a loud screech was heard from the tip of the bluff. There the raiding party was celebrating their victory and rubbing our noses in it. Volsung shot up yelling, "I'll kill you bastards!" as he vaulted onto his steed. Unkar tried to stop him, shouting at him not to go for the bait, but Volsung kicked him out of the way as he sped up the hillside. Troy quickly mounted and scrambled after him. Unkar yelled at Michael, "Get the horses!" and took off after them on foot with Manuel close behind. I ran up the opposite hillside to see what was happening.

Volsung with his large sword in hand was plowing into a group of Navajo and swiping a couple off their mounts. Then an arrow pierced his back, then another his side and still another his abdomen. Finally a yelling Troy trying to capture their attention smashed into and dismounted one of the horsemen. Troy slashed fiercely with his sword at the remaining men. He severed one's arm but it wasn't enough. Close up fighting only worked well for sword fighting. He too was brought to the ground littered with arrows before being stabbed by the Navajo whom he had knocked from his mount a moment before.

The scene was more than I could bear. I cried out, "No! Please God no!" Through tears, I saw Unkar reach the mound only to find the fleeing foe and his brethren butchered before him. He knelt at the side of Volsung who gasped for air and tried to say something as he collapsed in his arms. Manuel was at Troy's side. He too was dead. Arrows had pierced his chest and side; one went through his jaw. It was now Unkar's turn to cry, this made me weep harder seeing such a battle hardened man as him in such a state. But weep he did, as he cradled Volsung's head in his arms.

When the sun finished rising that morning, it found us far from the scene. Unkar had decided it was best for us to leave immediately, leaving our dead as they lay. Tesha did not want to leave Lance this way and I helped her cover him with rocks from the river's bank until Unkar demanded that we go. Troy's horse had not been taken by the Navajo, so I had packed and loaded it for myself. We galloped towards the pass that Volsung had told us to follow. Still weak from lack of food; we camped that evening at a high mountain lake. Michael and I fished and found the lake full of trout. We caught enough to last a couple days.

The next few days as we climbed the air became thin and cold. The scenery was bleak. Most of that part of the forest had been burnt up in a fire some time ago—an endless sea of blackened stalks giving me a foreboding feeling of doom. Tesha rode in silence, her face barely visible with her blanket wrapped around part of her head. Unkar having yelled at her to mount up, refusing to hear her words seemed to have wounded her when she scurried to cover Lances body, or perhaps is was just the loss we all suffered, whatever the reason it was as if a part of her died there with Lance on that rocky creek. She even refused to eat the fish that first night. The next day, she fainted when riding up a steep incline. If not for Manuel's quick response, she could have rolled off the steep embankment.

Michael had tracked a group of elk and came back on the fourth evening with two sections of meat. Tesha asked him where the hide was, the first words she spoke in half a week. I think Michael was so shocked to hear her voice that he wasn't sure what to say. He just shrugged his large shoulders.

The next day we traveled over cottonwood. The snow was not all melted and the horses were having a tough time getting through the heavy stuff. We had to stop often to let them rest in the thin air. By mid-afternoon we made it to the tree line on the opposite side and it was all downhill from there.

Unkar said it was sacrilege not to stop at the hot springs, so we rested for a full day when we reached it. I never thought water could feel so good. It was magical; it seemed to erase all your problems and concerns…and seeing Tesha walk in totally nude sure took me by surprise. If was as if she just didn't care anymore. She held her head up high as she lowered herself into the water. The men tried not to blatantly stare, but rather glanced occasionally from the corner of their eye after she disrobed before them. She then gazed at Unkar and spit out; "Why didn't we bury those men back there, that's more sacrilege than some spring!"

"My duty is to protect the boy's life, everything else is secondary. I was told no matter what the cost Meno was to make it back to Tolemac unharmed and that he is to be quickly removed from any and all danger."

After Unkar said this they all began staring at me. Unkar, quickly turning away and trying to distract his men, said, "It's only a couple days to Tolemac from here, hopefully there will be no more surprises!"

10
TOLEMAC, 2046 A.D.

I could see the village of Tolemac in the distant valley as we descended. Some Tolemac guards eager to learn of the trip greeted us as we approached. Volsung's helmet on the back of Unkar's horse made them all stop and remove their hats. They bowed their heads as we rode past. No words were spoken.

Tolemac was larger than I had realized. There were endless fields of grain growing on either side of the road along with rows of large wind turbines, all turning like huge airplane propellers. There were no fortress walls like I had been expecting, just an endless sea of the most interesting structures I had ever seen. Huge glass domes as big as athletic fields. A very tall tower with a silver disc-shaped room at the top was hard to miss as it glimmered in the sun.

"Michael, what's that building that looks like a water tower?" I asked.

"The guard uses it for an observation deck. We also collect atmospheric data there, but primarily we use it to give children a fun ride in the elevator."

I looked quickly at him to see if he was kidding. He just grinned without a hint. By far the largest structure of glass was a huge pyramid located in the middle of the village. I figured this to be the Center that Tesha's grandfather had spoken about.

The first building we came to was a guard outpost. Unkar had to check in and said he would be a while, so Michael took us through the check-point. The city was alive with all types of people scurrying here and there, many on bicycles and small electric scooters. We passed through two very large pillars that had Tolemac's name etched upon them and a bronze plaque stating the year of the founding and some of the founder's names. In smaller letters across the bottom, a quotation read; GOD IS LOVE, LOVE IS LIGHT HERE LIES TOLEMAC TO GUARD THEIR PLIGHT. Under the words was a small circle with two polished triangles touching at the center.

We stopped at a short cone shaped building. A couple of gray haired old ladies behind a window took information down as Michael filled in the details, pausing occasionally to ask us the correct spelling of our names, dates and locations of birth and past illnesses. From there Michael took us to a small adobe doctor's office where we showered and changed into gowns for a medical examination. After the physical we proceeded to a dentist for another examination, for more probing and prodding.

Michael was waiting for us outside the door when we finished. "Just one more stop then we can all grab some grub," he said. My belly growled its agreement. I hadn't realized how hungry I was. Tesha and I both quickly took Michael up on his offer. As we rode through town all eyes seemed upon us, I just shrugged and looked down pretending not to notice. We stopped in front of a long, low, lackluster structure that was partially underground. The sign on the door read "Welcome to Ellis Island." We stopped at the first door and were greeted by more questions about who, when, where, and why. Then we were handed wristbands to put on and led to another door to receive our temporary quarter arrangements.

A thin elderly women offered to show us to our rooms. Michael said he would meet us in the mess hall afterwards and pointed in its direction. The rooms were small, with a bunk bed and small desk. I lay on the bed momentarily and looked out the window on the ceiling. It had a long string on it that attached to a locking mechanism. I pulled it and the window swung open as if by itself. I pulled it again, and it snapped shut. I thought that it was quite clever and played with the apparatus until it no longer amused me and then headed over to Tesha's room to see if she was ready to eat, but she had already left.

I found the mess hall, as Michael had called it. There were long rows of tables and benches and the air was heavy with the intoxicating aroma of cooking. At the far end was a banquet with all types of food. Tesha was eagerly piling an enormous amount of food onto her plate and I happily followed suit. The food tasted excellent, but neither she nor I could finish half the food on our plates, it as if my stomach had shrunk up at a most inopportune time. Michael on the other hand got up for another plateful.

As we ate, Tesha asked Michael if all the food was grown in Tolemac.

Michael replied, "All you see has been grown here. Tolemac has its own dairy farm and we raise chickens, turkeys, hens, and ducks. We even raise the fish in large ponds. But this is only the beginning. We also have hundreds of bison grazing in the south pastures and many greenhouses growing all types of vegetables and herbs."

Tesha's eyebrows rose when she heard the magic word. "Herbs, what kinds of herbs?"

"Herbs for spice and herbs for lice, all kinds of herbs," Michael sing-songed.

"I really would like to take a tour of the greenhouses," Tesha replied.

"As soon as you have had your orientation and decoding completed, you can spend as much time there as you like," replied Michael as he continued stuffing his large face.

Tesha furrowed her brow. "What's orientation and decoding?"

"I'm not the best one to be answering that question but I'll tell ya what I remember. The decoding is done with the small sample of blood you gave at the doctor's when he pricked your finger. From that small drop of blood the lab will analyze your genetic history. This is gonna tell 'em a great deal about your strengths and weaknesses—from which foods to avoid, to which drugs and diseases could be fatal to you. They also scanned you when you laid down in that large cylinder. The scan was sort of like the old MRI hospitals used to use, but these scans take much more than a three-dimensional picture. They tell the staff 'bout things like body fat, bone density and organ longevity. They also measure and chart the body's circulatory, lymphatic and endocrine systems, as well as brain chemistry, neurotransmission rates, and electromagnetic frequency!"

"Orientation takes two weeks. The first few days you'll get a look at the entire complex with an escort who will explain everything in great detail. Then for two days you'll attend an examination of sorts. This is not a pass fail exam, just a method of determining, again, your strengths and weaknesses. The followin' week you'll be in the care of the one we call the wizard. The wizard will debrief you and then blow your mind."

"What do you mean blow our minds?" Tesha interjected with a surprised look on her face.

"What I mean is that they don't call that old guy the wizard for nothing. But don't worry, it's all quite painless. Now after two weeks' orientation you get a week off to do as you please while they collect all the data and build what is called a matrix. The matrix has all the technical information compiled to formulate what is then called a manifest. The manifest is what you show the director in any department in which you may choose to work. From this he can ascertain your qualifications."

"Is it like bringing a resume to an interview?" Tesha asked.

"In a sense, but you can still work in any department you want for a trial period, even if it's against a director's best interest, provided there is an opening—and there are hundreds of choices. You see, the manifest will put it all into layman's terms for the directors and counselors, but it is the counselors that will always be there, like family to help you find something that is rewarding and productive. Counselors will see that you are also educated to the capacity of your manifest description. You can always be learning at Tolemac if you choose to."

Tesha began to ask another question but stopped at mid-sentence when Unkar appeared at our table. Unkar nodded at us and then turned to Michael. "Check in with the marshal, he needs your testimony for the record before the memorial can be scheduled."

Michael got up, quickly finished his drink, briskly waved goodbye and left the room.

"How's the food?" Unkar said as he squeezed his large frame into Michael's spot.

"Great," we both said.

"There's someone I want you both to meet," Unkar said. He beckoned to a women of considerable age, who had just come through the doorway. Unkar introduced her as Moora and said, "Moora will be helping you both for the next few weeks as your mentor until you are assigned your permanent counselors. Now if you'll excuse me for a moment, I'm going to get me some of that great food."

As Unkar made his way to the buffet, Moora sat down in the chair next to me. She was dark skinned and had deep dark eyes and very long gray hair in a braid. She wore the same jumpsuit that I had noticed many others wearing. She held instead of shaking our hands and said with a smile and a heavy Eastern accent, "Unkar told me of the losses you all suffered on your long journey to be with us here at Tolemac and for these I am sorry. Your next few weeks may not seem as exciting as your last few were but I guarantee they will have their moments."

"How long have you been at Tolemac?" Tesha asked.

"I came from Kashmir, my native country in 2012 to get away from that war torn land. I came with my then new groom, who made a sizable donation to the Tolemac foundation to help fund their ongoing public works projects. We were looking for a new way of life; a life without all the controls that most countries have, a life where we could be at peace without constant battling and bickering over lands and religious beliefs."

"Miss. Tooniqua, I knew your grandfather Jay Tooniqua when he was a strapping young lad. He was so very handsome!"

"You're kidding, oh my god!" Tesha said holding her hand over her mouth.

Moora continued, "We used to call him Spiderman, and if you ever saw him working on the high webbing over the greenhouses you would know why. He was a natural and helped build most of the superstructures here."

"That's amazing!" Tesha said.

"We will have more time to talk about old times later. Now it's getting late and you both need your rest. Tomorrow morning I will meet you here for breakfast at first light, which means that if you see the sun rising over the hillside you're already late!" Again Moora graced us with a beautiful smile as she got up from her chair.

"After a big breakfast, we will begin the sight-seeing tour," Moora said and slowly exited the room. Unkar now came back and began finishing his meal, then said that there would most likely be a memorial for the fallen guards sometime over the next week or two and that it would be good if we could make it.

"Where will it be held?" Tesha asked.

"At the Center. You will be informed through Moora and she will show you the way there." Unkar stood up. "My job is finished here. After the ceremony you will not see me around very much. My responsibilities lie outside the village, so that's where you'll find me." Unkar took a long look at the two of us and added, "It has been a pleasure serving you both. I wish you both a rewarding future here at Tolemac."

Tesha gave Unkar a teary-eyed hug and thanked him for all that he had done. As he turned to go I yelled, "Wait, wait one minute, I'll be right back." I ran to my room, grabbed Harold's old sword and sprinted back to the mess hall. As soon as I reached Unkar I held out the sword. "Please take it. It belongs in the hand of a true warrior."

Unkar took the sword and said, "I am truly honored, Meno." He bowed his head. "Remember that my offer for a place in the guard still stands if you're so inclined after your schooling...but I think the delegation has bigger plans for you." He saluted us both by crossing both arms over his chest, then left the room.

We walked back to our rooms in silence. I was just starting to realize that tomorrow would be the start of another life and I was feeling apprehensive of what the future held. That night I dreamt of my mother and father; they were very happy for me. Then my old grandfather showed up, patting me on the head like he always used to do. We all gathered around a fire to sing the old song and as we sang, more and more familiar faces gathered to join in the song of our people, a people that, aside from me, were no more.

11
A WORLD APART

The next day I awoke to a large whistle. The skylight showed a dark sky, and I gathered all my will to force myself out of bed and to the bathroom. The long corridor was dark, but the moment I commenced down it a soft indirect illumination at the floor and ceiling preceded me until I got there, going off in areas I already passed. I got to the bathroom and as I entered the lights once again turned themselves on. I looked around in amazement expecting to see someone playing tricks on me.

The ceramic floor of the bath was unexpectedly warm giving one a cozy feeling, and although the surface looked hard, it seemed to give slightly to cushion ones feet. The sink area was a trough with a long clear pipe that sprayed water in a fine mist as you approached. The water temperature was somehow regulated for comfort. I spotted myself in the mirror agape for a brief moment. The person staring back at me bore a strange resemblance but was as yet a stranger. The long shaggy hair and narrow face caused me to shake my head in disbelief. Even the missing tooth I had was now replaced and I seemed taller.

As I checked out the rest of the room with all its strange features I saw what resembled a shower in a glass cylinder. As I opened the curved glass door a strong fine mist of water sprayed from the top and bottom. Even the toilets were different, working on some sort of vacuum when the lid was opened as I sat down to relieve myself. Warm water greeted my bottom, cleansing it. When the water stopped, the vacuum from below seemed to dry me as well. I gazed up at the ceiling but could not find any light, yet the room was suffused with a bright white illumination.

After getting acquainted with my new home I dressed and headed to the mess hall. Moora, along with a few others, was picking from the fresh buffet of fruits, grains and dairy. I piled a plate full of fresh fruit, my mouth watering at the sight of it all, and began gorging myself as Tesha came over and soon joined in.

After breakfast Moora said, "First things first, we need to get you both new clothes and some personal care items so let's go shopping shall we."

We followed her outside to a small glass enclosure that had an elevator for going down into the womb of Tolemac. We boarded and went down a short distance to some sort of underground tunnel platform. The tunnel was narrow, perhaps six feet in diameter.

If not for the shiny metal walls reflecting the light as if by mirrors, I would have felt Closter phobic. Moora pressed a large red button that caused a red light to start flashing. She then pushed buttons on a large map on the wall, which made small lights flash at the locations she selected. Within a few minutes a pointed, tubular vehicle with no driver pulled up. Its clear top opened up, revealing six seats and a luggage compartment. Moora climbed in and Tesha and I followed. The clear lid closed and the vehicle zoomed down the lighted tunnel surprisingly quickly and smoothly.

After passing several similar platforms the car stopped automatically. Again, the clear top lifted and we got out. The tiny train zoomed away and I looked around. We appeared to be at an underground work facility. Every door lay open, and within each of the rooms there was the inconsistent whine of sewing machines and bustling activity. We stopped at the room on the far end and sat down on a bench as Moora waited at the counter for a young lady to come over and take our measurements for clothing. The lady admired Tesha's deerskin dress while she wrapped a cloth tape around her thin waist. The room was humming with the sounds of seamstresses at their worktables. Moora placed the order for our jumpsuits, but we got to choose our own colors. I always wanted a light blue suit.

Before re-boarding the transporter I noticed something I hadn't before: it had no wheels, or tracks of any kind. It just sort of hovered in the air. Moora saw the look on my face and said, "It's electromagnetic Meno. One day you're sure to learn all about it."

The entire first day we visited many different places, chatting with people before zooming off through the tiny subway to yet another new sight. Moora showed us the Center; a huge complex recessed about twenty feet in the ground and caped with a large clear pyramid. Hanging from the apex of the pyramid was a large crystal star that glimmered in the sun. The center was bustling with people and activity. There were musicians and actors practicing on small stages. People were walking their dogs in the central park, where many large trees grew around a small pond. Some people were actually fishing. I saw gymnastics and martial arts and yoga type exercises with slow, difficult movements. There were even food vendors there, offering their latest creations—all for free!

Tesha and I tried one of the chef's inventions. He called it the medley roll. The first bite tasted like a hamburger on a bun, but as I worked my way to the end, the tastes changed to French fries and then to sweet cake. When Moora stopped to rest at the fountain, we relaxed in the grass, if that's what it was. It seemed more like the stuff growing on golf green, short and soft.

"In a couple days we begin examinations, but these examinations are not like what you would find in a normal school. We don't care about your I.Q.; we only want to get to know you more in detail, from your head to your heart." Moora said.

Examinations, no matter their purpose bored me, so I changed the subject.

"Moora, why is the ground always warm wherever we go?"

"It's the hydrogen propulsion system that we use to power the village. The water used to cool it is circulated under the entire village, including the streets and parks. It keeps us warm and melts any ice or snow. Come on I'll show you."

We headed to the transport and traveled a short distance to another platform and set of elevators. We took the elevators down further than before and came out in a large underground cavern with a huge round metal globe in the center. A man came forward and talked a short while with Moora. He gave us a guided tour and explained how the hydrogen was created through thermolysis and what the series of pipes were for. I must admit I understood very little of what this man said, but it was all fascinating regardless. After the tour Moora told us; "Tolemac had begun with mostly solar and wind generation systems, which was plenty for a small village but as the population increased they needed something more substantial and began experimenting with parabolics and methane before settling on hydrogen, which was created out of water and electricity, or electrolysis." She called hydrogen "God's great atom," and it would be years before I understood what she meant.

The next day Moora took us through the two of the many greenhouses throughout Tolemac. These greenhouses were large enough to get lost in and completely covered with canopies of webbing and a glass like material. Automated irrigation systems ran under the rich soil. Some plants grew in slurry-like soil; usually the vegetables that were in high demand and needed to be harvested quickly. The humidity in the greenhouses made my long hair stick to the back of my neck and there were many workers cultivating and harvesting. Tesha was beaming as she tried to control her excitement and continually asked Moora questions about everything from fertilization methods to seed gathering. I noticed that both of the greenhouses we visited had large rabbit populations penned up, and again it would be years before I understood how those rabbits played a role in the fertilization of the plants.

The following day we visited the observation tower, which was by far my favorite part of the tour. An observation deck with large telescopes let you observe a stranger riding a horse a mile away or you could examine the peak of a distant mountain. There were even telescopes strong enough to gaze at the Milky Way on a clear night. Even without the telescopes the tower gave a breathtaking 360 degree view of the gently rolling high plains and the distant windswept peaks. We visited some of the large fishponds that they used to raise fish for consumption, then a large farm and watched butter being made. We even rode bicycles around the outdoor park.

That night before bed, I asked Tesha if I was dreaming. It was truly hard for me to digest all that I was seeing. She answered,

"I never in my wildest dreams imagined that such a place could exist. I can't understand why my grandfather would ever want to leave such a place."

After the first day of examinations, I was perplexed. The questions seemed so easy: What's your favorite animal, mammal or bird? What are the colors in a rainbow? What's your favorite food? How would you describe love? What is an emotion or belief, or cultural beliefs? They even asked if I thought I was smart, handsome or pretty, and asked me to describe my attributes. The next day the questions got a bit harder with questions about my views on government and politics, my opinion of war and even death. They wanted to know my religious or cultural beliefs and asked me to explain them. They asked me to explain what God is and my understanding of evil and what an ego is. But the hardest question of all was when they asked me to explain human nature. I was stumped I must admit, I had no clue as to why they needed us to answer such crazy questions and began to think of it as some sort of a game.

The following day Moora brought us to the Center to unwind. We listened to live music in the amphitheater and sat in on a class on "love and emotion" that was being held by one of the members of the Star Delegation. Moora insisted that we stay since it was quite rare that a member of the delegation, and in particular Abigail, held class.

The class was unlike any other. The lady teaching the class was older, very fair and pale with long blond hair and a subtle demeanor. She was talking about unconditional love as we walked in. She approached us and looked at me closely with light blue eyes that seemed to go through me and said in a soft voice. "Welcome children. Please make yourself comfortable and please listen very carefully." Then continued staring at me as if she recognized me, then switching her gaze to Tesha who looked at me as if I held the answer. We all sat and listened in on her lecture. There were several people in the room with us, of all age groups and some were taking notes, including Moora. It was so new to me, but I still remember so much of what she said.

"Your heart is much more than a muscle that pumps blood. It is the emotional, vibrational and magnification center for love, a divine source of creation and manifestation, a biotransducer that's only limit is the mind's ability to empower it. The physical world that you see before you was indeed conceived out of love, which therefore makes it the most powerful creative force there is. The water that you see in the physical plane is what sustains the very life breath of all that exists, but to add it all up would be the equivalent of only one tear shed for the very love of creation."

"There will be perversions of this divine source in the minds of man, but they are only temporary, for love always returns to its source. Then there's science, full of the quantum theories of atoms, electrons and photons. Scientists will spend billions of dollars and countless hours of life as they ponder the external reasons behind the quantum leap or the collapse of the probability wave, but the mystery is really no mystery at all—just love. For light is the vehicle while love is the substance."

"There will be religions of old and new telling great stories of a supernatural and external force. A force not to be ignored or reckoned with, else a vile wrath shall overcome you. Once again, the external force they fear is only love."

"The great irony of love is that in spite of it, you can search the external corners of the universe trying to capture, dissect and explain it or create statues, institutions and cultures adoring it, while never truly getting any closer to it than the day you were born, for all you have done is to pervert it."

"It's all we are, our intellect and our emotion spring from its source like the fountain of youth. Physical matter itself is little more than light vibrations condensed to a lower threshold. It works through you and for you. All light vehicles, portals, and pathways that access divinity are only accessible through this cosmic vibration and this is why only the saints and sages with the purest hearts gain access to higher mind. The very God some fear is indeed love and light in its purest form. So now,

when someone asks you what's the matter, you will know to say,——
'Love!' For matter as you know it is little more than a vibrational
frequency of light sent from a cosmic triad of love."

"Perhaps you thought it something different——a romantic interlude
or courtyard courtship. Are these really examples of love in the truest
form? Not at all; these are emotions, simple feelings of want or
constituted need. Can emotions be a form of love? Of course they can,
and they are, as are all aspects of creation, but it's important to
understand that although emotion may contain love's energy for divine
manifestation, it's a universal misconception that emotion is all that
love is in its entirety, a simple commodity bought and sold upon every
emotional whim."

"When we romance something, someone, or some place in time, we
must first create an image or a vague idea of what it is that we find
emotionally stimulating, or the deep rooted vibration that comes in
want of physical expression. The physical body derives its experiences
from the senses of touch, taste, smell, hearing, and sight for aiding its
sensual and emotional stimulation. But it all starts with an idea
construct—the mental image that we breathe life into by adding color,
texture, and style until it becomes a fantasy or imaginative dream, and
this dream if extremely vivid can cause the emotional energy to gather
up the universal forces of love to manifest a physical facsimile."

"Unconditional love means then not to hold love back until you find
someone or something worthy of love, but rather to love all,
understanding that even the things you don't like stem from a belief,
attitude, or judgment. A trial by jury is ruled by the notion, Innocent
until proven guilty. I say; love all you see until you find a stronger
motive not to. For when we hate, anger, or envy, we stop the flow the
very energy that is struggling so hard to perfect itself. The problem in
most instances is that we are not tuning in and tuning up the misdirected
energy emanating from self."

"And now I think its time for a break." Abigail gave a small nod and
smile before gliding out the room.

I asked Tesha, "Do you think she meant that I should have loved
those bad men who almost killed us?"

Tesha said, "I don't know, Meno. I don't really know the subject well enough yet."

"How could she know if love vibrates or not?"

"I don't know Meno, ask her she's the teacher this is all news to me as well." Tesha said as she got up and proceeded to walk about the room.

Abigail soon returned and once again sat in front of the class on a tall wooden stool, "There are many emotions and all contain electromagnetic energy, which can be considered seed energy for the creative forces, but none are equal to the energy of love. When we combine love's divine energy with the desire force, we co-create whatever we are intuiting unconsciously and effortlessly. Unfortunately the negative emotions can also become seed energy. Fear and hate are good examples since humanity has all but worshiped these. Judging from the current state of our nation, it goes without saying that these are indeed part of our misdirected culture"

"There is really only one true energy. All other emotions that seem to be at odds with the emotion of love, such as fear, hate, anger, or sadness are born out of the very substance they seem to oppose. You see when we fear, it is usually that we are fearing the loss of something we love. It may be your life or way of life, but it will still come back to love. Hate and anger work the same way, but sadness is slightly different. You see sadness and sorrow come from the illusion that you have lost someone or something close to you, when it is just a temporary frame of reference."

"Your heart is symbolic of love and your emotional center, and this is no illusion. The heart is like a huge resonating transformer waiting for you to push the on buttons of desire. So from now on you should all be self-evaluating these feelings and analyze them, so as to put them into the proper context. Then you will soon enjoy a life far greater, when you understand that these feelings can come and go with greater compassion and understanding as well as mutual benefit to you and the world you create."

"Tolemac was founded on different ideals, ideals that are not fear based or materialistic. We don't have a regimented, adulterated way of living, learning, or working. It is what we consider a natural way of life. We all keep busy taking care of each other without fear of losing our jobs, without fear of going hungry or not having the opportunity for personal growth through education and evolution."

"We try to work in harmony with nature and its bountiful resources, for we understand that we are not separate from her and all that we do to harm her only comes back to harm us, for she is a beautiful expression of love. A good example of this neglect from our past ignorance of these truths would of course be the heavy use of fossil fuels, nuclear energy and chemical and biogenetic catastrophe, all contributing to global destruction and contamination. It has only been within the last twenty years that our oceans went dead from pollution; over-fishing, and wild temperature swings. The polar ice caps are now melting so quickly that we all seem to be living on borrowed time and this clock is in the hands of the very nature we took for granted for so long."

"Perhaps now you can see the importance of loving your environment down to the last blade of grass to the smallest insect hidden there. Now, before we can love all that surrounds us we must learn to love ourselves. This is not as hard as we make it out to be. First we must take a good look at who we are, a self-examination of sorts. We should see the grand beauty and perfection that we are if we first lose all the judgments, beliefs, and attitudes that have somehow obstructed the beautiful view. We must listen quietly to the emotional self, our inner barometer that is more a part of us than the largest of the physical brains. You know that your heart has more knowledge than any physical brain could ever hope to, but it doesn't work on logic, it works on passion and knowing. How can you rationalize with a vibrational energy that is pure and unadulterated, especially when it's a similar vibration that brought you here in the first place?"

"If you had a body that was emotionally bankrupt and could never feel pleasure or pain, love or loss, or desire and disgrace, you would then feel, or rather think that there must be something more to life than living like a machine. It is those very energy currents that we call emotions that give physical life meaning through experience and opportunities for growth through sense based expression.

However, some of us tend to get a bit carried away with emotions, instead of identifying with them, learning from them, and using them as a positive tool for achievement, awareness, and creativity. We sometimes let emotions pull us around like a big dog on a short leash, dragging us through the corn and the cabbage. Now there may be an element of fear and doubt lurking behind such problems, but that will be the topic of next month's class. I hope to see you all here. Thank you all for coming, and go with love and light. Good afternoon!"

Abigail slowly meandered out of the room, while I tried to process what she had said. Most of the words were unfamiliar, but I did seem to follow where she was going with all of this. I decided that I knew even less about love now than I did before we sat down.

When Moora took us back to our quarters that afternoon we were very quiet, deep in thought about we had heard in Abigail's class, as we whipped down the subway as if on air. I realized I had a great deal to learn about Tolemac and this thing called life.

12

TINY, THE WIZARD OF TOLEMAC

It was the day of rest and reflection, which was sort of like a Sunday. Moora was meeting us at the center for the ceremony and eulogy for the fallen guard. We spied a few large Magpies pecking the ground as we walked through the common grounds in route to the center, they did not fly away as we approached, just stared quietly with their ebony eye's; I wondered if they were tame. Moora explained the strange dwellings that everyone inhabited; they looked like giant ant hills. Tesha said they reminded her of huge Kivas.

The pods, as they were called, were circular earthen mounds with small holes, which were windows. When I got to the top of the hillside I could see that the center of the pod was covered by a round clear dome and all of the dwelling units encircled a central open space. Moora told us that each adobe pod was like a tall building within the ground, with many levels reaching deep into the earth. Each pod had its own center in miniature and they were very active places to be.

Upon arriving we found the Center very crowded. We squeezed in as close as we could, right behind a hundred guards standing in ranks in their bright dress uniforms. They all stood with their arms crossed on their chests; the way Unkar and his men saluted, while an elder guard of higher rank spoke over them. I could see Unkar among the guard there, as well as Michael, but Manuel was not visible. On the ground before them were five mock bodies wrapped in linen to represent those who had fallen in battle. After the captain of the guard finished his speech a member of the Star Delegation led the procession. He said words over each of these victims and then invited all of us to do the same.

It took an hour before we were able to say our formal goodbyes. Tesha kneeled before the bodies and began to quiver as she held her hands over her face, with the memory of Lance and the others still so fresh that one could almost smell the blood. She soon rushed out alone. I felt strange looking at those figures in linen, almost guilty. Images of the men and their fate swept across my mind. Was I really worth such a cost? A sullen, hollow feeling overcame me and the tears came without warning as my now trembling lips spread to gasp, letting enter the salty dew.

Unkar came over after the ceremony and put his arm around me as if he knew the very thoughts going through my head. "Please do not feel responsible for those men. If anyone should feel responsible it should be me. Accepting responsibility would be admitting guilt of wrongdoing, but since there is nothing wrong with defending oneself against man and nature accepting such guilt would be a dishonor to those who have fallen. We should remember them for how they lived and shared their lives with us. Death in the line of duty is an honor for a guard. One day you will understand this."

Moora interrupted; "We should go, seeing this sort of thing may be a bit much. Tomorrow I need you sharp as a tack for when you meet Tiny."

"Who?" I replied.

"Tiny, the wizard of Tolemac. You are to begin his classes tomorrow morning."

"Wizard? Aren't wizard's just made-up imaginary people from old stories of castles and dungeons?"

"Yes," said Moora, "and Tiny is no different. You will know what I mean after the coming week is over. You will enjoy Tiny. There's really no one quite like him anywhere."

That night, I tossed and turned with images of small wrinkled wizards flying around a classroom, with a high pitched laugh and

108

wearing a long frock coat and a funny hat that resembled a flower pot. I finally got this character out of my head when the reoccurring scene of all those linen-clad bodies at the center began to replay. When I awoke, I somehow felt more tired than before I went to bed.

That morning Moora escorted us a short distance from our temporary quarters to a low cinderblock structure with a long dimly lit hallway.

"Go into the seventh room on the left and wait inside for your lesson," were her only instructions.

We could see the doorway as we walked down the hall, a bright white light emanated from it. As we walked in there were three others already sitting in the class; one old man and two young girls who looked like sisters. The younger one looked to be about my age. She had a smile that seemed pasted on her unwilling face.

We took seats in the front of the class with the others and I looked around. The bright white walls and ceiling made my eyes squint, while the floor was pitch black. A short desk with a very short chair, alongside a short podium, sat in front of the class. They all looked very old, but the scale of the furniture was almost child like. Suddenly the air was pierced by a high pitched voice.

"Good morning class!"

Out from behind the small podium came a small wrinkled old man with a funny hat, long gray hair and a beard that almost touched his feet. His old frock was fastened by a rope, like some medieval monk. His large grin and dark, beady eyes looked almost animated.

I nearly fell off my chair when I realized that he was the same wizard that was in my dreams last night? *That's impossible!* I thought.

The small wrinkled old man came forward, examining all of us as if we were experiments in a jar.

"Hello, my children. My name is Enoch, but most here refer to me as Tiny. I have come here today to help all of you pry open those ironclad minds of yours. On your desk you have a pad and pencil to take notes, and to write down any of your questions for the question and answer period at the end of the day."

I was sure I had just overlook the pad and pencil on my desk, which were very much in front of me now, although Tesha had the same surprised look on her face as I.

Tiny continued, "We will discuss many things over the next five days. Some of these may shock you; some you will refuse to believe, but most of it you already know, beyond those palpitating little hearts. I want to get to know each of you, but first I will tell you a little about myself. My age has no reference here, so we will skip it as well as where I was born, or when and where I came from. The only thing that is relevant here is what you see with your own eyes and what you hear with your own ears—and most importantly what you feel!"

"I have been with Tolemac, or perhaps I should say Tolemac has been with me from the beginning, when it was just a thought in its infancy. I crystallized and fertilized this star seed to help this specie of fallen man once again, to perhaps create another opportunity for you to prove yourselves worthy of existence and evolution."

"I am small by your standards but very big by other forms of reference. Some regard me as a wizard or magician. This I consider an insult, but if this is the best they can do to understand me, then I will just have to live with it. I am a multidimensional being, capable of existing on many planes of what you know to be time and space. I have no true physical existence, only vibratory energy held in place by a thought form through an electromagnetic frequency of light parallel to yours. Perhaps we will discuss this more in detail as your capabilities for understanding such matters increases in due time."

"Now let's see who we have here with us today, please stand as I call on you and give your name, age, and where you're from, as well as a little bit about yourself."

Tesha was called on first. She stated her name, age, and that she was from Washington, then sat down quickly. She kept staring at Tiny with her mouth partially open, as if she could not quite grasp it all. He then pointed to the other two girls, who said they were from a place called Nova Scotia. The youngest one was Sarah, who was eleven with lots of freckles, long auburn braids, and a strange accent. Her sister Kate was fourteen and had never seen a whale like her father had. Their home was under water. Their family escaped with another on an old sailboat that made it to the Gulf of Mexico before sinking. They survived on an abandoned oil rig until they could make a raft out of oil drums and paddle the long distance to shore. Their Uncle Vince and Auntie Helen were Tolemac residents of twenty years.

When Tiny called on me, I told him that I was from a small group of islands off the coast of Alaska. "My home was also consumed by the sea, but I saw a whale after my father and others from the village hunted it down about four years ago. Even then it was a rare occurrence."

I looked behind me where the old man had been sitting when we came in, so he could know it was his turn, but he was gone.

Tiny said, "I'm deeply sorry for all of your hardships and losses, but I am truly glad that you all managed to beat the odds and make it to your new home at Tolemac. Now you may begin learning how to create a better tomorrow for yourselves."

Tiny pulled some papers out of thin air and flipped through them. He looked at me and said, "Meno, the answer you gave on your examination regarding the nature of man was brief but accurate. Man's nature is indeed goodness! This simple premise gets overshadowed by layers of doubt, fear, greed, and envy, but even with all those negative qualities the goodness within still rises to the top in most of us when needed."

"Now, Tesha, your answer defining the meaning of time is absolutely correct as well as absolutely incorrect. You see, time measured by seconds, minutes, and hours as well as days, months, and years is a correct analogy; however, the idea of the existence of time is but an illusion manufactured for the purpose of physical reference only, so you may organize your past, present, and future in a 'timely' manner—He-hee!"

"Let's for a moment take the belief of time out of context, shall we? Do birds know what day it is? Do squirrels care if it is six o'clock? Would our hair still turn gray if there were no instrument to tell us that we were old? Perhaps we could live twice as long if no one ever told us what our life expectancy was. Do you think a clock should tell you when to eat or rest, or should you listen instead to your body? Here at Tolemac you will find no clocks or calendars of any kind, and although this may seem a bit strange, in 'time,' you will learn the benefits. Nature carries with her at all times an internal clock that never misses a beat! Isn't that neat—He-hee!"

"Now then, Sarah had answered the question, 'what is a belief,' by stating that a belief is a story someone told you, a story we believe is true. This answer is remarkably correct, and you my child get a gold star."

Tiny took his hand from behind his back, revealing a brilliant gold star brightly twinkling on a short rod as if it were a star out of the very heavens above.

Sarah grabbed the rod with a face full of joy and wonder. We all watched as the star's energy slowly burned out until all that remained was a smoldering rod in Sarah's hand.

"Sorry child, but stars burn up in your atmosphere —He-he-hee!" Tiny said with a large smile and high pitched giggle.

"Now then, Sarah's answer was a good one because it not only was simple, it was also true. You see beliefs are indeed created by the stories we hear and accept as truth, and this is where the trouble begins. Truth as you know it will not always set you free but can imprison you behind the walls of your beliefs. Let me elaborate a bit here:

"There was this German child whom we shall call Albert. Now Albert was a very slow child, or so the people thought—a bit dyslexic the parents assumed. Teachers said that that there was little hope for little Albert, who seemed so far removed from the classroom. His peers assumed that this absent minded little boy could indeed be troubled; he was expelled from school with little prospects."

"One day a young man from the local college came to visit Albert's family, having no prior knowledge of Albert's handicaps in the field of learning. The two had an in-depth conversation about science. The young man was so impressed with Albert that he left him a special book on the subject of physics. Upon his next visit to Albert's house, the young man found that Albert had studied and understood with incredible insight the entire volume, so he gave him yet another book to read. Albert once again surprised the young student by learning the entire book's theory and application and even began to hypothesize his own ideas.

"Today Albert Einstein is known as the man behind the theory of relativity and the unified field, and one of the greatest scientific minds of all time. The belief that he was inadequate almost caused him to take a different path, and what a shame it would have been for science—and mankind."

"Your heads are so very full of beliefs about what you cannot do, with plenty of self doubts about your abilities, and all because of some story you were led to believe. Well then, it is time to set the story straight, and clear up all this nonsense about who you are not! As if you forgot —He-he-hee!"

"Now, Kate, in your answer to the question regarding evil, you stated that evil comes from the devil. I will tell you now with great certainty that no such entity exists, nor will ever exist. This would be a good example of a belief that has no basis. There are no red men with horns on their heads waiting for you in your mythical Hades; however, there is something that I consider just as bad, and that is ignorance. Ignorance can be considered evil due to false assumptions that stem from false beliefs. These false beliefs can lead to alternate realities; however these types of alternate reality are as weak as the minds that created them."

"The absence of love and light can also be considered a personal hell, for when we are without love and light, our negative aspects of mind can become dominant energies. But if you are a loving being, which you all are or else you would not be here, you have nothing to worry about since like-energy attracts like. Now if the energy that you are sending out is something less than positive, then that is exactly what you will receive in return…something less."

"You see, my children, life is just a big game, but knowing the rules of the game makes it much more fun to play. Now I would like for you all to play another game using the 'image-nation."

Tiny wrote this word with his finger in the air and to our amazement sparkling letters appeared momentarily, then soon faded away.

"The image-nation is something like your imagination, the place where we create and fantasize. We shall refer to it as the image-nation from now on, since the old word has taken on an improper meaning that does not do justice to this area of creativity."

"Now before we get started, I would like you all to understand that the image-nation is a magical place where all of our stories can become real, so we would not want to create a bad story. We must search our hearts for the story that we really want to create; the story about your life! What we would like to do with it, how would we want to live it, where you may want to live, and with whom, all the way down to the smallest details about the animals, plants etc. Now remember, you must not set limitations to any of your creations. Anything goes in the image-nation."

"You are now all to become wonderful artists! Your creativity is the paintbrush, your level of emotion will leave you with either vibrant colors of intensity or drab shades of inequity. The canvas in which you may color your life is the mind itself so size should not be a problem, so be bold and daring and let intuition and feelings fill the landscape. Please don't look at it as work, or you may stifle yourselves. Have fun with it, like a child playing with dust particles in the morning light. This way we lubricate with joy those gears rusted from years of fears, my dears — He-he-hee."

"Now, you may take the pad and pencil with you and work anywhere you like. This is today's lesson, now I will answer your questions."

I raised my hand eagerly, and when he called upon me I asked why he calls love, love and light?

"Because my boy, one will never be found without the other, for light is the vehicle and love is the substance!"

Now Tesha had her hand up, and when he called upon her she asked," What do you consider light?"

"Without light there would only be night, there would be no sight nor guards of plight, nor fight, nor sinister smite, not even the right. 'So let there be light,' declared God with all his might —He-he-hee!"

"Now, now my dear, I was just having a bit of humor at your expense for humor is the great equalizer bringing all consciousness to the forefront uniting it in expression. The truth of the matter is that light is not a concept that is easily understood at the mental level that humanity is currently experiencing, but I will try to put it into laymen's terms so you have a mental picture for your physically oriented minds. Imagine if you will a huge ocean engulfing the universe in which all material substratum exist, yet this is not an ocean of water but rather one of light; not light as it relates to color but rather in invisible wave or frequency, yet not particle in nature but the fertilizer for its existence; Just as sunlight provides the plants electromagnetic fertilizer for photosynthesis. Now this subtle energy is an energy that knows, for within this awareness and pure potential lies a latent yet powerful and all knowing source. From this universal mind of intelligence all matter is born for without the source there would be no matter, for matter is born out of love and its desire for expression, which leads to the self perpetuating inertia of creation itself and the evolution of planets and all life forms herein."

"You see my children there really is a unified field of intelligence or consciousness and any separations from it are self imposed, and all past and present thoughts and experiences remain in it like memories in an ocean of mind, and just as you can easily recall experiences that carry the gravity of emotional energy so to with the universal mind."

"Now all life forces are aware on one degree or another but there are principal beings such as humans that are aware that they are aware, which means that they are utilizing more light, and that there capacitance for such light is far greater than they may know as well. This means that they, although physical in nature, are not only in the light but of the light and connected to the source making them true light beings with unlimited potential, so the goal here at Tolemac is to remind you all of this important fact."

"I will hope to see you all back here tomorrow morning with your renderings. Good day children, good day," Tiny said as he walked off into a white fog that mysteriously appeared behind him, soon vanishing with it.

We all left the bright classroom and walked down the long hall. I was numb yet alert still not quite sure what just happened. I headed to my quarters to be alone in thought as the others went their own ways. What kind of a person was this small wrinkled old man and what manner of teaching was this? To create a story for ourselves and use whatever means possible, on a canvas of mind. It sounded so hopeless. What was the benefit, I wondered.

I searched my thoughts for a reasonable story, one that I would truly enjoy and one that I would love to be in. I thought up a story of piloting a huge rocket ship, flying around the universe meeting different types of beings, learning from these distant beings of better ways to live and grow, ways that did not disrupt nature. Maybe I could find another planet to immigrate to, but the thought crossed my mind that immigrating to a new planet would be a waste of time if our destructive ways never changed. As I lay back I dreamed up my imaginary life in vivid detail and color. My juices began to flow as adrenalin began to pump up the support of my emotionally vibrant experience, while the images floating across my mind were taking on a life of their own. I for a split second found myself in the cockpit of a large craft falling towards earth, the experience was so realistic it caused my whole body to be jerked awake. Had I just been dreaming, my heart was pounding the inner walls of my chest and my face was covered in sweat. I realized that I had my first taste of the image-nation and was now hungry for more.

Tesha was also in my heart, but I could not bear to let her know—not now at least. The time was just not right. How could the affection of a ten year old do anything but flatter in the weakest sense of the word. The next day as we walked into class, Tiny was sitting in mid-air as if a chair supported him. We all ran over to try and find wires or something. He just sat there laughing with that trademark "he-he-he-he!" like an overgrown child. Once we took our seats, he started the lecture.

"The stories you've created are personal. Therefore I will not require you to tell the rest of the class, but I will review them later and return them to you tomorrow."

"I trust you all had pleasant dreams and are hopefully still having them. Yesterday's exercise was just that—an exercise, however an important one. I want you to start getting used to the idea of creating with your image-nation. This is not something to be taken lightly. No, no, no! This is very, very important."

"Now the stories that you have begun are indeed rough drafts and will require more concentration and fine tuning until they make harmonious vibrations, like that of a finely crafted flute. You should dwell within your image-nation for a short while each morning or evening, adding a bit here and removing a bit there, until it becomes as much a part of you as the nose on your face."

Tiny pointed to his nose and it began to grow, and grow, and grow, until it was at least a foot long. It snapped back with such force that we all jumped and started to wail with laughter. Even Tiny joined in.

"You see, the mind is a wondrously beautiful instrument of creation. We are all painting upon the canvas called life every waking and sleeping moment, without even the slightest idea that we continually surround ourselves with our own artistic endeavors, yet our thoughts are like seeds awaiting cultivation."

"Let me illustrate: if you are continually wishing for apples and know that only apples will do your heart justice, you may wake one day to find an apple tree in your garden. The mechanical means to its materialization are of little consequence. If you are continually loathing apples, however, you may find that same tree in your garden as well. Why is that? Because both thought catered emotions will still bring out that artistic talent in you. Both thoughts are composed of the same mindful energy. The only difference is that there was a change in attitude, or belief, although both apple trees were created with a thought carried on the winds of emotional desire. The cosmic energies of creation will not discriminate between morals or reasons—that would be judgment, but it is you who are constantly reaping all that you sow."

"Let me clear something up for you before I go much further. The mind I am referring to is not that little wet noodle between those funny looking appendages you call ears."

I couldn't stop a laugh from bursting out of my mouth—but I relaxed when I realized the whole class had sunk into giggles with me. Tiny waited for our chuckles to subside, then continued.

"No, the mind I speak of is what you refer to as the soul and spirit, but without mind there is no need for the latter. Now I know that this sounds strange to you, but it's just word symbolism that has become confused. You see, at one time the ancient Greeks referred to the soul as the psyche, but now the psyche is referred to as the mind, or perhaps it was the brain... Regardless, it's all word symbol confusion. Why would you want to confuse the mind with something you call the bottom of your shoe—the sole? This could lead to great confusion indeed!"

"The brain that you have been led to believe is the mind is more like a delicate instrument of reception for the mind's incredible resources while maintaining bodily functions. It also acts as a fulcrum to balance the emotions that can run rampant within your physical body as well as regulate the powerful glands that help color your world. What I'm trying to say is that the brain is no more your mind than your shoe is your foot. That is, if we of course subtract the soul from the foot, or perhaps it's the foot from the soul. Then again the sole of your shoe would be an appropriate metaphor for how humanity tramples all over their true beingness—He hee! In any event, if this is not clear make a note and we shall elaborate using a whole new set of symbols. Phew, I'm sure glad that one's over."

"Now I know much of what I tell you may seem at first to be a bitter pill. This is quite normal, considering that you have spent your entire life learning the opposite from trusted teachers and loved ones and are not about to jump ship so far from port. It would be a bit easier if the seas were not so deep, but it's the leap of faith one must take if we are to expand our awareness to higher levels."

"Now some of you may have heard of the word consciousness before. The word is no doubt used in many different methodologies. So perhaps it would be better to de-fine the true meaning of the word and then try to avoid it so we don't confuse matters. Being conscious is being aware or understanding whatever it is you're into; however; this is superficial since there are several different levels of understanding and awareness. Consciousness may be likened to something slightly different, like a sense of who you are or perhaps an acute, sensitive, spiritual nature. Both consciousness and being conscious, however, point to awareness."

"Then there's unconscious, which may indicate someone who took a nasty bump on the head and is lying there incoherent, or someone who is simply unaware. The there's awareness, but of what? Maybe you will achieve an expanded awareness of some hidden mystery and become content sitting in the rocking chair of your mind and patting yourself on the back. This all comes back to our beliefs, assumptions, and attitudes. Which are self-perpetuating filters of light or awareness, typically born out of emotional experiences and ego centered habits. It is these filters that keep us from understanding our awareness of the truth, and within their matrix are the ego's close allies, being greed, envy, lust, fear anger, loathing, control and many others."

"Our entire level of understanding is screened to fit our individual parameters of thought. Now if your awareness level keeps you opening doors and asking questions you should be well on your way. Still, there may be one problem with this equation— which doors are you opening and what questions are you asking? These will be dictated by current assumptions and beliefs."

"Now let's illustrate this to give one a better understanding. There is a one year old babe who is crawling around and saying gaga goo-goo. There is a ten year old boy saying that he loves one year old babies. Then there is the fast asleep mother of both of these children. Can you guess which of these subjects is more aware?"

No one raised their hand as he looked around for an answer.

"The correct answer would be the one year old babe. Why the babe? Because the babe has not yet been exploited by the assumptions and beliefs of those around him. Let me elaborate: the mother while sleeping is only aware of her idle thoughts, while the ten year old boy is consumed by the feeling for the one year old babe. The babe however is in a state of pure joy, wonder and happiness that is not associated with any known symbol. This state of being is a natural state derived directly from the source—the universal mind or light; just because the babe cannot speak with your symbolic gestures does not make the babe ignorant. The babe has plenty of reference material available through its mind. The babe's ignorance will begin much later, usually around age five. This is when the persona begins to develop. Some refer to the personality as the ego, and this is another area of self that must be well understood if we are to begin to pry open your ironclad minds."

"The ego, or personality, is like a character we develop in the great play called life. It is the bodies escort into the physical world. All human physical bodies are represented by one, and each are as different as the physical particles that make your worlds. The ego temporarily separates you from your all-knowing self; your true essence, so that you can experience the physical world like a child in an amusement park, full of wonder and amazement. But in the earliest of times the ego was necessary for survival, when the rational part of self was in its infancy, and although there has been much growth in this area for humans there is still a long way to go before the ego is understood enough to control it adequately."

"Here at Tolemac there is something called the Imputable Impetus. It is our declaration of self independence. To us, that would be *ego* independence. You will hear others refer to it often, for it is full of the truth and wisdom of the people of Tolemac. One of the statements of the Imputable Impetus states, 'Truth is the only separation of man and mind; ego is the only separation of mind and truth.'

"There are ways to overcome the ego's powerful grip, and the first one is to be aware of it. The second is to not try to overthrow it like some small governmental coup. The ego serves many purposes in life, and you would be boring without one, without its many dramatic expressions and artistic forms. It is much better to watch your ego as if you're watching something external from yourself, and then learn from it by noticing what makes it respond so intensely to external stimuli. The best way to do this is to acknowledge emotional responses to such stimuli and question whether they came from one of the many ego allies or from one of your true essence whose allies are compassion, empathy, selfless acts, and unconditional love."

"Most of these types of responses can be traced back to assumptions and beliefs that you have been exposed to and are now part of your personality in the form of accepted truths."

"This shall take a concerted effort, with lots of practice, but in the end it will be a most worthy endeavor. Form a wonderful partnership with your ego by taking advantage of all its strengths. At the same time, dissolve those weaknesses that stem from false assumptions and fears that have undermined the ego's ability to be the pure vehicle for expression that it truly is. After all, you created the beast, so keep it on a short leash before it bites you or your neighbor!"

Tesha burst out laughing, but I was too busy struggling to understand Tiny's lesson.

"Now, there is one more area to cover before we break for the day with our assignment, and that is truth and understanding. You have heard it mentioned many times, and perhaps it's time I elaborate a bit on this subject."

"The Imputable Impetus claims that a life of ignorance and despair is a life in vain; a life of truth and understanding is a life— Enjoy."

"A truth is a timeless component of all realities, hidden or not. Its meaning is an inherent aspect of *mind* that is unarguable, unquestionable, and undeniable. There are physical laws that govern all nature; these could be called truths of nature. But there are forces behind all of nature that are also considered laws or fundamental truths. This is a bit too technical for you at this time, but as you learn here at Tolemac, they will become part of your curriculum."

"I will tell you though that your *mind* is fully aware of these truths, and that sometimes truths are confirmed through the body with feelings and intuition, something we will go into more detail about tomorrow."

"I sense that many of you are drowning in the sea of words and need an adjustment period. Why don't we break for your questions before the assignment?"

Kate was the first to eagerly raise her hand. "Is there such a thing as death?"

Tiny replied, "Yes, the physical body does return to the sea of matter from which it was born, and many false beliefs die with it. However, after a brief period of transition, the ego loses its independence, and we are once again *mindful*."

Now Tesha raised her hand. She asked Tiny, "If the spirit was considered to be the mind, then what is your definition of the Great Spirit?"

121

Tiny replied, "Your many meanings and symbols of the word spirit have a tendency to obscure the real meaning. Let me illustrate: You, Tesha, are a very spirited young lady, and I know, because of this spirit you have, you don't like being referred to as a child. But you must not take this so personally. Here at Tolemac, all the student body (which is the majority of people here) are considered children until they become self-realized beings, at one with themselves, true participants in their own evolution."

"Then there are the spirits in the attic that keep us awake at night. These are sometimes personalities that refuse to relinquish their identities; they hang on to the physical tooth and nail by the means of emotional energy. They are stuck from the assumptions and beliefs that have become their alternate reality."

"The spirit of your body is on occasion humanity's idea of some sort of abstract energy or identity separate from mind, but this is an illusion. There are no separations from mind other than the self created ego, which is really only a temporary assumption. Now calling the mind 'spirit' is just another way of getting lost in the confusion of word symbolism once again. If you look at yourself in a mirror you see a reflection of your physical self and it is only the physical self you see. In truth you are casting many local shadows of a similar nature but of a higher frequency vibration, not visible in your light spectrum; however, the reflection in the mirror would not be seen if not for the light, and it is through the Father's light that your spirit brings forth the reflection of your soul or mind."

"Now, the great-spirit is just one culture's way of saying God, the ultimate presence behind all, that is."

Now Sarah was raising her hand. "If there is no devil, who is Lucifer in the Bible and isn't he evil?"

Tiny replied, "An Angel who was born out of, and composed of love and compassion. There are many fallen luminaries of the brotherhood of light. Some are the requirement for in the world of duality there need be a nemesis. Some are beings that alienated themselves from the Father's master plan with their own agendas and by taking matter into their own hands when it was unlawful to do so. The stories in the Bible are always left to one's own interpretation. Let me illustrate with biblical verses of Lucifer from Isaiah the prophet:

"'Thou sealest up the sum, full of wisdom and beauty."

"Thou art the anointed cherub that covereth; and I have set thee so. Thou wast perfect in thy ways from the day that thou wast created, till iniquity was found in thee. But says the prophet, "Thine heart was lifted up because of thy beauty, thou hast corrupted thy wisdom by reason of thy brightness."

"Of course there is more verbiage, but as you can see, there are many possible contradictions even with these few verses. Also, a fallen member of the cherubim is not always as evil as one assumes. They just get a bit big for their britches; however, there are those who like to manipulate and control species of incarnate form when they're able. You must understand that these were beings who had a great deal of control before their fall and maintain a great deal of knowledge, while no longer permitted to incarnate into the physical realms, but can use there *evol* ways against man, to keep you from your evolutionary birthright; from ascension to higher dimensions of *mind*; for once you do, they will not have dominion over you, and will be powerless among their pantheism. Just do not attract them; keep love in your hearts and minds, and you will always be a step ahead of them. It's that simple."

"The Bible is a trusted historical record of many a creed and I will not try to remove words that have become very sacred and special to many sectors of humanity that would be injurious and accomplish little. But the fact remains that the meanings of words change over time, so without interrogating the prophets it's sometimes hard to tell the meaning cloaked in barriers of language and time."

"Now the second part of Sarah's question referred to the word evil, which is love spelled backward: e-v-o-l. That's exactly what it represents, a sort of backwards love, or the absence of the love and light of the Father. It could be the love of revenge, or envy carried to extremes, or even an overabundance of smothering affection that suffocates the life out of the one being manipulated by it. But evol's basis is not so sinister as one may believe. It's just love, confused and misdirected by the power of a misunderstood emotion."

"In the physical world, there are the physical laws of polarities, or opposites. In order for *evol*utionary growth we must have the ability to choose, and that choice must consist of opposites: good, bad; light, dark; love, evol. It will not always be easy to choose, but without these choices the cream would never rise to the top and your growth would suffer. This is why some might be led to assume that one of the Father's most beloved angels is so sinister, where sinister and evol would seem to meet the requirement for duality."

"There are many texts here at Tolemac, some religious in nature and others that are equally as beneficial, from great spokesmen that came for the purpose of teaching. But nothing can be gained in truth that has not already been acknowledged by mind. The world is full of many ideologies and many institutions of religious beliefs. If you feel yourself being willed into one, it would benefit you to learn of it, after you have gained an objective viewpoint by becoming self aware and mind full, then and only then can you interpret the knowledge handed down through the ages. The Imputable Impetus states, 'forcing a system or belief upon the minds of your contemporaries is contemptuous.'

"Since that is the end of all the questions, we will stop for today. Your assignment for this afternoon will be simple. Rewrite your story with your new level of awareness considered and give me the definitions of the following: What is mind and what is ego. Have a good day!"

He was gone, within the blink of an eye, but to where? We searched the front of the class and found nothing. I was confused as we walked down the hall and asked Tesha how it was possible to disappear into thin air?

She replied, "I don't think he's real. I once read about a computer generated hologram at the World's Fair in 2020. The hologram was so incredible that people would say excuse me when they got too close to it, thinking that it was a real person. The hologram had some flaws though. One was that it couldn't carry on a convincing conversation unless it was close to the audio controller, and it became almost see through in sunlight."

I told her that Tiny was so close to me when he introduced himself that I could feel his breath when he talked.

"Maybe he's a good magician. I saw a magician make a horse disappear once," she replied as we walked out of the building.

Moora was waiting there for us. "Do you want to go to the enrichment baths with me?" she asked. "You can do our assignments later."

Our ears perked up at the sound of such a place and we eagerly agreed.

13
THE ENRICHMENT BATHS

We all changed and met back at the shuttle platform. Moora said that we had been working too hard and we needed a break to recharge. And in Tolemac, the baths were the best way to do that.

We arrived at the large doors that entered the cavernous structure from underground, as we strolled through; an immense cloud of steam engulfed us. There was a large circle of rock walls, lined with tiled benches and floors with vibrant colors and mosaic designs. In the center was a large clam shaped wading pool with seating along the perimeter. There was a beautiful center island with a large palm tree growing half the height of the structure.

Tesha asked Moora why the water was cloudy as they both removed their clothes, baring themselves before me. I tried not to stare but was in the state of shock until Tesha elbowed me. I looked around and could see that there were others in the pool that were also nude. I waited until there was no one looking before throwing my clothes off and jumping in and cowering in a corner.

Moora lay back in the water and said, "Can you feel the whitish powder on the bottom? That silt is a mixture of rich clays and sodium bicarbonate, which is another way of saying baking soda."

The baking soda and mud squished through my toes as I waded through it. I thought it was a bit odd to be soaking in mud and a baking powder, but the water's warmth immediately consumed me. I stared upward in a constant float, gazing aimlessly through the vapors. At the very top of the building was a skylight of a pyramidal design but more faceted, like a prism. A huge crystal orb hung from the apex on a copper braided line that continued downward into and through a large inverted funnel, also made of copper. The copper braid ended in the center of the island, where there were other devices. I asked Moora what all this was for.

"It is an ion accumulator and that's all I care to know at the moment. You will have to ask Sergy about how it works, I get lost in his technical explanations."

"Who's Sergy?" I asked Moora now floating on her back with her eye's closed.

"Sergy Ivanovitch is the director of science here at Tolemac. You will meet him when you are ready to learn what he has to say. Now no more questions, just relax your body and mind."

We spent nearly an hour in the bath. When we left, my entire body was tingling, the way certain parts of my body used to on the island when I had been thawing after too much exposure to the cold.

"I am definitely coming back. I feel like I have a new body," Tesha said.

Moora told us to go rinse off and change and get ready to accompany her to the Center for dinner, so we went back to our rooms to prepare ourselves. Upon arriving there music filled the air. A group of what Moora called minstrels roamed the park with violins and one mandolin. They sang and played music I had never heard. We loaded our plates at the food bar and made our way to a bench under a large aspen tree. As we ate we watched several small children playing at the edge of the pond giggling as they played with toy boats. A tall, slender man with a rather large dark mustache came over and began talking to Moora. She stood up and introduced him to Tesha and I. His name was Artemus, and he was a mentor. Before departing he gave me a smile and said, "I will be seeing you soon, Mr. Olikai."

I thought it strange that he knew my last name when I never gave it. The next morning we were back in Tiny's class and he was sleeping in midair when we walked in, but Sarah's giggling woke him.

Tiny quickly fell to his feet and yelled, "Good Morning! We have a lot to cover today, so I hope you are all awake and listening closely. Please pass your assignments forward. Today we will be exploring that wonderful world of emotions, feelings, and intuitions.

Now, let us first talk a bit about feeling. A doctor would probably tell you that feelings of pain are caused by sensitivities of a certain part of the body, sending nerve impulses to the neural transmitters in your brain. The transmitters in turn ring the alarm bells that pain has been identified in a sector of the body, which must be pulled back before the entire body comes under attack. But I am not a doctor, and that's not the type feeling I am talking about. Everyone knows enough to keep their sensitive fingers out of the fire; that's animal instinct, but do you know how to keep that sensitive ego out of the fire?"

"Understanding the ego is a hard mountain to climb, but if we are well equipped it makes it a lot easier. The first thing we must understand about feelings and emotions is that they are, once again, the overwhelming response to assumptions and beliefs that lie hidden within the matrix of your personality, or ego. Let me illustrate:"

"Let's say there is a monkey who lives in a tree. We'll call him Jo Jo." Tiny now imitating a monkey—screwing his face into scrunched features and bouncing in ape like ways. We all began to laugh as Tiny went ape up and down the isle.

"This monkey loves bananas but has none in his tree. But Na Na, the monkey in the tree around the corner has more than she can possibly eat. Jo Jo will not go to Nana's tree because his mother told him that the monkeys in Nana's tree were crazy and would become violent. So Jo Jo would go far out of his way to get his bananas. One day a bad storm hit when Jo Jo was far, far away hunting for bananas. It was raining so hard that Jo Jo got lost in his panic to get away from the loud thunder. Lightning struck so close it caused Jo Jo to quickly climb the nearest tree, fearing for his very life. Jo Jo was very sad, lonely and scared, but the storm soon departed, and the sun began to filter through the clouds and into the trees. Jo Jo could now see that this enormous tree was full of bananas and he began to eagerly collect them. He was just about to begin eating his bananas when he saw another monkey in the tree swinging down from the higher branches. Jo Jo froze. The other monkey swung over toward Jo Jo, quickly grabbed the bananas that lie next to him, took one and peeled it and handed the peeled banana to Jo Jo and then began to peel one for herself. Jo Jo was not sure what to make of this behavior, but then Jo Jo suddenly recognized the monkey and the tree he was in as the one around the corner, and this monkey was none other than Na Na herself. Na Na had been sad and lonely for many years and could not understand why no one came to visit her and share all her bananas. She would cry whenever she saw Jo Jo pass her tree while hunting bananas. Jo Jo and Na Na fell quickly in love and lived happily ever after in the banana tree."

"Now Tesha, can you tell me the moral of this story?"

"Don't judge a monkey by its tree!" she quickly interjected with a smile.

"Very good, he he—— we don't want to judge a monkey by his tree or a banana by its peel, but the key word here is judge, it seems we have a tendency to be the judge and jury without a trail let alone sufficient evidence for due process."

"Now I know this may seem like a silly story, but as you can see, Jo Jo's sadness, fear, and frustration stemmed from a belief handed down possibly from one generation to the next without questioning it. This now caused Na Na to suffer for no good reason."

"If we are to live in a state of joy we must question our feelings over and over until we find the root assumptions from which they spring. If we can not find any reason behind our actions and feelings, we must contend that these feelings have no basis for existence and therefore should be relinquished."

"Fear is another emotion that is very misunderstood. It also can cause people great mental anguish that is quite unnecessary and can carry a great deal of weight, which causes people to change their physical worlds in a way that caters to the very things they seek to avoid. Now do you remember the story I told you about how the apple tree grew when it was loathed or loved? Fear and hate can both reach a level of intensity that can create by other means. This is why we must seek to develop our emotional understanding, to live life in a natural state of being, full of love and enjoyment."

"You all have an incredible ability to create and organize the physical world around you to suit your needs and desires, but it is a difficult concept for you to understand because you believe the exact opposite; you believe that you are indeed a product of nature, when in truth it is nature that is the by product of *mind* Now the details of all this are not as important as the fact that you believe or have faith in this, just as some of you now carry a faith in God."

"When you meet Sergy, he will explain our longstanding joke about the phrase 'What's the matter?' I will touch lightly on the subject, so we don't get to far off course here. It has been humanity's historical and religious assumption that the physical body is at the mercy of the physical world, and there is little we can do about it except pray. The external God has free reign over our soul, being judge and jury over our every action, like the kings of the kingdoms, so you should fear him above all else."

"Although this was not always humanity's assumption, this belief seemed to grow to epic proportions during the Age of Ignorance, which was right after the destruction of Atlantis. The demise of this continent was no accident; your specie at that time had knowledge of the sacred sciences of light and color and used it against one another, as well as consorting with the fallen cherubim, breaking the laws of the cosmos. Parts of your Bible were written by scribes that were descendents of these advanced cultures, but the Age of Ignorance was long, and most of the stories that were handed down were confused and abused. Now if you knew your history, you would know of the millennia when a great number of religions were formed as the Age of the Sage and Prophet."

"During this period, humanity had a great deal of assistance to try and turn the tide of ignorance back to the fundamental truths and laws that were derived from our vast inner kingdom connected to the eternal mind, to help raise all to a level that was much more natural and enjoyable. While there was some progress made in small circles in ancient Egypt and Greece among others, the majority of humanity failed to understand the concepts or never wanted to adhere to a disciplined life. This led to a new set of beliefs and assumptions that infiltrated most religions. These beliefs have a lot to do with self-indulgence, intemperance, and self-righteousness."

"The root assumption that we are all victims of a cruel physical world controlled by external gods who are not all loving stems from the Age of Ignorance, when the ego forgot that it was a part of mind and went searching for external substitute truths to confirm upon its longings for the inner truths of mind."

"Your science, while looking through the microscope at creation in hopes of better understanding the riddles of physical matter, unearthed the biggest riddle of all: that matter is not what people have always assumed it to be. Matter simply does not exist in understandable orthodox parameters of science. So the standing joke 'what's the matter' has left science at odds with itself after spending billions of dollars on particle accelerators and space programs. They have reached a level of paradox that's being called 'Albert's anomaly,' after our German friend who was the first one to make the assumption that quantum mechanics, the brain child of one of his contemporaries by the name of Bohr, was a waste of time. Now, although there is no such thing as a waste of time, I would agree with this statement to a certain degree. My opinion of such science could be summed up in this riddle: Why does the kitten chase its tail? Because the pursuit of the distraction provides an interesting experience!"

"What I mean is that Albert was the first physicist that had a hunch that the viewer is working in a joint partnership with the view. Simply put, one could not exist without the other; our assumptions and beliefs predicate our physical world. Now how can you get to the bottom of the riddle of matter when you peer into a telescope or microscope with assumptions and beliefs, when such beliefs are possibly tainting the discovery? Simply put the riddle of matter cannot be solved with matter, only mind."

"So what's the matter, why do they scatter or grow fatter, it makes my heart go pitter patter and then I'm mad as a hatter. Oh please tell me what's the matter, it comes and goes making billions of O's yet nobody knows from whence God throws—He heee!"

"Now let's talk about feelings, shall we? The hunch that Albert had is another way of describing intuition. Intuition can be considered inner wisdom unfounded by assumptions or beliefs. It's a positive feeling about something when you are believed to have little knowledge of it in your local noodle, forgetting the connection to the unified field of intelligence. Now normally this inner knowing is circumvented, or second guessed by the ego because the ego loves to rationalize. It is only natural for an external part of self to pass judgment upon any stimuli that it does not control, the end result being that most intuitive thoughts and feelings never get the opportunity to bare fruit. All because of that big fat ego!"

Now Tiny was not so tiny anymore but began to expand like a balloon——a big balloon. We all stared in shock as he became a blimp, then with a large gale came from his mouth that blew my hair back and lasted until he was once again normal. The room was silent, we were all utterly speechless.

"Now that you've seen the illustration of a big fat ego we can get back to business. Intuition is a knowing that is connected with the mind by way of the heart, not the ego, but if you have a working relationship with the ego, intuition becomes a close and respected companion. Let me illustrate here:

"You are riding down a river in a canoe when suddenly you see a nice comfy spot under a tree where you would like to take a nap. The feeling is there, but you criticize it and continue on only to be thrown into a rocky ravine where you loose your canoe and almost perish in the process."

Tesha and I looked at each other with eyes as large as saucers. *"There was no way Tiny could have known about that event"* I thought to myself.

Tiny smiled at me and said, "There are actually no secrets of thought or feeling. These are merely the handicaps of the ego."

"Now, the story that all of you are working on may appear to be fictional, but there is a fine line that separates fiction from potential realities. What I mean to say is that the world you are living in at this very moment is by my standards considered fiction while you see it as reality. How is this, you may ask? It all comes back to the difference between my level of understanding and yours."

"We both create in the same fashion, with the only difference being that I am aware of what I am creating, but this is soon to change. The exercise that you are doing must not be taken lightly, for it has the power to transform your world just as the sun has the power to create light. Let's illustrate again, shall we?"

"When we cook a stew we use all the necessary ingredients that make the stew palatable and enjoyable. Without these main ingredients, it is a flop of slop. We create the stew by means of thought, then help it along with physical intervention. We don't look upon this as anything special—it seems quite ordinary to make a delicious stew—but let's analyze the process a bit further, shall we?"

"Before the stew, there has to be a thought, a thought with a feeling attached to it. The feeling could come from the memory of the delicious stew Grandmother made when you were a child, or it could be something less significant. This begins the process of an organized mental effort to create this thing called stew, so we 'stew' over the idea of assembling the list of creation, then we acquire said ingredients. Once all the necessary ingredients are acquired, we commence to create the object of our desire, stew! Now sometimes we substitute ingredients when necessary, or forget to add some, giving us a stew that is a bit unlike Grandmama's but still basically what you desired."

"Now then, when we create with mind we use the same format, but we change the ingredients a little. If my heart's desire is to become a pianist, doctor, or to sail the high seas, I must first recognize the desire that is present. Sometimes these desires can be quite strong and cause great dissatisfaction with any substitutions. We then take this desire and add thought to it, and this is where the ingredients make the difference. If you are a good storyteller or detailed artist, your creation will be as perfect as the one you created in the image-nation. If you are too vague and leave out important ingredients, your stew will be a close representation only and sometimes leave a bad taste in your mouth."

"Regardless of your skill in the image-nation, one of the main ingredients that you must add to the story is faith. If you are not sure without a doubt that this is what you desire and if you do not have faith in its ability to manifest, then it is all a waste of time. What we believe, we achieve, and what we deliberate, we create. It is that simple! Now many fool themselves into failure at this moment because they lack the proper understanding of this word faith, they think they can just pretend or be semi committed and this is where they fail. You must believe with your heart and mind for this to cause a spark. There are two kinds of faith one that is easily acquired through experience and developmental understanding and what we call applied faith or one that grows through sharpening one's skills. Let's illustrate again shall we:"

"There are two female vocalists that show up for an audition for the lead part in a musical. One is named Fleebie and the other Fleebo. They have both had a dream to become lead singers since childhood and both have faith that they will get the part but during the audition Fleebo hits many flat notes and can't seem to carry a tune for very long, while Fleebies voice resonates with such power and harmony she wins the part unanimously. Afterward the director of the musical looks at their manifests and reads that Fleebo had been dreaming of this part all her life while Fleebie had been in active pursuit of her passion with every opportunity that passed her way having a list of credits as long as her legs. Now Kate why do you think Fleebies faith was stronger than Fleebos?"

"Um, because she practiced her dream instead of just dreaming about it!"

"That's right she practiced and as we all know practice makes perfect, and this is what we call applied faith; you actively apply yourself again and again until your faith is as strong as iron. Another ingredient that will help speed up the process is emotional intensity or passion. Passion will grow as the picture in the image nation becomes clearer; the closer you hold the idea to your heart, the better the music will be. If you learn to love all without judgment like me, it will all come quite effortlessly."

"You may practice your will over smaller objects of desire first if you like. These are manifested much quicker and will give you more faith for the larger projects. If you can master this art in the physical, you will always be a *mind-full* master and never again be subject to external manipulations."

134

"The art of manifestation is great fun, and it's not as complicated as one may think; all of you are already creating your tomorrows to a certain extent by your assumptions and expectations today which are well seasoned with faith. The desire force is another contributing factor in manifestation in which we consciously draw in what it is that we feel we need. The ego likes to control this aspect of self and will send you off on wild goose chases if you are uncertain of the difference between desires of the heart and those of the ego. To ascertain this one must look closely at the object of desire and trace it back to its root, if it is discovered that this desire is rooted in fear, anger, vanity, envy, greed, vengeance or animosity, you can be certain that it is not of the heart."

"These very teachings are an everyday occurrence at Tolemac, for the Imputable Impetus states: 'only assumptions of mind created intuition by way of the heart are worthy of belief!' Now we shall answer questions before today's assignment."

This time I was the first one to raise my hand and asked "What if I have no desires?"

Tiny cocked his head to one side as he looked at me with those little black eyes and droopy hat and said:

"Then my boy you are either lying to yourself or incoherent. There is no living thing that does not desire at least something to eat, and there is no aspect of mind that does not whish to evolve and expand. It is an inherent aspect of creation——of all creation, otherwise genesis would be a waste of time."

Now Kate asked, "Do we reincarnate?"

"Yes, reincarnation hmmm… One life would seem to be an awful waste of artistic talent, wouldn't you think? Why settle for one suit when you can have an entire wardrobe and within each different suit of clothes an alter ego, complete with an entire new cultural view? I know of no actor who is satisfied with one role, no, no! We must play the roles of kings and queens as well as beggars and buffoons if we are to gather the true essence of physical experience and the fine art of expression. However reincarnation is a term that is misunderstood for we may reincarnate but you cannot, and again this may be a bit technical so I will try and put it in laymen's terms. We are mind but you are ego; a dew drop separated from the ocean eventually evaporates and returns from where it came, as does mind, you see your individuality is a physical characteristic not a spiritual one."

"Mind knows where it has come from and where it is going. There are no accidents; all lives are prearranged—including the most tragic, for pain and misery must be experienced to truly appreciate love and wealth. The biggest misconception is in the idea of the past life, for there is no past as you know it. Time and space are illusions of physical matter, and life a mere programming, but we will not go any further with that one until you are capable of understanding such concepts."

Now Sarah asked, "What is mind?"

Tiny was silent for a moment, looking at her closely and squinting as he scratched his long-bearded chin.

"Mind is a highly technical subject young lady, but I will try to give you something to chew on. Mind can be referred to as the awareness that seeks to express itself through forces in and beyond nature, occasionally using nature for expression and a sensual experience. But mind is no more a product of the phenomenal world than your tongue is the sweet taste of sugar. Mind is a sprinkling of light from the Godhead."

Now Tesha raised her hand. "If what you said is true, then where does that leave God?"

Tiny smiled and said, "I'm glad to see you are paying attention! God is a subject rarely comprehended in physical terms. There are not enough correct word symbols to paint an adequate picture, and even if there were, it would prove very difficult and you still would not comprehend it. But I will try to give you a piece to chew on as well."

"If mind is the ultimate awareness that seeks to express itself by forces in and beyond nature. Then God could be likened to the ultimate force behind all mind and awareness that needs not express itself independently, for it already exists in all that is. Phewww! Please save any more questions till tomorrow, he-he-he!"

"Now your assignment will be this; re-landscape the paintings in your minds to include the concepts you have learned here today, and include definitions of the following: feeling, desire, intuition and faith. Good day!"

Tiny then painted a small black door with his fingers then opened it and walked out of sight, the door slowly faded away into nothingness.

That afternoon I went to my room to be alone. All this mind stuff was making my head hurt. How could it be that if we create a picture in our mind that it would all come true? It just seemed so hard to accept, and to think that if I hated something enough, it might also come true was even harder to understand. What sort of a man was this Tiny—if he was a man at all, and how could he know about what happened on the river? Many questions remained unanswered. It seemed like the entire world was once again being shaken up, but only this time from the inside out, and yet I still had two more days of mind bending. I could only hope my sanity lasted that long!

14
TINY'S GAMES

The next morning I awoke to Tesha shaking me. I had stayed up too late working on the perfect picture in my mind and the copying it all down on paper. Although my dream of flying through space seemed a bit farfetched, I still maintained faith in its possibility.

Tesha went ahead without me, and I rushed to get ready, grabbing an apple from the fruit bar on my way out and chewed as I walked. When I got to Tiny's class, he, or rather part of him—his head—was sticking out of the wall, and he too was still asleep. I guess I wasn't the only one who overslept. Tesha, Kate, and Sarah were all just standing around his head whispering. I walked over and said, "How's that possible?"

Apparently, my question startled Tiny, who pulled himself effortlessly out of the wall, as if it were made of liquid. He stood, yawned, then smiled. "What? You've never seen someone sleep before? I can over sleep just as well as the next guy!"

Once again, my surprised eyes met Tesha's.

"Please pass your assignments forward! Today I will try to cover a large area of ground by talking about different subjects but not going so deeply into them that you get brain damage, which would really prove quite impossible, he-he-he."

When tiny laughed his wrinkled face bobbed exposing his little teeth and making his nose protrude even further, giving him the impression of a giant rat. It really was quite amusing and made me giggle even when I did not understand the joke.

"I realize that the last few days have been difficult for all of you, and it is not any easier for adults. You see adults have it quite a bit harder because they have many more assumptions and beliefs to contend with. The majority of adults will never become the clever creators that all of you will, simply because they lack the faith. Now that's not going to make them become monsters or anything; it just means that they will struggle with life more and enjoy it less."

"Some of you presently struggle with these concepts, but please keep in mind that your mind has full grasp of what has been said. It is only your ego, not your age that is a bit narrow minded. When we admit to ourselves that something is beyond our grasp, it becomes just that— too hard to comprehend. Now if we find ourselves beginning to think and feel thoughts of lack and limitation, we will unfortunately begin to turn the tide against us before we have the opportunity to paddle through it."

"The best way to get through something when you feel that you may have misunderstood it is to simply allow it. Struggling is not allowing. Allowing is simply relaxing your thoughts with the inner confidence that you are mind-full and that the thing that's troubling you is a temporary lapse of memory. Which indeed it is!"

"The ego's always trying to rationalize, control, and cast judgment over everything. The more you understand about this greedy and insecure part of self the less control it has over you. When you encounter conflict or trauma use your understanding to search yourself for the motivation or feeling behind it. You will find that time after time you are infesting yourself with negative emotional energy due to one of the ego's many insecurities."

"Allowance is not a word that humans are well acquainted with, yet it is a pivotal act of redemption. Just live and let be, without passing judgment or trying to control the situation. The very thought of allowance goes against human nature. Why? Because it contains what some would label as weakness. These feelings will trigger self-doubt—again, those feelings of lack and limitation I mentioned earlier. The self-doubt will in turn help you build a nice, solid wall between you and whatever it is you wish to become one with."

"Let me illustrate. There are two small children growing up in the same pod. They are the same age sex and weight; they are both well cared for. The first child's name is Bongo; the second, Chongo. Bongo's mother loves him very much and is very concerned for her son's 'mind' and encourages him often, but would never criticize him. Instead she teaches him how to avoid mental traps that destroy self-confidence while keeping him exposed to a great many things."

"Chongo's mother also loves her son very much, but instead of caring about his mind, she cares mainly for the welfare of Chongo's body. She constantly feeds him and fusses about what he wears and how he looks, criticizes him when he wants to express his individuality, and keeps him away from external experience for fear that he may get hurt. This causes him to lose his self-confidence and gain excessive weight. With feelings of inadequacy, he becomes too shy to enjoy social gatherings."

"Both graduate school with honors, but one day there is a terrible storm and the floodwaters sweep them both out to sea. They each find refuge on a small island, and each is unaware that either is alive on another part of the island."

"Bongo quickly begins building himself a shelter and gathers food that is plentiful on the island. Chongo is scared, cold, and hungry. As his thoughts dwell on his losses, he waits on the beach hoping for someone to help him. Bongo is quickly learning how to spear fish and make fires with two sticks. He collects wood to build a raft. But Chongo feels helpless. He ventures into the forests to find food but is overcome with fear after hearing strange noises."

"Months later, Bongo paddles his raft off the island. He's pushed by the current to the other side of the island where he finds Chongo's bones bleaching in the sun. Bongo yells out, "I can't believe it, my mother was right! Everything I wish for really does come true!" Bongo quickly grabs the valuable bone material and sets down to the business of making the tools needed for his journey. Now Meno, what would the moral of this tale be?"

"Um, your mother's not always right?"

"No, the moral to this tale is that we can be a Bongo or we can become tools for his journey —He-he-he."

"Now there is another disruptive energy that you must become aware of as well; it's called forgiveness. Now I know that many are thinking that forgiveness is not bad, and you would be right in this first assumption —to a point."

"To forgive is a highly noble and compassionate act in hindsight. To forgive enables one to wash away the mental traps created in a web of judgment. However, if you were allowing, instead of judging and controlling in the first place, you would not need to be forgiving anything or anyone. The biggest problem with forgiveness is that people don't practice it enough for it to do us any good. Instead we are like garbage collectors who gather all these negative feelings, and soon our minds and bodies begin to resemble huge garbage dumps."

"You loathe so-and-so because of? You can't stand water because of? You get sick when you smell flowers because of? And on and on. All this rubbish gets mixed in with our assumptions and beliefs when most of it should have been reassessed for what it really is—an experience—and then reconciled within our heart—forgiven."

"When we maintain an inventory of such rubbish, we slowly cease to live our lives the way they were intended to be lived. We become like puppets on strings, jumping and jerking to every beat of the very drums we created. It's time we cut those strings and put our feet once again on solid ground! To do this is quite simple but will prove time consuming if you have a great deal of rubbish to contend with. We first put all thoughts except the subject at hand out of mind. We relax and put our mental bodies on a slow rewind, unlocking every emotional event that was ever stored there, from the present to as far back as memory takes you. Relive those tragic moments and find the lesson hidden behind the emotion. As the lesson surfaces, forgive that which you assumed trespassed upon your person, be it a person or the will of nature."

"This is difficult and at times painful, yet a most powerful method of cleansing rubbish. All supposed injuries happen for the greater good, for our personal and collective growth. It's just hard to think in these terms when we are overcome by emotion and self pity, yet realistically it is the ego not the essence that has been wounded, so the wound is superficial. These superficial wounds are supported by a thin vale of emotional energy, which is mostly composed of injured pride; fear based anger, or unfounded guilt, when we learn their true nature. You see this sort of trapped emotional energy never really goes away; it just festers like a dirty wound. The skin may seem to heal over the wound, and as years go by you may forget about it, but know this; that wound is now like a silent poisonous snake waiting in the weeds and willing to strike at the slightest threat. So lets shed that snake skin and allow the luminous you to shine through, shall we —He-he-he!"

"Now let's review one more human hang-up; the illusion of wealth and power vs. passive poverty. The illusion that mountains of gold will buy your happiness is hard to disperse after so many centuries of acceptance. We have dug up the hillsides and polluted the waters that are so vital to the natural world, and all for the greed of gold. The indigenous peoples would scratch their heads in wonder, while the white man slaved his entire life away in a small hole in the ground for a soft yellow rock that you can't eat, sharpen, or use for tools."

"There was once life without gold, if you could imagine such a thing, and the people lived very happily and had lives full of experience, love, and laughter. These people did not even have words for things like greed, wealth, or poverty. They were quite comfortable with mere existence and the basic essentials of life and mostly lived together intimately, never trying to control or pass judgment upon their environment. Your planet has suffered greatly for the ignorance of man, and now the opposite shall be the case. The plunder of resources once plentiful has prematurely brought about an expedient cessation to the very home that cannot be replaced. Once we break the chain linking mind with monetary madness, mind and matter recover."

"The value you place on minerals seems to be out of proportion with the value you place on creation and is also in direct conflict with the value you place on mind. With each jewel, the ego gratification gains strength until you are all but lost in the luster. The biggest problem with this sort of obsessing is that it confuses the heart. While you were trying to quench the desire of the heart, you began thirsting after the vehicle used to help produce your desire. Before long, you confused desire itself with its tools of expression and creation. This all comes back to the belief of lack and limitation. You see, when we feel externally insecure, we try to balance the scales by the accumulation of the external symbols for abundance. These symbols are gold, silver, or extremely large physical objects. The truth of the matter is that you are rich beyond words, regardless of the accumulation of these symbols, but fail to understand how this could be. If we begin to understand mind and realize that it is mind with which we create, we will soon learn the futility of external obsessing. The act of obsessing after something can also build a wall between you and the obsession. For when you obsess about something, you in turn admit that you are without it, and keep this fact for faith. This assumption will not quench the thirst of desire."

"We must first understand the tremendous wealth we hold within mind, only then can we understand faith's ability to create the heart's desire effortlessly, and only then take advantage of all our riches. This is the law of abundance!"

"This works the same way with power. If we were not powerful, we would not be having this conversation in the wonderful creation called Tolemac. Instead there are at times a craving for power and control. One could only guess what your world might have become if the Romans had put as much effort into their internal realities as they had within their creative pursuits of building and conquering. Then there are those who try to gain power over the external world by the means of the black arts, meddling in alliances and affirmations of supposed evil to gain abilities that are, in reality, substantially less than what a mind full of truth has to offer. They trade in the inner truths of mind for a second rate illusion, or by befriending some unknown spirit who is attracted to their life force. The real shame is that these power seekers have not recognized through true awareness the fundamental law of cause and effect or the cosmic truth of conscious coercion. They would tread much softer if they knew these profound truths."

"You see, you need not search for external magic, for if I can be considered a wizard, you can easily be considered great and wise magicians! The capacitor that stores this magic elixir is the heart, carrying within it the charge of mindfulness, while the resistor being the judgmental, doubting, and questioning ego. A well disciplined ego, however, will accomplish all that it sets its '*mind*' to."

"We must also take into consideration that all of creation was manifested with these simple timeless philosophies, that your only handicaps are self imposed, and that these tools I am sharing with you are indeed keys to the great doorway to salvation. So let's reset our hearts and minds to the high frequency mode and tune in our well sculpted, vibrantly colored and emotionally stimulated dreams and goals. Step over the threshold to the image-nation and dwell within for a moment; can't you see them, now I want you to feel them, now smell them, now taste them and hear them and you are there. Isn't it wonderful, it's all yours and more."

"Now we will take a short break and when you return I will answer any questions on the subject at hand before we resume with the lecture."

Tiny disappeared in a puff of smoke before our very eyes, yet his childish giggle lingered faintly. I was almost getting used to these tricks of his but they still amazed me and the others. I followed Tesha and the girls over to the cafeteria to get a cold drink, few words were spoken between us; as if there was little else our minds could think of.

Tesha was smiling at me as we made our way out of the doorway.

"What?" I asked

"I'm having a tough time following what Tiny is saying, but I can at least catch the general idea, but do you understand any of this?" She asked before sipping her paper cup.

"I don't understand some of the big words, but I know what forgiveness is and I know that I'd rather be Bongo than Chongo!"

Tesha laughed into her cup spraying its contents, then said, "yeah me too."

As soon as we were all seated Tiny began to grow out of the floor, steadily rising until he was once again whole. His toothy grin made us all once again snicker.

"Your questions please."

Sarah was the first to raise her hand and be selected. "How can I forgive someone if I hate them?"

"Well my little flower petal you must first understand that we must first defuse the energy of such a word, how such words as these take root I dare not ask. We simply dislike the actions and behavior of those that offend us. What lurks behind the motivating forces of these acts are at times more offensive than the acts of the perpetrator. Perhaps the sufferings of such an individual seek to be compensated by the sufferings of those they have contact with and who are somehow vulnerable. What ever the reason is not as important as how such indignities self perpetuate in a vicious cycle where all become victims, yet forgiveness alone has the power to free, you see —He-he-he!"

Now Tesha was the only one with her hand up and asked, "Would praying be the correct method of creating what we want?"

"When we pray we say 'I don't have,' and we in turn are asking outside entities to give us or someone else what it is we believe they are in need of. This conflict's with the law of abundance and can also create more problems than its trying to solve. You see we are not always the best one to be judging what another needs, and could do more harm than good by gumming up the works. If you feel the need to pray you should do it somewhat open ended, by praying for the best possible outcome for that occasion instead of making a directive, see. Now if we affirm with faith we understand in our hearts of mind that just because we cannot see something with the naked eye does not mean it does not exist, for true existence must occur in mind before its equivalent expression can manifest on a material plane."

Now I asked Tiny," If I wanted to see someone who died could I bring them back?"

"Not unless you're Dr. Frankenstein, but you can sometimes communicate messages to those you wish to when they are mind-full enough to receive them"

Kate blurted out, "How do you do all those magical tricks?"

"What like this one?"

Tiny opened his mouth and his tongue kept getting longer and

145

longer until it touched the floor before it curled back up into a little ball in his mouth. Then he sat there smiling back. We all busted out laughing once again.

"The truth is that if I was physical like you I would have a tough time performing them, but my physical presence is an illusion, it is only my mind that is consorting with you. Now then let's continue with today's lesson shall we."

"When we set out on our journey to become great mind-full magicians, we must travel light. What I mean is we want to loosen the mental load a bit, so we can concentrate clearly on our destination of mind. Many of the mental traps that I spoke of earlier will need to be cleared out. Dwelling in the past or future is fine for recreation, however getting stuck in these time frames keeps mind out of the creative mode. The Imputable Impetus states: 'Now is the only time for mind-fullness, for tomorrow is a contingent, concurrent, and contiguous by-product of today.' You see, when you are obsessing about future, you can't create it. When you're obsessing about the past, it no longer is in the past because you just brought it into the present. Even if you dwell on either past or future, you truly only dwell in the present, for nothing ever changes but a state of mind."

"Yet these states of mind can be counter productive. When we are incessantly obsessing over a traumatic incident in the past, we are choosing to torment ourselves by replaying the event in our minds, as if it were going to correct itself; it never does, but you continue like a cat chasing its tail. While misery sits at the helms of tomorrow, today is born sufferable."

"When we obsess about tomorrow—will the sun come up, will I find the pot of gold, will I die—we lose today and tomorrow. Remember the story about the apple tree? Then we must understand that if we send out the wrong energy, we may get the wrong creation or the very thing we feared could happen. Another problem with obsessing, or wanting, is that if you believe that you don't or can't have something then this belief will actually push it further away."

"A magician who lives in the now is the alchemist who creates the picture perfect now—whether past, present, or future—with absolute faith and expectation, as if it had already happened, with only the actual event needing to be experienced in the realm of time and space. Now that you know the method, here is the secret ingredient: passion! For without this simple yet ever elusive ingredient, you will surely fail in your attempts to be mind-full magicians."

"Now for your assignment. Tonight I want you all to take a trip to the dump in your minds, to discard old useless data. As I mentioned earlier, we must clean the old trash bin that thwarts mind. An hour or so before sleep relax yourself and put your minds on rewind, re-witnessing all the emotional events of your past. When you come to an unpleasant memory, try to determine what the lesson was and forgive all involved and continue on to the next one. Within days you will clear out an incredible amount of mental and emotional rubbish. Try to work your way all the way back to when you were only a small child before you stop the process."

Sarah was again holding her hand up in earnest before Tiny called on her.

"Can it be harmful to others if I get angry at them?"

Tiny made his usual smiling nod and said, "Only if you hold it in your heart. You see all reactions are just that—reactions. We soon recognize them and quickly release the energy through understanding. If we search for ways to get even or take on a personal vendetta against another, we cause the wheels of desire to turn. So yes, you can hurt another if you devote yourself to their misery, but more importantly, you hurt yourself even more because energy is like a wheel that always returns to its hub. So give it up. It is a waste of time. If this sort of desire force is from the heart but not of it, expect repercussions to follow. This comes back to the laws of cause and effect. The Imputable Impetus states; life is the effect of mind's causation. Give it a whirl and cause a sensation —He-he-he!"

"What this is trying to say is that whatever type of energy you are sending out into your mental environment, you are getting that same type back like a reflection in a mirror. Mind energy always returns in equal harmonies. Simply put, if you are not sending love, you are not living it! I will see you all back here in the morning. Leave your pads and pencils at home, for where we go tomorrow, words have little value."

Tiny once again vanished into thin air, and this time there were no body parts sticking out of the walls...if he even had a body. When we came out of the building, Moora was waiting for us with some documents—manifests for Tesha, Kate, and Sarah. She said that mine wasn't ready, and then led the girls back into the building to explain their manifests. I moped back to my room feeling a bit left out, wondering why I was not selected yet, but these feelings were soon replaced by pangs of hunger. I stopped at the buffet to eat and think about what Tiny meant when he said, 'where were going tomorrow, words had no value.' *He must be up to something being it's the last day of his class*, I thought. After dinner, I went back to my bed and lay down. I began to search my thoughts for highlights of the past year's events to try to rid myself of some rubbish. Only a few memories with feeling came. The first one was the death of Lance the guard. Somehow I felt helpless. Seeing Tesha in shock had made me angry that I was too small and weak to have made much difference. I could not find any lesson with this feeling, but I forgave all those involved who I thought to be the enemy; mainly the Navajo who made our lives so miserable during those few days. Yet I still could not understand why, or find the lesson there. Those men we encountered on the beach at Bear Lake were the meanest I had ever known and would have surely killed us if not for Unkar's quick rescue, but since they all paid for their crimes with their lives I forgave them as well, even the one who hit me so very hard. The only lesson I could find here was what Tiny called cause and effect. The next was the scene of my father's bear attack. It was all so clear now in my mind. I could smell the fresh blood and feel the bear's claw in the back of my leg. Suddenly I was once again overcome with emotions and could not continue with the exercise. I asked myself, what kind of lesson could I hope to find, other than pain?

The next morning Moora came and sat next to me while I was eating some cereal. "Is everything all right, Meno? When I walked past your room last night, it sounded like you were having a difficult night."

I glanced up quickly. Moora had heard me crying? Her eyes were kind, but I couldn't bring myself to do anything other than shrug. She put her arm around me and said, "My door is always open if you need someone to talk to." She insisted on walking with me to Tiny's last class. Moora said, "You will enjoy Tiny's last class, he is always so full of surprises."

"Is Tiny real?" I asked her.

"He's as real as he needs to be," she said staring down at me with those big brown eyes.

"But how is it that he can pop out of the walls and floor, or disappear?"

"Meno, very few people know the answer to that question and unfortunately I'm not one of them, but I do believe it's more about science than it is illusionist magic."

I entered the class and there he was, that same old man sitting in the back, the one that was there the first day. Tesha and the girls were there, but there was no sign of Tiny. As we sat there, a strange wind began to pick up in the classroom, coming from the front of the class and growing increasingly stronger with each passing moment. We began to hear Tiny's childish giggle. I forgot to leave my notebook at home and was now trying to hold it while simultaneously grasping the table, which seemed unaffected by the gale. Sarah began to scream, and the wind suddenly stopped as if to answer her. Tiny was now grinning in the front of the room.

"Good morning, children. I just wanted to make sure everyone is awake. Now today is fun and games. These games may seem a bit different, but they can all be played in mind. The only difference is that you will be experiencing my mind more than yours. If you get scared, just open your mouth and the illusion will cease, but I must warn you that your fears will diminish the fun. Remember, these are only mind games."

As Tiny was talking, he began to multiply in number. Within a minute there were at least a dozen Tiny's in the front of the room, all speaking and acting exactly as he was. We all began to laugh, but the spell was broken. It was Sarah again; she began to get scared. Her sister scrunched her face and told her to start playing along.

Tiny was now flapping his arms in the air like a big bird. "Who wants to go flying?" With Tiny's first flap, the walls and floor fell away, and everything in the room—including us—seemed to be floating in midair. I could still feel a hard surface under my feet, but my eyes were telling me that we were climbing high above Tolemac and starting to soar through the air like a flock of seagulls, albeit a flock of seagulls seated at desks. Tiny was still standing in front of us waving his arms and laughing. Sarah, who had been holding her hands over her eyes, now uncovered them and began to scream, and we spontaneously found ourselves back in a walled classroom as if it had never happened. Kate once again gave her sister a dirty look, but I was secretly relieved. I had almost begun yelling myself when we began to pick up speed; I could feel it in the pit of my stomach like some carnival ride.

Tiny was still laughing and said, "Perhaps this is a bit much for some of you. Let's try a different game."

Tiny was now shrinking as he laughed and did not stop until he was the size of a doll. His voice was high-pitched and sounded funny. We all began to laugh hysterically, including Sarah. Tiny was back to his normal self within seconds and immediately asked Tesha to meet the future Mr. Olikai. When Tesha looked at me, her hand flew over her mouth. The girls were all looking at me as if I were someone else. I stared at my hands, but they were just the same as always. Before I could solve that mystery, the floor and walls once again fell away. Now we were looking down upon Earth from outer space. Suddenly we were in a desert with large sand dunes. This quickly changed to a forest with huge redwood trees, which gave way to a canyon. The images picked up speed, flashing through almost every possible environment. At one time we were at the bottom of the ocean, and I feared to breathe. In seconds, we were in a whale's belly, then in a rocket headed for the moon, then we were on the moon. These changes were like living pictures that lasted for an hour, and then we were back in our classroom as if nothing had ever happened.

Tiny was now grinning in his imaginary chair. "Are we having fun yet?"

We all agreed it was great fun; even little Sarah was clapping wildly.

"All that you have witnessed was created by me in the same fashion that you create with mind-fullness; the differences being that you do not yet believe in your mind and have not yet begun to understand its power. You too can travel through space or swim under oceans if you are a good artist in the image-nation. There is little you cannot experience here. It is here in the playground of mind that we begin to create our fiction of mind. The mind has power, but when you combine it with the heart you create the golden elixir of the alchemist. The Imputable Imputes states; the light of mind is brighter than one thousand suns when charged with loving passion."

"You must always and forever follow your heart's desire. If you follow this simple rule, you will live a life worthy of mind. Any other course of action is not worthy of you. This is why you must continually study your stories and edit their content, changing details until the picture is perfect and clear. When we focus on the image-nation, we focus on the things that make us feel. If there are no deep rooted feelings at the center of your image, or behind the ideal, you are barking up the wrong tree."

Now Tiny changed into a small terrier dog with his face being the only thing recognizable, he ran over to a small tree that materialized and began barking up it. Before I could finish laughing he changed back.

"A story that is not yours is a story that shares no personal vibration with you, and therefore you cannot create it, or at best you will miscreate it. The story that's found within your heart carries with it a resonance, and only through that resonance shall your heart dance in harmony with mind."

"Yea, the charade, thy musical parade, singing of character and heart, chasing emotion through blind devotion, shall only keep thee apart, He-he-heee!"

"If you have questions, speak or forever hold your peace."

I was the first one to raise my hand this time and for some reason I just blurted out, "Why do people you love have to die?"

Tiny came very close—so close that I got my first good look in his eyes. There were no pupils, only blackness with small white dots swirling around like the Milky Way.

"My dear Meno, your word 'die' is a bad choice. It sounds so hopeless. You must change the word's meaning to what it truly represents before you can understand it. I prefer the word 'pass,' for we are passing from one place to another. There are more wonderful worlds to dwell in than your present localized vibration called Earth, so why would you want to get stuck in the muck of the physical? Do what you have come to do and get out of here. As for the love you share with those you have chosen to be close with, this love was there before your physical birth and shall remain long after you pass, for love is as eternal as the heart and mind from which it flows."

"But where do they pass on to?" I asked.

"That depends largely on the their state of mind when they passed, a great many have a tendency to linger close to the only world they remember along with its emotional attachments. But as the emotional energy dissipates they find that they are once again mind-full and full of eternal essence, not tied down by the physical weight and mass of a body, and are free to travel by mere thought. Where they choose to go depends largely on where they want to go and their level of understanding of how to get there. Many who have dwelled on the earth plane for eons will remain in close proximity awaiting their next opportunity to return."

I was somewhat satisfied with this answer and nodded in agreement, but the concept was still a bit out of reach.

Tesha now asked, "Are you going to be holding classes for us in the future?"

Tiny replied, "I thought this was the future, do you know of another one? Tesha, my kindred keeper of cardamom, you should by now know that the future is created by today's desires, and the better the understanding of this, the more control you have over that future event!" Then he turned too little Sarah, who was jumping out of her seat. "Yes, my deary, please speak clearly! He-he."

Sarah began speaking a bit loudly, "Will I ever be able to go home?"

Tiny now cocked his head, as if to acknowledge her, while his beady eyes contemplated the question thoroughly. "Yes, my sweet little Sarah, you will one day go home, and this home will never be lost to you, and at this home will you ever love and be loved, for this home is not the birth place but the place of birth, and you know it like no other."

Now kindly and softly, grinning in a manner that that held irony and sadness at once, he said, "Yes, Kate, go on."

"I just have one last question. Who was Jesus, and did he really do all those wonderful things told in the Bible, and are there really angels?"

"One last question?" Tiny smiled. "It's a good thing it wasn't three! OK, you're Bible and its teachings of Jesus. What a wonderful man, so full of timeless wisdom and weight. Who was he? Perhaps he was a great teacher sent to a culture bent on ignorance and licentiousness; perhaps he was trying to teach truth to a world that had so distanced itself from their own origins that it would take such a mind, so full of charisma, contrivance, and love, to aid hearts and minds ready for change. But again I must contend that you never invest more into an external event, place, or book than you do upon self."

"'I am in the father, and the father is in me.' What I mean is that I am the truth, the life, the way. I am that I am. Now all of you say that last phrase."

Collectively we chanted, "I am that I am."

"Yes you are, and you will always be, and never let an external illusion get between you and your eternal truths because we are a universal I and it takes someone with a great deal of awareness to understand this. Now as far as for the angels, I can assure you that there is one among us in this very room!"

We all began to look around with astonishment, hoping to catch a glimpse of such a holy sight, but saw nothing more than the few familiar faces.

"Children, the only thing that keeps you from seeing the angel in this room is your limited expectation of what an angel should look like. This pygmied, winged cherub painted on the ceilings of cathedrals is a delusion of painters who painted too often with lead tinctures. The angels that serve and protect are workers, constantly giving through selflessness for other causes considered far nobler than self-indulgence. One in the flesh may have a similar calling."

Tiny was now starring at me with a strange grin, as if it were a clue in some game he was playing.

"Now it is time for me to say goodbye to you, my beloved children, and need I tell you that you hold your future within you? Perhaps I have helped you all to better find the way home, for after all we are all on an incredible journey."

I raised my hand in hopes of getting one more question answered.

"Well, I almost made a clean and timely departure. Yes Meno, go ahead, laddie. Speak your piece, loosen those lips, and quack your query quick, for the universe is unfolding and there are those who are needed for molding, he-he-he!"

"What is the jewel of the rainbow?"

Once again he came so close to me that I could see in the depths of his eyes, eyes that were not human, but like a vacuum inhaling all they gazed upon. These were not eyes, but windows that crossed into unknown parameters of space, and vast untold dimensions. Suddenly I got a glimpse of something. It looked like a body with a rainbow pouring out of it, but the image was quick and fleeting, and I was unsure of it.

"The jewel of the rainbow you say. That is a good question, isn't it? Unfortunately I cannot go into the explanation in great detail for reasons that lay undisclosed at this time. However I will give you a few hints, and in ten or so years you can ask Abigail to elaborate further. The jewel of the rainbow won't be found among external creations and cannot be pondered while duties demand, but search for it not and it will find thee in time, for there is no hourglass quite like the one at hand. He-he-heee!"

He was gone in a flash. My heart sank with the realization that I might never see the small wrinkled old man with the long white beard again. We all quietly left the room. When I got to the outer door, I realized that I had left my notepad on the desk and ran back in. I got to the end of the hall where the doorway had been to Tiny's class, but there was only a block wall. *What, how could this be?* I thought, and then I began to head back down the hall peering through a doorway at the opposite side of the hall. An old man who was doing maintenance work on a long machine with huge copper coils turned to me and smiled. It was the old man who I had seen in Tiny's class. I had a funny feeling that he knew something, but I was afraid to ask. Instead I smiled and headed back to my room where I found my notebook on my bed.

I wanted to write Tiny's riddle down before it was wiped from my memory, so I snatched up the notepad and a pencil. But when I opened the pad, there the riddle was, already written in my own handwriting too. I couldn't stop myself from saying aloud, "That's impossible!"

15
MENO'S MANIFEST

It had been nearly a week since Tiny's last class, and I still had not received my manifest. Tesha and the girls from Nova Scotia had already moved into pods. Tesha now shared a pod with another woman and was already working in one of the greenhouses.

When I asked Moora about it, she said only that she would check into the delay. Another week had gone by before I heard back. She told me that Artemus—the mentor we'd met at the park—would be coming by to explain "the situation" in a day two. I wondered what kind of situation she was referring to. I began to get a bit worried.

The following morning Artemus was knocking at my door and asked me to join him for breakfast. He was taller than I remembered, his head nearly touching the top of the doorway and his eyebrows were like two giant caterpillars. After a long quiet meal, he said, "There are some complications with your manifest, but they should be resolved soon. There appears to be some sort of variation in your DNA, which has the lab working overtime to understand it. It seems they have never seen anything quite like it."

"What's a DNA?" I asked.

"I will try to explain this in simple terms. The term DNA is short for deoxyribose nucleic acid. This nucleic acid is part of the building block of human cells. You see each cell in your body carries within it a fingerprint of who you are. Everyone's so-called 'fingerprint' has a slightly different pattern, and these are stored as DNA in what's called genes. Your genes are what make your body look and act like it does, the same way my genes make me look and act differently. They also help us to avoid sickness, but sometimes they can carry a potential sickness within them, causing the person to die or suffer. This is rare, but it does happen."

"Does this mean I have a sickness in my genes?" I quickly interjected, stretching my neck and searching his face for any changes.

"Meno, I don't believe you have a sickness, but I do believe you are a very rare breed. Now this could be a problem or a wonderful solution to some unknown problem. We will just have to wait until the lab investigates a bit more. So please be patient. I'm sure we will all have the answers we seek soon."

It would be many years later before I learned the truth of what was going on behind the scene's from the director of the Lab Wendell Scott, he told me the story in his own words;

Wendell was running out of answers and was chewing the erasers off his pencils repeatedly as he struggled for hours on end to understand what he had. He had been mapping my DNA for over a week, while other assistants were checking the history of the Human Genome Project's large backlog of data. The supercomputers were cross referencing for days and had not found one recorded case of a human genome having an extra pair of chromosomes and a code structure like this. Even the mitochondria was perplexing. After Wendell took some of these typical sample cells and introduced them to cancerous cells and cells of well known diseases the results were unbelievable. Wendell repeated the tests in the most sterile atmosphere available, and still the results did not change. The mitochondria had the most unique survival and defense mechanism he had ever seen. Instead of mutating or dying off, it actually multiplied, attacked and neutralized foreign cells, then cloned itself.

Wendell knew he had an enigma of the rarest form. He sat back in his office chair trying to grasp what he had just witnessed. Thoughts rushed through his mind about the possibility that it could be genetic, but he knew better. *Could it be divine intervention?* He thought. He rushed a memo to the Star Delegation in hopes that they could shed some light on his findings.

Wendell was sure there must have been a crossover, quantitative inheritance, or genetic variant to explain the anomaly, but he could find none, nothing to explaining the situation. Two days later he received a message back: "The boy carries the perfect gene. Take more samples and test on all known diseases to confirm, then have his hypothalamus checked for enlargement."

"The perfect gene; that's impossible!" Wendell exclaimed to no one in particular.

I was called in for additional samples of blood, they also asked me about past diseases, but I could not ever remember having any. They asked me when the last time was that I had a cold. I could not recall. They wanted to know the last time I had a serious injury was. I told them about the bear attack and showed them where my leg had been injured. To my surprise the scar was gone, yet they kept asking me if I was sure I remembered correctly, as if I had been making it all up. I finally got fed up with this repetition and raised my voice claiming for the last time that this was the location of the injury.

They performed test after test, then sent me back to my room to wait for the results. Why all the fuss? What was the big deal? I was becoming very confused and shook my head vigorously, mentally denying them any more probing and prodding. What were they after?

That night I thought about the leg wound. I could remember it hurting for about two days—until I found Tesha near the lake. I can't remember it even hurting after that night. Had I forgotten all about it? When I got skunked and was spreading myself with mud, I didn't recall seeing a scab or scratch marks. It was as if the deep claw had never slashed my calf. I remembered back when I was in Unalaska, one of the school bullies had thrown a rock at me because I had been on a swing he had wanted. The rock struck me with such force it knocked me backward off the swing, cutting my head open and covering my face and hands in blood as I tried to stop the flow from blinding me. I was rushed to the nurse's home, and she cleaned and bandaged the wound and told me to come back in a few days for another examination. When the nurse removed the bandage, she was shocked to see that the wound had healed. Only a light mark remained. She called it a miracle.

The next day Wendell came to see me and asked a great deal of questions about where I came from and about my parents and grandparents and any relatives I could think of. He asked me how it was that my eyes were such an unusual light gray. I told him about the story of the Russian fur traders and of my grandfather's eyes being the same color.

"Meno I had infected your cells with some of the worst diseases of the century and found they were immune to all of them. What we have here is nothing short of a miracle. There has never been anything like this in the history of man. I just wish we discovered it twenty years ago. We may have saved a lot of lives."

"How could my fast healing help others, I don't understand all this, and when can I get my manifest?" I asked Wendell whose eye's seemed to be staring at me as if I were one of the experiments.

He replied raising and shaking his hands like a Sunday preacher, "You have an advantage over others Meno. You have been given the gift of what some would consider immortality—the ability to maintain health in the most severe circumstances imaginable. You may even live twice the age of normal humans, all in good health. I think we will find out many more interesting things about your DNA before long. You see, everyone has twenty-three pairs of chromosomes; you have twenty-four pairs. These chromosomes are long strands of thread holding DNA. Each DNA strand carries its own genetic code, which are basically a sequence of amino acids, the building blocks of proteins. Simply put, our genes make proteins and the proteins make up the body. We find small inconsistencies in genetic codes, which are normal, but the genetic coding throughout your DNA has no inconsistencies. All the patterns are identical and predictable like some sort of model DNA. Simply put, you have perfect DNA!"

Wow! I thought, perfect DNA, I won't get sick. I was glad that they found me so special but still I didn't feel any different and had a hard time sharing Wendell's excitement. Again it had been many years before Wendell filled in the gaps of the meeting they had to discuss there findings. The members of the meeting consisted of Sergy Ivanovitch the director of science, and Abigail of the Star Delegation, along with the director of medicine and the director of biology. Wendell briefed everyone on the DNA dilemma. He concluded;

"I cannot even fathom the possibilities. I don't even know where to start with such an unprecedented situation."

Sergy looked at Abigail and asked, "How much does the Star Delegation know about the boy?"

"We have known for some time that a child with great abilities was to come before the cleansing, and that he would be the chosen one to continue the next human cycle. We knew that he had a gift-like memory and special skills for survival and that he would be heavily influenced. We located his birth place off the coast of Alaska, but we were too late. The polar melting had already claimed his home. We established communication with him by other means, and then sent Unkar to retrieve him. The DNA only proves our assumptions—that he is indeed the correct messenger for the program."

"What sort of program did you have in mind for him, and what do you mean that the boy is 'heavily influenced?'" Sergy asked.

"A program that offers as much exposure to learning as he can handle. There cannot be a single bit of knowledge left out. The influence that I am referring to is one of light—a vibratory capability beyond other humans. You see, it is through our very chromosomes that we receive our transmissions from the crystal sea of illumination. Our frame of reference is mostly one of reception from the heavenly spheres, in conjunction with the biotransducing capabilities of our primary resonator. This is why I wanted to confirm the size of Meno's hypothalamus gland, and the test confirmed my assumptions: an oversized gland is indeed present," said Abigail.

"After all this training, then what?" Wendell asked, pleading with his hands.

"That's where the space program comes in," Abigail replied.

"What space program?" Sergy asked with eyes as big as saucers.

"The one that starts today, now that we have our primary

passenger," said Abigail. "It is to be the primary focus of Tolemac over the next twenty years, and all of you will be apart of it."

"We don't have the manufacturing capability required to do this," Sergy snapped.

"No, not yet, but we have been working on solutions. There were reports of a carrier shuttle crash landing in the northern Rockies just after the revolution. Without the assistance of ground crews, the shuttle, on its way back from Jupiter's moon Europa, got off course and landed there. All we have to do is locate it and retrieve it."

"Retrieve it, with what?" Sergy threw his hands up in the air with a surprised expression.

Bianca, the director of biology, pushed her oversized glasses down to the edge of her nose and peered over their top. "I don't understand where we are all going with this. Why is all this necessary?"

The others in the room now were looking in surprise at Bianca. Abigail turned toward Sergy. "Why hasn't Bianca been briefed about the Nemesis?"

Sergy, looking guilty, said, "She only took the position a year ago. With her so young, I just didn't have the heart to tell her."

"What's the Nemesis?" Bianca burst out.

Sergy replied, "Bianca, please understand that I was only acting in your best interests. Sometimes the less we know, the happier we are."

"Sergy, don't treat Bianca as a child. She is now a director and privy to all our findings," Abigail scolded with a stern look and a pointed finger.

"I know. You're right. Bianca, please forgive me. But please keep this confidential. The people of Tolemac have little to gain by having such knowledge and will be told when it is necessary for their own defense."

Bianca was now squirming in her seat in anticipation.

Sergy continued, "The Nemesis is the name of a rather large black hole that has been discovered in our Milky Way. I realize that this is not a great concern in itself, but the concern is that our solar system trajectory will come close to the magnetic influence of the mass, in our not too distant future."

"What does that mean?"

"It means that within the next twenty to fifty years our planet is going to get the largest face-lift since the end of the age of the dinosaurs."

Bianca was now silent and staring blankly at Sergy. After a prolonged pause, she asked in a low tone, "How long have you all known about this?"

"The Star Delegation has known about it for as long as there has been a delegation, but it has only been for the last ten years that Sergy has been able to get a visual on it to confirm the inevitable." Abigail said in a low and soothing tone.

"So where does the spaceship come in?" Bianca asked.

"The ship will be needed to seed the new world for the continuance of our evolution through the next dimensions in space and time, until we become self realized specie." Abigail said.

Dr. Renaldo, the large, gray-haired director of medicine, now spoke up. "Bianca, I personally believe that this thing won't affect us for many years. We have most of our lives ahead of us yet to enjoy, so please don't let this thing get in the way of that. If you need anything to help you sleep, let me know."

"Could we please get back to the boy's DNA?" Wendell interrupted.

Abigail replied, "The boy's DNA will be studied, but for now we must get this boy a manifest, so he can get on with his life. I will meet with the director's of education and housing today to get this organized. We will talk more about the space program and the shuttle at our next scheduled meeting, but as for now, let's just be thankful that we have Meno. We must understand that he and his DNA are here through divine intervention and that we now have a great responsibility before us."

16
MENO TURNS 21

I was amazed how fast the years flew by at Tolemac. I celebrated each long winter of extremely heavy snowfall by putting one more notch on the wall of my bedroom. With so many things to learn, I could barely believe it when I scribed the tenth notch into the wall.

That winter, I had heard rumors that their was to be an expedition into the northern territory. I was not sure of all that was involved, but I knew I needed to escape Tolemac for a while, before my head exploded. The last few years seemed to be the hardest of all. Artemus just kept insisting on these classes that were real mind benders. The math alone would keep me up for long hours into the night.

I also wanted my own place. The pod with my temporary parents was a cramped two bedroom. I filled out an application with the housing department for a single room pod, the size other student workers my age were living in. My new parents could not understand the need, but they were not the ones with hormones on a rampage.

My foster mother, Yoshi, was a great cook and one of the most caring people one could ever meet. She had a frail delicate demeanor, but it was an illusion, for she was a powerhouse. Mother taught exercise, gymnastics, and martial arts at the center every morning. I once saw her illustrate an open handed attack by slamming her open hand into a large mans abdomen so hard that he flew into the air and landed quite hard. She also loved to have me there when she was giving demonstrations, which hurt until I learned how to fall, roll and not resist her when she was bending my hand in an unnatural direction, causing me to flip or roll.

My foster father, Kam, was a very studious and serious man. He worked in the lab before transferring to the space program last year. I personally thought the space program was ludicrous since we had little resources and a space program seemed so unobtainable.

Kam and Yoshi emigrated from China just before the revolution, after he had won the internationally recognized Gates Award. He was on the team of researchers that concentrated on immune disorders. Their findings developed into the cure for AIDS, which had been sweeping across Asia like a wild fire.

Father never talked about his research much. Whenever I asked him what he was working on, he would just say it was routine stuff, too technical for me to understand. One day I asked him about the expedition to the northern territory. His eyes got big, but he told me he had no knowledge of such an expedition.

I told Artemus that I knew that they were forming a work party to go on the northern expedition, and that I wanted to go. He too pretended he had no such knowledge. Finally, I went to visit the guard station to see if I could get some answers. A fair number of new recruits were training in the yard. I asked one of them if he knew where I could find Unkar. The man told me to try the stables.

As I approached the stables, a man on a horse trotted towards me looking all business. I recognized him right off— the sandy long hair with those soft blue eyes. It was Michael.

He took a long, hard look at me and shouted, "My God! That can't be Maeno?" Michael through his right leg over and slid from his saddle and lifted me off the ground in a giant bear hug. He laughed, stood back, and said, "Let me look at ya. I can't believe how you've grown, boy. What brings you to the old guard house?"

"I'm looking for Unkar. I heard there's an expedition into the northern territory, and I want to be on it."

Michael said, "Unkar is out riding a newly broke horse, but he couldn't help you anyway. You need to talk to the captain of the guard, who's up in the tower. Follow me, I'll take you there if ya promise to come by tonight and have supper with us, some of the boy's would sure like to see ya."

"I would like that Michael, I'm drowning in homework, but I will try to slip away after dinner if I can."

The captain's office door was closely guarded by an armed sentry and a secretary who had more questions than I had answers. While she cross examined me about admittance without an appointment or authorization, the captain came out.

"What's all the commotion about?" he thundered causing me to take a step back

The secretary briefed the captain.

"What's your name, son?"

"Meno Olikai, sir."

He paled. "Michael, leave us. Meno, why don't you come into my office?"

I nodded and followed him in.

"Make yourself comfortable, Meno," he said, motioning me into a chair. The captain however, nervously paced near the large windows that gave him an incredible view of the hillside. His large, dark head bobbed as he asked, "Meno what can I do for you today?"

"I want to sign on with the expedition this summer to the northern territory, sir."

The Captain raised his bushy eyebrows creasing his forehead as he sat down behind his sleek metal desk. "The um— expedition. Huh. Tell me what have you heard of the expedition."

"I overheard some talk in the center about a team being sent up north to retrieve an aircraft of some kind and the hustle and bustle out at the guard's quarters seems to indicate the same sir."

"Meno, this expedition is for trained forces and scientists and is quite dangerous. There is a small labor force going as well, but you are neither prepared nor qualified, not to mention you must have a written recommendation from at least one director and your councilor since you are still under his tutelage."

"If I were able to get the signatures, could I then go?"

After a pause he slowly nodded. But from the curl of his lip, I could tell he was assuming that I would never get them. Later that afternoon, I found Artemus and told him what the captain had told me about the signatures.

He said, "Meno, even if I gave you my signature, finding a director to approve it would prove impossible. Do you really think they will allow such a rare and precious person as yourself to be put in harm's way when they have future plans for you?"

"What kind of future plans?" I asked seeing a sudden freeze in his expression.

"I'm not sure, Meno, but do you think I would have put you through the kind of educational hell you've been under if there weren't good reason?"

"Artemus is there something you're not telling me. I mean is there another reason you don't want me to go?"

"Meno I'm late for an appointment, we'll talk about this another time." He said before shuffling off.

That night I tossed and turned. I wished I never had this DNA crap. I just wanted to be normal—not some damn science experiment! But as I wrestled with the covers, I remembered what I learned from Tiny. *I should be able to make this dream come true as long as I put forth the desire with enough faith and emotion to spin the wheels of creation in my favor.* For the rest of the night I concentrated on the result I wanted with great detail and clarity. I created the entire expedition in my head, right down to the color of the horse I would ride. The next morning I awoke with a great idea: the star delegation took questions and suggestions. I would submit my own suggestion, and if they were as understanding as I had heard, they would grant my request.

Two weeks had passed and I had still not heard anything. I was beginning to wonder if my attempt had been in vain, I was becoming obsessed with the whole idea. Still, I would not let this get in the way of my belief. I was going, and that was the end of it! I said slamming my hand down on my desk full of neglected homework. The following day, Artemus called me out of my foreign language class. In the hall, he gave me a gentle smile. "Meno, Abigail wants to see you down in the sub-center."

"The sub-center?" I asked. In ten years, I'd never even heard of that place. "Did I hear you right?"

Artemus laughed. "Yes, the sub-center. Get off at platform S and ring the bell."

This could be my lucky break, I thought and began to feel anxious as Artemus walked off. *But what if it was just more excuses by a third higher ranking party.* I could no longer concentrate on school work and nervously chewed my pencil.

That evening I took the shuttle to platform S. There was very little light other than the illuminated button next to the door. I pushed the button and waited for a short while before an elderly man opened the door.

"Can I help you?" he asked.

"Yes, I'm Meno Olikai. Abigail is expecting me."

He led me down a long, dimly lit arched brick corridor to a double door. He opened the door for me and waved me into a room vaguely illuminated from a skylight. He told me to have a seat, that Abigail will be in shortly, and then he shut the door behind him.

I looked around the room. It was completely empty other than a few chairs and a table in the center. The ceiling was shaped like a dome, and there were fish swimming past the skylight. I figured we must be under one of the ponds.

Abigail entered the room and smiled as she held out her hand. She was wearing a long shear gown that was somewhat transparent. Her figure was illuminated as the light from the skylight reached her, giving her a ghostly iridescence.

"Welcome to the private chambers of the Delegation, Mr. Olikai. The reason I wanted to meet you privately was to personally give you a response to the letter you sent. I also thought it was time we got to know each other better, please make yourself comfortable."

I sat down in one of the cold leather chairs and rubbed the gooseflesh from my arms as she sat across from me never letting her eyes leave mine, with a sublime expression that never changed.

"Your letter was very persuasive. Even though you still are not aware of what this expedition entails you want to go no matter what. I think you need a break from the pressure we have been putting you under. Perhaps you could care less for such small details as who, what, where and why. More importantly, I think it's time we leveled with you, Meno. You are a man now and should be able to handle the facts, and those facts are to be confidential. You must understand that this information could cause a great deal of discomfort within the confines of our little sanctuary here, so I am instilling a great deal of faith in your ability to understand the sensitive nature of this material."

Abigail went on and on about the Nemesis and the fate of humanity and of our planet as I listened intently and squirmed in my chair, at times wishing I had not been so hasty. She told me about the downed shuttle and how they had already sent a field crew a few years back to locate the ship, to assess the damage, and to map out a practical route for transporting it back to Tolemac. She explained the need for the space program and the cargo shuttle and emphasized how important it was to make everything operational before the storms began. Abigail then told me that I had been selected as the pilot of the shuttle that would leave Tolemac for the wormhole in about thirty years, depending on our progress with the program and the climate.

"What, why me?" I asked in shock, feeling a lump rise up in my throat.

"Because no one else has your qualifications, but don't worry we will make sure you are well equipped and well trained. We wouldn't want to gamble with the future of the human race. Your shuttle training won't happen until we get closer to that time, but you are to learn as much as possible in all pertinent areas. You will have a rare opportunity to preserve the efforts of mankind for eons to come. Meno you have not realized the potential of your own capabilities, but in time you will learn a great deal more about them. You're photographic memory and fancy DNA is only the beginning."

Abigail then said, "The reason you have been getting a cold shoulder from everyone about this expedition is because losing you now could doom the program, and when you step foot outside Tolemac we can offer you only the protection of the guard when there are other concerns. You see there are what can be considered negative entities that would like the human race to be exterminated, however, if you still want to go, I will not stand in your way. The Imputable Impetus states; rational exuberance and judgmental opinions can't hold jury to the power of will."

"What other capabilities do I have that I'm not aware of?" I asked in earnest.

"Meno we as transitionals are here for mankind's education of truth, law and divine light, to help them see there divine essence and to increase awareness before the end time's. You came here as a human bridge to carry the children of tomorrow to the next stage in the evolution of the specie; to the next dimension in space and time, where fears give way to love and matter gives way to will."

"If this is true then why don't I remember any of this great plan?"

"Self realization is not spontaneous for any who incarnate, you must first identify with the body and its needs and wants. You must first be the learning human to gather as much information as possible about what they need to exist, to survive and to evolve, so that you can pass on these requirements without incident. As your human lessons are ending, your true nature will begin to reveal itself forming a culmination of the two, at this point your human nature will no longer be able to hide the truth that you are an emissary of light."

"An emissary of light? You mean like Tiny?' I said jumping to the edge of my seat.

"Well, perhaps in the form of a teacher, yes."

"If fate has anything to do with it," I answered, "my going on this expedition will only be an asset to the crew."

Abigail smiled. "I figured you would maintain your position on the matter. Here." She handed me a folded piece of paper.

"Give this letter to anyone who questions you. You have my recommendations and my love. Have a safe journey."

That night I got no sleep at all. Every time I closed my eyes, I saw black holes and speeding shuttles. "*My god, this was my dream from Tiny's exercise in the image nation!*"

17
THE EXPEDITION

For two weeks before the expedition, I stayed and trained at the guard house. Artemus had insisted that I learn the fundamentals of weaponry before leaving. My parents, on the other hand, were still trying to convince me not to go, telling me stories of the tragedies that lay outside our village. Such Stories were powerless against my determination; I wanted to go regardless of the cost.

Before reporting to the guardhouse, I went to see Tesha at the center with Sonia, her roommate and the youngest sister of Lance. Sonia was a heavy girl and giggled most of the time, or at least when I was around. The hellos didn't take long, and I didn't have time to build up gently. Finally, I just blurted out, "Tesha, I can't go to your engagement party."

"Why?" She said with one eyebrow raised.

"I'm going on the expedition to the Rockies. You know the one that everyone keeps whispering about? I'm in. I leave in two weeks."

She jumped up and said, "Meno, are you out of your mind? How could you sign on to such a dangerous expedition after what happened to us last time? Who authorized this suicide mission, and who or what could it possibly benefit?"

I was shocked and could not understand why she was so mad.

"Meno answer me!" She stared at me sternly and tapped her fingers against her folded arms.

I felt bad enough as it was that the only women that I ever loved was getting engaged to some pretentious plant python that honked when he laughed. *"Who does she think she is anyway, the queen of Tolemac?"* I asked myself. *I don't owe her any answers.*

"Have fun at your engagement party," I told her.

I walked away ignoring her condescending raving. I wasn't sure if she had been exposed to the wrong type fungi, but with her fiancé on the scene, I was sure she was the one losing her mind. I was glad to be getting out of this place—the timing couldn't have been better.

I trained hard everyday with the split bamboo sword, which was more of training in humiliation littering my upper torso with bruises. Archery came more naturally after brushing up on the fundamentals, I even learned how to load and shoot an old muzzle-loading rifle. On the other hand I had a long way to go before I could master a horse well, but Unkar and Michael would come by often to assist with sound advice. They had wanted me to learn hand to hand combat, but I threw the instructor on his back the first time, countering one of his moves. My mother's training was indeed better than anything he could hope to show me.

The preparations for the trip were extensive. We were taking an old truck frame, pulled by a team of twelve mules and loaded with provisions and tools. There were two engineers, one medic, three from the space program, two surveyors, and one geologist—not to mention a dozen or more laborers, including me, and four four-person guard units.

The direction of travel was due north over some of the roughest country one would ever traverse. The destination was the Beartooth Wilderness of Montana, just beyond Yellowstone. The shuttle was in the mountains somewhere between Grasshopper Glacier and Glacier Lake. Obviously, with names like that, I packed my winter gear. The trip to the site was to take at least a month.

If everything went well, we would be back sometime in the fall. I kept my fingers crossed that we'd be home before the harsh winter weather set in.

Unkar was to lead the expedition along with Clarice, the head scientist of the space program. Clarice was a quick witted disciple of

Sergy Ivanovitch. She was tall and thin with pointed features and less hair than I, but she knew her stuff. Before we set foot out of Tolemac, Unkar and Clarice began locking horns. Clarice shuffled over to Unkar who was already saddled and screeched;

"I need you to bring more horses for additional water and supplies!" Unkar gave her a stern look as he pulled in his chin to his chest and said; "I'm not providing more horses for a commodity found everywhere half the guard would be on foot." .

"Well then how about some more wagons, one truck frame is hardly adequate for all our supplies," she argued.

"This isn't 1900. We don't have prairie schooners and buckboard wagons!" Unkar scoffed.

"Well, what do you have then?" Clarice retorted.

"One old truck frame, but I know where we can find more of the same. It'll mean a slight detour to an old town's bone yard."

"How much of a detour?"

"About a day and a half, unless you have a better idea," said Unkar. He looked at Clarice and asked, "Have you ever traveled on horseback?"

"No. Why?" She snapped back, with lightning speed and a disgruntled look.

"Just a word of advice then. Shorts and tennis shoes won't cut it. Get some boots and pants and perhaps a pillow for your rear, and tell that to the rest of your company. We leave at dawn."

"Oh please don't concern yourself with my rear," Clarice belched out, slapping her thigh.

Unkar turned his horse, smirked, and shook his head in disbelief as he rode off. Michael and I were laughing as we peered out the window of the tack house. Michael was letting me ride the old nag, as he called his old paint. He was taking one of the newly broke horses. He even gave me his old worn-out saddle, with the promise that it was still a comfortable ride, and a sword with a side-mounted scabbard. I rode the horse around the corral a few times. That "old nag" could turn on a dime. I felt ready for just about anything, then Michael interrupted with. "It's chow time. Let's get a good last meal. One never knows what lies out yonder."

We quartered the horses and headed for the mess hall. Halfway there, Tesha came running up to me, her green grower's apron still on. She threw her arms around me, and I noticed with surprise, and a bit of smugness, that her eyes were filled with tears.

"Oh Meno, I'm so sorry about last night! I would die if anything ever happened to you. Please forgive me. You are like family to me. Please be careful." She pulled back, put a leather necklace with a shiny stone around my neck, and gently kissed my cheek.

I tried to think of something to do or say in return, but I was dumbfounded. Before I could open my mouth, Tesha turned towards Michael and said, "Please watch over him for me."

"I will guard him with my life as always," he replied.

Tesha walked away with a small, watery smile, and Michael and I finished our walk in silence. At dinner, I examined the polished stone. There was a small carving of an owl on it. I thought about the work she must have put into such a small carving, and it reminded me of the totems they used to carve at my village. I wondered what it meant if anything—knowing Tesha, there was bound to be a hidden meaning somewhere.

The next morning the entrance road to Tolemac was chaos. The guards waited while all the labor crews ran around like chickens to fulfill the last minute orders of Clarice and her crew. By the time we were moving, the sun was upon us. Unkar and Clarice argued for a long while about sending a small party to Buena Vista to find another truck frame. Unkar would not risk separating the party, so we all headed to Buena Vista—precisely the opposite direction from our destination— to find more transportation.

We reached Buena Vista by sunset and camped on the Arkansas River. Clarice and her crew had a large tent to share while the rest of us camped under the stars.

I was envious…until the winds kicked up in the night and brought the large tent down. We laborers just stayed put and laughed silently while they all squirmed to find the exit. The next day Unkar took six of his guards and six laborers, myself included, through town to find what little was left. The town was charred. Only a brick structures, nothing more than hollowed-out shells, remained standing. One guard mentioned that most of the buildings were still intact just a few years earlier. Unkar said his best guess was that lightning had started the fire that had clearly swept through town.

We reached the bone yard, as Unkar called it. Acres and acres of junk autos, trucks, and buses rusted away in the field. Some had been there so long the erosion had half-buried them or aspen trees had grown through the engine compartments, as if they liked the protection. Unkar found an old military transport truck that had the motor removed as well as the hood and fenders. We began to remove every part that was not needed, to lighten the weight. I worked on the doors; others removed the glass. Two laborers lit a torch to remove the drive train and exhaust system. Three others were sent in search of an inflated truck tire to replace the flat on this one. Only one thing—aside from the chassis—remained totally intact: the brake system. Unkar insisted on keeping it so the heavy truck would not descend out of control on steep grades.

Within five hours, we had a custom trailer ready to roll. The guards, using makeshift harnesses out of wood planks, cut tires, and some cable, had made a pulling team out of four of the laborers' horses. Without our horses, we got to ride in the truck cab. We made it back to the camp before dusk and got the applause of the entire crew. The pack animals now became a team and their loads—along with a great deal that others had been temporarily packing—were put onto the new trailer.

The next morning we headed north to Independence Pass, our first obstacle. The expedition planners assumed it would be passable, due to the lack of snowfall we had over the winter. A few of the guards, however, whispered it was a big gamble so early in the season. All afternoon, we were buffeted with heavy winds, which eventually turned into a cold, driving rain. That evening the campfires were a bit larger than average as we tried to shake the chill from our bones and to dry our soaked bedrolls.

The following day, the pass greeted us with a seven-foot snowdrift—at least a hundred meters long. We had plenty of shovels, and we all shoveled the thick snow. Even Clarice pitched in to help; none of us wanted to be stuck on that high pass after sunset. We made it through and tramped halfway down the pass before it got too dark to continue. The day after we traveled through a ghost town, its only marker a rusted sign that proclaimed it to be Aspen. Although in a dilapidated state, it was no doubt at one time a beautiful place. As we slowly rode through, an eerie feeling came over me, I felt as though we were being watched but by what I was unsure. The others must have sensed it as well since no one made a sound. We didn't bother stopping. I felt as if we were trespassing upon a burial ground.

By the fifth day we made it to a town called Glenwood Springs. Glenwood Springs was a welcome contrast to Aspen—a small settlement built around a thriving trading post started by a couple of brothers. Although there were only a dozen or so living there, it was a good start. There was even an old hot springs still functioning, where we all had a nice, hot bath. That came in handy for I was not used to the rigors of a horse's back, and my backside cried out a silent confirmation

The trading post had nice furs as well as leather goods, Candles, soap, apple cider, jerky, and certain hand tools and knives. I wanted the fur-lined gloves and hat that they had, but I had nothing of value to trade. I just shrugged and headed for the door, Michael walked in.

"Anything you need, Maeno?"

"No, not exactly. It's just…" I hesitated. I certainly didn't need the gloves or hat, but I certainly wanted them badly. "Well, the gloves and hat over there sure would make the expedition a lot more comfortable. But I don't have anything worth trading."

. "You just go and pick out whatever it is that you want and let me deal with the trade." Michael grinned. A few minutes later, Michael traded his compass and an extra set of spurs for the hat and gloves.

"Michael, I swear I'll pay you back when we get back to Tolemac," I promised.

He just smiled and said, "Don't worry about it. That old junk has rattled in my saddle bags for years." Turning to the trader, he changed the subject. "Any trouble from travelers or Navajos around here?"

"Over the last couple of years, there have been few Americans traveling through," the trader answered. "Mostly foreigners and Amish. Take my advice; head north after the town of Rifle to avoid Navajo. They now claim every thing west to Salt Lake and don't take kindly to trespassers. They believe that that area is some sort of sacred holy ground, which is just another way of sayin' we ain't welcome." The trader said exposing a chipped set of green teeth.

We traveled a few days north and came upon a large Amish settlement in the town of Craig. The people were very hospitable and allowed us to stay the night in their large barn. I was amazed how these people thrived. They were very industrious and seemed to prosper in the arid climate. I tried to make conversation with a young woman who came in to milk a cow. Her hair was hidden under a strange cap, and she wouldn't say a word. She just occasionally looked up at me and giggled. Before she left the barn she said something in a strange language and slightly bent her knees in a curtsy before walking away, still giggling. A turned up nose and high cheekbones with a big bright smile had my heart palpitating.

The following morning I saw her again in the dawn's early light at the bucket well. I quickly tucked my shirt in and combed my hair back then walked to the well. She was humming a pleasant tune as I approached. She turned to face me and screamed, placing her hand over her breast, obviously startled by my presence. She then quickly smiled as she sat back against the stone well gasping for air.

"Water?" she asked with the bucket in an outstretched hand.

I took the bucket. "Do you speak English?"

She shook her head no, indicating with her fingers that she knew little or little words. I had no idea how to continue our conversation. To buy some time, I drew some water and took a long, slow drink. As I let down the bucket, I saw a large man with a long beard running towards me. *Oh great this must be dad, and he's not happy!* I thought. He must have heard her yell.

The girl quickly turned shouting something at him as he approached. He ripped the bucket from my hands and gave it to her, shouting and gesturing at her to leave. He stared at me with his chest extended like a gorilla defending his turf, his big brooding eyebrows made his eyes barely visible. Laughter drifted toward us from the barn. I turned my head to see Michael, holding his stomach as he wailed. The noise caused Clarice and her crew, partially clothed, to run out of their tent to see what the fuss was all about. The big man turned without a word and marched off. I went from being enchanted to terrified, to totally embarrassed, all within thirty seconds.

As I approached the barn I could now hear Unkar shaking the earth with his deep laughter. Michael had spilled the beans to the entire guard, making me the laughing stock of the day. I could not wait to leave, cute Amish girl or not.

We headed north for another few days, passing through many deserted towns, before coming to a large town called Rock Springs, on the river. Surprisingly the town was busy with people. There was even a store selling all types of foods and supplies, and a large church that was just letting out as we passed. These people had migrated here from northern Canada.

While Clarice and her crew bartered for more equipment, Unkar tried to learn about the road ahead from an elderly man. The rest of us set up camp in their playing field, which had running water and a privy available. Some young boys were standing near by bouncing a ball and wearing long faces. It was their day to play ball where we had camped, and so they began playing right next to our camp in a narrow strip of grass.

I was glued to the sidelines of the game of kickball they were playing; it was very fast and aggressive, with the boys banging into each other in pursuit of the ball. I remembered playing a similar game when I attended school as a boy in Unalaska; I remembered how much fun it was and for a moment felt a bit cheated. I wondered why I never had seen any such activities at Tolemac—I mean there were some games but nothing that got as physical as this. I tried to ask Michael why, but he gave me a noncommittal answer and told me to ask Clarice instead.

That evening I walked over to the tent. Clarice was sitting on a folding chair looking over a map with a small but very bright hydrogen lamp. I cleared my throat to get her attention. When she looked up, I asked, "Michael told me you could give me the answer to a question that's been bothering me. Why aren't physical sports part of the Tolemac program?"

"You must have been watching those boys this afternoon. I was too, and I enjoyed the action. Still, Tolemac has many reasons why contact sports are not recommended. The first is that we don't have a lot of physicians or a large facility to care for cripples and paraplegics. The second is that this sort of sporting activity caters to the ego and holds no internal benefit to the mind. Many would argue that sports of this nature help build character and confidence, but we disagree and find that most that play are left with a feeling of inadequacy, due to the performance of another. The few who excel at their game bolster an ego that gets in the way of mindfulness.

You see Meno the world is full of these old dogmas of healthy competition between countries, teams, and religions. We are called the human race, as if in a contest, but in truth there can be no winners in such a race. Competition is never healthy when the goal is making the other race, team, or person seem inferior. The Imputable Impetus states; "An ego separated from mind has much to prove; an ego that's mind-full finds no insecurities." Clarice now walked over to her horse to remove the saddle, which I took as a sign of my dismissal.

"Thanks Clarice. I get it now."

She turned and smiled, nodding her head. On my way out, I noticed she took Unkar's advice after all; at the back of her saddle lay a small pillow. The next few days we headed north into some very rugged mountainous terrain. The roads became almost un-passable where erosion had covered them or made large gullies. I was soon introduced to the back breaking labor I'd volunteered for, (road work). Some dreary areas we came upon had miles of charred forest, but there was hope—a great number of small saplings were taking root. Snow began to fall on the third night, and the wind howled through the canyon as we quickly prepared the camp. The following morning I awoke to a surprisingly warm blanket of snow which covered my bedroll and began melting through. The snow-covered pines and craggy rocks were a wonder to behold, and I stood momentarily awestruck at the might of nature's splendor.

As the camp came alive with breakfast and team preparation, I slipped off to the edge of the campsite to relieve myself. A magnificent horned owl landed on a branch not ten meters from me. She began flapping her large wings in a manner I thought most out of character, but then I was no scholar of the habits of the horned owl. The owl stared at me with large eyes of gold, let out a large screech, and turned her head south. Again she repeated the action, and then stared at me before flapping her large wings. Once again she screeched loudly at me, turned her head left, and then swooped down towards me screeching loudly as if to attack, before taking flight in that direction. I lost my balance as I ducked the beast while trying to keep my hands on the business at hand and fell over.

I never had a conversation with an owl before, but knew this owl was trying to give me a message. I recalled the bitter-sweet moment Tesha put the owl pendant around my neck. I wondered if it was just a strange coincidence or if Tesha was indeed trying to protect me with some sort of owl spirit, or better yet what if she was trying to warn me about something. She knew that if she believed in the ability of the owl to protect me, the reality would manifest. The only question was what was the warning regarding? I wracked my brain. The owl kept looking south before flying in that direction. Had something happened at Tolemac? No, I felt it was something else. *It must be telling us to go back, that some sort of danger was ahead!*

I ran back to tell the others and approached Unkar as he was saddling up his horse. I told him of the bad omen. A man who knew nature well, Unkar did not take the situation lightly. "For an owl to behave like that is a sign of a greater knowing." We headed for Clarice's tent. I told Clarice exactly what I had told Unkar, but she became tight lipped and began shaking her had in defiance. She yelled, "Do you realize that you are asking us to travel a week out of our way to regain the trail because you saw some woodsy owl flapping his wings, what am I supposed to tell the others huh?" "Sorry gang we have to take the long way because of a crazy Owl that might have just sat on a thorn or perhaps was just trying to protect her young!"

Unkar now calmly spoke, "Clarice, listen to what Meno is saying. This is not superstition here; this is a message possibly sent by the Star Delegation telling us to change course. I am not about to risk the lives of my guards with this hanging over my head. If you want to continue, you go without protection."

Clarice sat down, rubbing her eyes, and remained silent for a moment. She took a deep breath and said calmly, "Okay. Let's compromise a little here. How about if we send a couple men up the trail to investigate the situation, and if they spot trouble or smell an ambush, they can ride quickly back?"

Unkar said, "I don't like the thought of sending my men into potential danger but it would be better than splitting up the group with a stalemate. Fine, I will check out the trail, but I don't feel good about it." He threw the tent flap closed not seeing me directly behind him, blinded I scrambled after him. Unkar approached Michael and said, "Take another guard with a fast horse up the trail a couple hours to check things out. If there is even a hint of trouble, hightail it back."

Michael asked with ears and eyebrows elevated, "Is there a problem?"

"That's what you're going to find out!" Unkar replied in a military manner

As we all sat around waiting for Michael's return, the sun came out. My eyes were almost hurting from all the bright glaring, so I fashioned myself some eye protection with a strip of leather by cutting a couple of narrow slits in it and tying it behind my head. It worked like a charm. One of the other laborers asked if I had more leather for his eyes, so I made him one as well. As I lay back on my bedroll after breakfast, I became a bit sleepy and began to dose off. No sooner were my dreamy thoughts quickly erased when I felt the earth rumble and then heard the thundering noise from up the trail. We all got to our feet and were ready to jump on the horses. Unkar already in the saddle called three of his guards to mount up as he raced up the pass. I ran to my horse and jumped in the saddle. I could hear Clarice yell, "Meno no!" but I was already gone.

A few miles up the trail, Michael's horse ran by us like a bat out of hell and its eyes told a tale of their own. Only a few hundred yards later, we came to a huge pile of snow and debris.

"My God! The avalanche must have buried them alive!" He yelled

Just ahead I could now see the entire valley floor covered with tons of snow, trees and rocks, at least twenty feet deep. We spread out and searched for any signs of life or belongings, but the snow was hard to walk in without sinking. We searched the entire area for several hours, but there was no sign of them. Finally, Unkar said, "Mount up. We've lost 'em!" with a stone face that hid all detection, I unfortunately could not maintain such composure. I lingered back as the others rode ahead, I didn't want them to see me weep.

We traveled the long way around the mountains. During that time— almost a week out of our way, I reflected on the avalanche. Unkar was visibly upset over the loss of so close a friend and spoke very few words. Clarice had tried to question him when we returned that afternoon, but he just slowly rode by her and kept on down the trail, not willing to discuss the matter.

I too had trouble coming to terms with the mixed-up feelings that consumed me. I kept hearing Michael's words before we left—when he told Tesha that he would guard me with his life. While I did not hold Clarice responsible for the deaths, I still felt a slight resentment toward her. I avoided eye contact as well as any verbal communication with her. She was said to be a brilliant scientist, and it is the unfortunate habit of science to question everything that has no proven formula or equation.

One evening Unkar sat at the edge of the creek watching me trying my luck at fishing. Perhaps he wasn't ready to sit among the others. Clarice came over and perched herself on a boulder next to him as he stared at my line in the water ignoring the intrusion.

Finally after several moments in awkward silence she spoke. "If ever I could change one day in my life, it would be that day at the pass. I know you may never forgive me for the loss of your friends, but I want you to know that I am deeply sorry." Clarice sat for a moment. Hearing no reply, she got up to walk away.

"Clarice, wait!"

Clarice turned back to face Unkar, a tear on her cheek seemed suspended in time as the evening light made it glisten, causing Unkar to briefly hesitate as his face lost all expression.

"Look Clare…I don't hold you responsible, and so there is nothing to forgive. I have been out here long enough to know that to worry about who, what, or why is pointless. I will not waste my energy with such nonsense, but all the logic in the world can't compete with the power of emotion. Sometimes we don't know how much another's presence means to us until its stolen from us, and I don't rightly know why this one has bothered me more than the others in the past, but I think that deep down I knew the moment I sent Michael and Rudy down that pass I knew it would be their last order, but still I let them go not having the guts to retract my order."

Clarice put her hand on the big man's shoulder. "I understand. You know I've heard it said that two rights can make a wrong but I never knew the meaning of those words until that day at the pass. But if we're going to lead these people who depend so much on our day-to-day decisions, we must not let doubt and uncertainty get a footing."

"You're right," Unkar replied. "I have been a bit selfish the last few days and have forgotten my responsibilities to the welfare of the crew. There's just one question that I need answered: what the hell are we doing out here in the middle of nowhere trying to find an old rocket?"

"I guess it's time you knew the facts," Clarice replied. She launched into the details of the future space program, the nemesis, and reason we needed the rocket. Unkar looked pale and perplexed, and Clarice asked if he was all right.

"My God, woman, I don't think I'll ever be all right after those words!"

He now stared at me and said with a disgusted look on his face. "You knew about this Nemesis thing the whole time too?"

I just shrugged and said, "Well not the whole time, I just found out myself before we left that I have been chosen to pilot the ship into this—thing."

"My God Meno, you know how insane this all sounds, geez now I know why I went through hell and high water to gather your hide back to Tolemac, what is it about you boy that their willing to go to such lengths to protect, or do I even want to know." He said as he now stared back at Clarice.

"To avoid all the technicalities, it's just important that we understand that Meno is very special in ways that we've just begun to understand and that we should just keep the faith in the Star delegations direction for him until more is understood. But for now I'm getting hungry and that smell drifting from the camp tells me its dinner time." She said as she slowly walked off.

By the middle of the following week, we were within a few days of the downed shuttle. Cody, the town we stopped in, was deserted, so we made camp at an old airport. One crew member came running back from exploring the hangars and said something to Clarice. Clarice in turn summoned Unkar over. After a moment's discussion all three headed to a large metal hangar. After what seemed like an hour, no one returned. With such mysterious proceedings, I could not wait a moment longer and jumped on my horse and rode out towards the hangar. The closer I got the more monstrous I realized it was. I slipped through the opening in the large corrugated metal sliding doors and was overcome by what I saw—it was huge! Underneath the belly of the monstrosity lay a small room with a window, and through that window I could see Unkar and Clarice's tiny faces. Wow! Was all I could think!

18
THE RETURN TRIP

I navigated the maze of rooms in the belly of the craft, finally following the long, winding hall to the front. Unkar and Clarice sat in some sort of huge cockpit and were joking and laughing like children with a new toy.

"What is this thing?" I asked.

They both turned toward me and laughed. Unkar jokingly said, "It's a flying watermelon."

Clarice laughed and said, "No, it's a Zeppelin."

"A what?" I asked Clarice.

"Just kidding, Meno. It's a flying airship and quite possibly our ride home."

They gave me a quick tour of the ship with my jaw hanging open. The ship had all the comforts of home, a kitchen and dinning area with lots of windows, and several of the compartments had beds. Unkar had even found some old wine stored in a bottom cabinet and opened a couple bottles to pass around. Clarice told me to run back and get George and the rest of the crew. Even before I reached the camp, I began to shout and wave my arms in excitement. Everyone ran to the closest horse, some riding double, and we made a mad dash for the hangar. Once there, I cranked the sliding door back further. Everyone entered with a sigh and a lot of oos and ahs. I showed George the way into the cockpit, and a large entourage followed. George just kept saying, "This is astounding—astounding!" in his strong Scottish brogue. I finally herded him all the way to the cockpit. Clarice was thrilled to see him and immediately started grilling him on what he knew about airships. George answered with raised eyebrows;

"Enough to know that what we have here is not just some ordinary zeppelin. This is one of the most revolutionary models to come out of Stockholm, Sweden. Notice this saucer disc design? It gives greater mobility in strong winds while enabling greater speeds with a smaller volume of gas required for lift. What is this incredible ship doing in a deserted hangar?"

"We believe that someone landed it here after a long trip. The log states that it was last operated by a family and their crew in 2032. They must have hid it here before falling prey to the plagues that surfaced around that time," Clarice said closing the log book.

"George, what sort of fuel does this machine require? Is there a possibility that we can use this to retrieve the shuttle?"

George now was in deep thought pondering the question, "If my memory serves me right, these later models were entirely self-sufficient with a little water and a lot of sunshine."

"Totally self-sufficient?" Clarice asked.

"Yes, the lightweight skin of the balloon is actually three layers of material that work together like a photovoltaic panel, generating an electrical charge when exposed to solar energy. Due to the size of the balloon and efficiency of the materials, the charge created is in the neighborhood of twenty-five to fifty kilowatts per solar day."

"Wow! This thing generates that kind of energy?" Clarice replied.

"Yes, and that's not all," George replied. "That's not the primary power source. The electricity is converted into hydrogen by way of simple electrolysis inside a large cook-tank, and it's hydrogen that fuels the engine and inflates the balloon."

George tapped his finger on his chin before continuing, "Now to answer your questions regarding the use of this ship in retrieving the shuttle we would have to do some serious calculations, but I think the possibility is real if we take some preliminary precautions."

"What kind of precautions?" Clarice asked.

"The first would be concerning the ballast. These ships use a ballast of water to decrease buoyancy and for later conversion to hydrogen, so we can't empty too much if you are going to do any extended periods of travel. And then there is thermal uplift—any mountainous terrain will have some of that. That's great if you're a hawk searching for prey, but not when you're in a balloon the size of a football field!"

"Then I guess we all have a lot of homework to do over the next few days, don't we? And I know where I'm going to sleep while we figure it all out!" Clarice said with a big grin on her face.

We lugged all the supplies and horses into the small hangar on the other side of the airstrip, where we camped while awaiting instructions from Clarice. Unkar decided some of the guard could go out on hunts for more food, since there had been a great number of deer and elk sightings near the river.

The layover was great after so much constant travel, and the shelter of the hangar provided relief from the ever present sun and wind. There was even an old water tower that made a nice temporary shower. Unkar and a few guardsmen made a new home out of the abandoned flight tower. Unkar said he liked the ability to see a mile in any direction.

After four days we finally had a plan. The first step was to pull the ship out of the hangar using horses and mules. Once in the sun, it could charge up for a couple days. Then we would try a test flight to get acquainted with it. Finally, we were to try test lifting different weights. The first two steps went fine. It wasn't until we tested weights that we got into trouble. We had piled anything we could find onto the old military truck frame, then attached the weights to the ship with large cables. The ship emptied a lot of water before it was able to lift the heaviest loads, but once airborne the cargo seemed to help the ship in the wind. George even got so confident that he and five others took the ship for a one-hour test flight with a huge truck full of weight. The flight was no problem, but when we unhooked the truck frame, the ship abruptly lifted off—shooting like a rocket into the air and lifting some men at least ten feet in the air before they let go of the lanyards.

The ship became a small speck in the sky before finally leveling off and descending slowly. George had apparently stumbled upon an emergency gas release that let out hydrogen from the balloon from a manually controlled lever. We all had a good scare!

But the good news was the plan worked—we were ready to move on, this time in style! The next morning we loaded the airship with provisions for Clarice and her crew and refilled the water reservoir behind the ship's gondola. We left the majority of supplies at the base with a couple guards and rode for two days through Dead Indian Pass and over Windy Mountain, then into the uncharted terrain of the mountains. The whole time, we looked overhead following the airship's lead. We camped at the base of a rather steep and jagged mountain with the airship hovering over us all night, tethered to a few large pine trees.

The next morning we began ascending the steep incline on foot with climbing gear and full packs, having left a small party behind with the horses and gear. The hard work wasn't a burden this time, though—the shuttle was at the base of the other side of the mountain, and we were all eager to reach our goal.

The climb was tolerable until we neared the summit. Then the path had almost fifty feet of near vertical terrain, culminating at a jagged top. One of the more experienced guards went ahead and anchored all his points. After a quick lecture on procedure and safety, the rest of us were extended a rope to climb. One at a time, we dug our fingers and feet into the cold craggy rock crevices. The laborer named Dan in front of me was having trouble with his finger holds as well as his confidence and lost his grip and began yelling as he slid down into me and catching his foot on my shoulder, almost sending me down with him, but I had a firm foothold and managed to push him back against the rock. I think the adrenaline must have made him try a bit harder after that, for then he seemed to fly up the cliff face. Descending was a lot easier. We could see the crash site of the shuttle, and having the goal in sight motivated me more than anything else had so far. It was a long but easy hike down to the valley floor.

Upon arrival, everyone ran to examine the craft. It was larger than I imagined it to be—at least fifty feet in length—and in better shape than

I had expected from a crashed vehicle. Only the top fin showed signs of damage, plus one window that was blown out. The cockpit, however, was filled with debris and snow, so there was little doubt that the ship had been there for a while. We began to toss everything outside that was not part of the permanent structure—snow, leaves, and then the original cargo—to lighten the load. We didn't have the manpower to position it onto the harness for transport otherwise. In the cockpit, we came across the four crew members; skeletons, still strapped in their seats. The pilot in front had a metal tag hanging on his tattered vest. Major P. Bennington, NASA.

"Sorry, Major, but this is my ship now," and tossed the body out the window. When I heard the crew on the ground holler in surprise I yelled back, "sorry!"

When we finally finished, I sat in the control seat and rested as the others went to help with harness preparations. The seat was surprisingly comfortable, considering what had been resting in it. I put my hands on the controls and could feel the power of the ship. I envisioned blasting out of Earth's atmosphere, then cruising to a distant planet. My God, this was my dream! But there was no time to waste. Soon I was outside with the rest of the crew, assembling the cable harnesses from our packs. The airship could be seen in the distance, flying low up the valley floor. As it stopped directly overhead, blocking the sun, a cargo door opened up on the bottom and a large cable was lowered. The cable was hooked to the front of the ship by Unkar. The rest of us all grabbed lanyards to try and stable the air ship. This maneuvering went on for a while, until the shuttle was properly positioned in the harness. Once the cables were winched tight, the main cable was re-attached to the other cables, and Unkar gave the thumbs up signal.

A torrent of water rushed down from the back of the ship, until the shuttle rose off the ground. The loud, whining hum of the large turbine engines filled my ears as the ship turned 180 degrees and slowly slipped out of sight. We all cheered it onward, jumping up and down at the amazing sight. Still, I wondered how we could have removed it without the airship. I don't think we would have made it halfway up that steep cliff, let alone over the summit. I began to see the perfection in it all. We would never had found that ship if we had taken the short cut through the canyon that morning. Although we lost two good men to the avalanche, it seemed to have ensured the mission's success.

We made it back over the ridge safely and camped again at the base before heading back to the hangar. Although the trail was downhill from here, I kind of wished I was riding in that airship. But that would have had me back at Tolemac in three days—and I was glad for the three-week journey that lay ahead.

When we got back to the airport in Cody, the two guards, eyes wide with shock, ran to Unkar. I slid over so I could hear the conversation. Apparently, while out hunting the day before they spotted two young men dressed in animal skins hunting the elk with spears. When the guards approached the boys, they ran in fright.

Unkar nodded in thought, his hard face slightly softened. "They're probably the surviving children of the families that once lived in these towns," he said. "This is their life now; it's all they know, just basic day-to-day survival. I'm sure there are others as well. We have become spoiled at Tolemac and have perhaps the best standard of living left on our continent, but it is our culture that keeps us as we are. I only hope we can maintain that culture and standard of living as the world dims around us."

As we rearranged our supplies, preparing to leave the hangar behind forever, Unkar suggested a detour to a place called Yellowstone on the way home. He had never seen it, and we were so close. One of the guards was quick to mention a bear problem.

Unkar smiled broadly as he said, "What? You don't like bear meat?"

We loaded the wagons and headed towards Yellowstone the following day. It wasn't long before I discovered the guard's fear of bears had merit. That's all we saw in Yellowstone, in fact there were black ones, brown ones—we even saw a mama grizzly with her cubs, and none of these bears seemed to be the least bit fearful. We camped in the open that night and did not cook. We also took turns alternating watch. The wolf howls throughout the night aroused even greater concerns. In the end, I decided Yellowstone was a beautiful place but it belonged to the bears. I think Unkar agreed, since we went an unusually long distance the following day.

We backtracked, avoiding the Amish community, but rested a couple days when we got to the trading post at Glenwood Springs. No one could get enough of those mineral baths. While there, we saw few travelers other than the occasional fur trader, Amish, and even a few Navajo trading skins for knives. We headed back over Independence Pass, surprised by what little snow was now present, and reached Tolemac shortly thereafter.

From the guard station we could clearly see that Clarice's crew had safely landed, for the huge airship was hard to miss. I was tired and saddle sore, so I barely said goodbye after dropping my gear off. Instead of celebrating the successful trip with the guard, I headed home. I opened the door to find Yoshi making a fuss about my return. She was ecstatic.

"Kam will be so happy you are home. Oh! I can't wait till he's back from work," she exclaimed.

I tried to smile encouragingly, but I was too exhausted. "I'm sorry, Mom. I just need to lie down for a while. Is that okay? I promise we will talk about my trip soon."

"Of course, of course," Yoshi said, as she ushered me to my room. But I never got the chance to relax. A moment after I lay down Tesha appeared at the door of my room. She ran in and hugged me and began shaking me in my bed, saying with excitement, "You got my message! You got my message!"

"Did it have anything to do with a large owl going insane while I was trying to relieve myself?"

Tesha laughed and said, "That's incredible! You know it was the strangest thing. The night after you left, I had this nightmare of an avalanche burying the entire crew. It scared the hell out of me, and I couldn't sleep the rest of the night. The next day I felt terrible all day and could not shake it, so that evening I used the image-nation to send you a message by way of the owl spirit. I did this every night until I had great confidence in its ability to manifest. About a month later I had another dream; this time I saw you riding home on a large owl."

I grinned and said, "It looks like I'm not the only one being delivered by birds these days."

Tesha gently rubbed her swollen abdomen as her face flushed with embarrassment.

19
TOLEMAC 2076

Almost twenty years had past since our expedition, and my dream had finally come true: Abigail asked me to report to the space station the following day to begin my training.

There was no stone left unturned in regards to Tolemac. The last twenty years proved exhausting as I struggled to keep up with all my studies. The years flew by as I was exposed to Tolemac's complex systems, working hands on in every department with the exception of the space program.

I even spent a year in sanitation, and it took another year before I could get that awful smell out of my system. The entire sanitation system was built as a large dehydration chamber, so that all of the nitrogen rich waste could be recycled as fertilizer for the greenhouses. The year spent in the power plant was an incredible learning experience; the genius behind its design kept Tolemac going after the rest of the country regressed to more primitive means.

The system was based on the creation and reaction of hydrogen. Thermolysis was the first step: huge parabolic dishes concentrated solar energy through water, which was heated to an extreme temperature to separate the hydrogen atoms. The hydrogen was then piped to two areas for use. The first was an enormous fuel cell that acted like a huge battery. Once the hydrogen came in contact with the electrolytic fluid, the atom split again causing electron movement and an ionic charge. This charged battery was then used to power several electromagnetic motors, which created enough current to supply the entire village. The excess hydrogen was circulated and used as fuel gas for domestic purposes.

A large heat exchanger in the hydrogen combustion chamber provided hot water. This circulated through the village underground to provide heat and domestic hot water. Auxiliary hydrogen boilers placed at the furthest points in the loop supplemented the heat exchanger and kept the water temperature up. Another back-up system was added more recently for the production of hydrogen, called a frequency harmonizer. The frequency harmonizer, when calibrated correctly, vibrated the tenacious hydrogen atoms free from the oxygen atoms in water, like a large tuning fork searching for the proper octave.

There were also old wind turbines used as a back-up system for extended cloudy periods. The turbines generated enough current to create hydrogen through electrolysis. Although it was not as productive as the thermolysis method, it was enough to power up the large cathode battery for generation. Tolemac did not have a substantial electrical requirement, since the heating was a byproduct of the hydrogen generation and all lighting was mainly chemical. Even refrigeration required very little power due to the advanced designs in electromagnetism.

The ventilation fans throughout the village and in all the greenhouses were technical marvels worked independently. Once hand-cranked to start, they would run indefinitely, unless the circuit was closed. They worked off some sort of atmospheric energy that operated by negative induction causing a bipolar charge that caused the attraction of opposing ions in the atmosphere.

My year in water distribution was by far the easiest. My only tasks were to change the occasional filter and monitor pressure gauges and reservoir levels. It was a good opportunity to catch up on my studies. Water conservation was essential and every raindrop was captured by way of roof drainage systems and positive drainage landscaping, which funneled all water back down to the cavernous aquifers far beneath

Tolemac. The distribution of water had been built at different periods of growth and therefore many separate systems existed. The green houses all had their own system to siphon well water out of the aquifers. To do so, wind turbines connected to small air compressors that pumped air into the small pipe wells. By aerating the water for buoyancy, water achieved the required lift to the storage tanks in each greenhouse, where it worked on gravity feed. The pressurized distribution system for domestic and commercial needs was a bit more complex, using solar heated steam pumps with a back-up hydrogen pump to keep the water tower full.

Most recently I had been working at the sub-center—the home of the star delegation. The star delegation was made of a handful of transitionals—knowing and loving elders who came to ease others' minds into a new dimension in space and time, as well as the space and time event known as the great transition. Despite being so few, they all lived a life far removed, except of course for Abigail. She was no doubt a transitional, filling in at the chamber when required, but she did this only occasionally. Most of her time was spent overseeing the group's needs and teaching others the greater truths, as well as keeping the directors well informed. The rest of the transitionals claimed to be part of an ancient and sacred brotherhood that were spiritually aware from the day they were born. After the age of puberty, they left their homes from all over the world to come to Tolemac, recognizing each other immediately for what they were.

The nine transitionals were easily recognizable, for they all maintained a similar facial expression—utter disinterest in the mundane while the eyes seemed to conceal some sort of inner excitement or expectant surprise. Their strange gazes seemed to look through your very soul with a loving demeanor. You could not segregate them by creed or culture, for they were beyond all these stereotypic structures of man. They cared little for the physical experience but a great deal about our evolution.

The chamber in which they resided was designed for isolation and vibration. It was a dimly lit pentagonal room quarried from solid granite. The floor was inlaid with a shiny metal pentacle and in the center was a small concealed pentagonal box that housed a large stone said to be a sapphire, and upon the flat center of the sapphire was etched the sacred name of God. Hovering directly over the box was a strand of five glowing multi-colored crystal orbs that increased in size as you moved downwards. The bottom one was about a meter in circumference. I recognized the scale as that of *phi,* a geometrical progression known as the golden mean that can be found throughout nature and the physical universe. The domed ceiling of the chamber gave the room an acoustic resonance when the orbs were vibrated by way of vocal resonance with the sacred name.

Five transitionals would reside in the chamber for days at a time without interruption. The number five represented each point of the pentacle. When one was removed, another took his or her place. At the start of each stay, the transitional always toned in by way of the orbs, a method held secret from all non-transitionals. This somehow put them back into resonance with the other members of the delegation before they drifted back into a catatonic state. I was not allowed to be present at the toning in. Abigail said that the high decibel level could cause physical and mental side effects ranging from nausea to headaches and even bone fractures.

The transitionals were hung from the ceilings of the room by a strange body sling that supported all the main joints and extremities of the body. This was also operated by a computer motorized cable and pulley system that would put their bodies through slow methodical, continuous movements.

Abigail had them all on IVs for feeding and catheters for waste removal. In fact, each member had permanent tubes that were medically connected to their bodies for this reason; all bodily waste was handled by a computerized machine. Their IVs were connected to another computerized machine that distributed the proper quantities and mixtures of what Abigail called "the formula." This formula was a mixture of proteins and carbohydrates and select herbs that strengthen the immune system and mildly sedated the body. Only the delegates knew this formula and would prepare it during their off times. I helped Abigail remove delegates that were connected for their three-day maximum, after which they had to get up and move the body and eat solid foods. To prevent atrophy, disconnection was necessary for at least two days while another delegate took the slot. Transitionals were beyond the vale of the ego. They were a congress of mind, not creating physical laws, but rather creating through their understanding of the imputable laws of creation.

One day I asked Abigail, "Why I was the chosen one?"

"You chose to be the messenger long ago," she said, "and although there is a temporal block of this information, you still carry a great deal of it within your heart in the form of knowing without symbolism. You are an angel of mercy who is here to carry the vibration of love forward to a new field of resonance, so that all can enjoy the new octave—just like your predecessor Noah. If this chain is broken, then human progress will be seriously retarded, or even erased"

"Is this the reason for my unusual DNA?" I asked her.

"Why, of course, my dear. Do you really think an angel of mercy would be anything less than perfect? You have more mind power than all of the transitionals put together. This is why you are the messenger. Anyone with fewer qualifications could botch the job. Your awareness will increase when you are less burdened with the technical aspects of your mission, freeing up the creative side of your brain."

The transitionals had been preparing the new world for me by removing any obstacles that threatened the transition. No matter who I asked; they would not tell me any details, claiming that I could cause interference through emotional mental projections. Too many times I heard one say, "Never worry about the unknown. Its creation is an act of faith." They would also say that all the changes yet to come are an all important part in the grand schema, and the grand schema has a divine motive.

I came to understand the laws of Tolemac—which were not laws at all, but rather the philosophies and truths taught by the transitionals. There were no laws to govern the people at Tolemac, nor courts, juries, or judges. No jails existed to hold felons, and no one could be held in judgment. If one were to judge another, the transitionals believed, the individual showed that they lacked understanding of the truths that were taught throughout Tolemac.

The Imputable Impetus states; The manifestation of a law governing the physical characteristics of an individual is not only born of fear but creates a need for government for want in its volition; Imputable laws already govern all that is and any perversion of truth only exists in spite of the imputable laws.

Abigail said, "If we look at the cultures with the largest nuclear weapons, we therein find the largest symbols of fear. The sheriff of this town is love and understanding and he has many deputies."

To further my understanding of Tolemac's philosophies once I asked Abigail why Tolemac did away with their monetary system, and she replied, "It was too Roman." Normally this sort of statement would have left more questions, but after taking several courses in history and religion, I understood what she meant.

The Roman way of life really never ceased to exist and was interwoven into modern societies. The Roman nation was one of conquering and controlling, which are both practices born out of fear. Romans exerted more control over the commodity markets of that time via currency, with the goal of dictating supply and demand of all trade goods of interest to the state. We even assumed their hierarchy's congress, the influential political archetypes. The emperors of Roman times had many similarities with U.S. presidents. They both were seen as rulers of a sovereign state, and they were constantly being chastised by congress.

Abigail continued, "Currency will always be a source of corruption and manipulation. It will always become more important than the goods it can purchase, and most people will fall prey to its belief to be a cure-all. Currency once was worth its own weight in a precious metal, which is only precious because you have been brainwashed into believing that it is. Without the so called precious metal, currency becomes a representation of that metal. Then we have a credit, which is another representation of a representation. Soon it all becomes nothing more than a misrepresentation by way of abuse of that controlling commodity. If we eliminate the commodity, we eliminate a great deal of fear and control, as well as corruption within the control systems, not to mention crimes committed to get back some of this controlling commodity. I think that just the removal of an external nuisance like currency will jump start any society into a more natural state!"

It took almost the entire year before I asked Abigail the one question I had promised myself to have answered while sitting in the big chairs of the sub-chamber: Who's Tiny?

"Enoch or Tiny is a multi-dimensional being who does not like the limitations of the physical body, so he influences the psyches of unsuspecting individuals to create mechanical contraptions of his own design that give him a temporal life. This way he can entertain in several dimensions at once while avoiding cultural identities or ego separation."

"Tiny works with us in unison to prepare the mind for expansion. He is one of the oldest and wisest teachers we have, and loves us a great deal. You see all the originators of this society were gently persuaded by Tiny in dreams and visions. He is a master of the art of transformation and knows no limitation of mind. When in his presence—mechanical or otherwise—you become instantaneously aware. The word symbolisms spoken after this fact are just his way of enjoying your company, for Tiny is love."

"Tiny has helped man upon the face of this earth for eons and is always there when a crisis prevails. It was he that the ancient Egyptians knew as Thoth, the god of wisdom and architect of the great pyramid. The Greeks knew him as Hermes and Mercury, and the Hebrews by Enoch or Kanoch, which meant the initiator. He was also called Taaut by the Phoenicians. Even this could not guarantee his teachings would be remembered, for the Scrolls of Enoch were not allowed into the Roman collection of scrolls called the Holy Bible. But the omission only goes to show that his teachings cannot be manipulated for the enslavement of man."

I told Abigail that when I first arrived at Tolemac, I had the opportunity to sit in on one of her classes about love; it was during that class that I realized that Tolemac was unlike any other place on the planet. Although I understood a great deal of what was said, I still didn't understand the basic essence of love, only its emotional stereotype.

"The true essence of love really is quite simple. You see there is nothing in the physical or mental planes of existence that are independent of it. It is the universal ubiquitous energy that pervades and invades the fabric of all creation and all thoughts of mind. You see, my forgetful little angel, for every thought there is a vibration that precedes it. For every act, every movement, every feeling, word, deed, and spectrum of light, there is a vibration that precedes it. As for our physical bodies, they are like waves in the ocean of time. This incredible vibratory source is that true essence we call love. So I ask you again, what's the matter?"

"Love!" I replied.

"Indeed, my love, indeed."

Abigail also taught me how to tap my own resource center for personal manifestation. Her method was very similar to what Tiny taught, but she filled in a great number of the details. She showed me how to blend emotional energy with the pictures created in the image-nation for greater results, and how I could entertain and amuse myself while experiencing these pictures as a latent reality, drawing more emotional energy to aid in its design and fabrication. She said that these were fundamentally the same techniques they used at the center. The only real difference was that they applied themselves liberally in whatever they were focusing on and were very organized and deliberate and had a very high expectation of what was to come to pass. Abigail would constantly remind me that it was all mind and that I was creating all of my tomorrows without even realizing that I had total control. She taught me that I could easily change course by changing my focus upon the image of my desire, which was mental, emotional, and driven by expectation. Any limitations were self-induced.

I asked her if she could explain what the jewel of the rainbow was.

She gave me a big smile. "I'm not going to make it that easy for you. Tiny had already given you a riddle to help you understand it. You just need to break it down into the sum of its parts and discover the true meanings of the words. Due you even remember the riddle?"

After so many years of pondering it, I could recite it without hesitation: "The jewel of the rainbow won't be found among external creations and cannot be pondered while duties demand, but search for it not and it will find thee in time, for there is no hourglass quite like the one at hand!"

Abigail stood up and applauded. "Bravo, bravo! You have passed the test and can handle the rest. Now I bid you a good night, my love," she said as she left me to ponder the meaning of it all.

The evening before I was to report to the space program my mind was too full of energy to retire to my pod, so I went to the center and walked in the park for relaxation. Some of the young drama students were practicing a play called *Romeo and Juliet*, so I grabbed a seat and watched them rehearse. Juliet was being performed by Gina, Tesha's daughter, now full grown and in every way just as beautiful as her mother. Looking at Gina almost hurt, for she reminded me so much of her mother the first time we met, but there was something else very familiar about Gina. It was in the way she carried herself and in her patterns of speech, something in the look of her eye's carried an uncanny resemblance to someone else. But I couldn't place who.

20
TIME WARPED

That night I wrote down the words to Tiny's riddle for a serious investigation. *The jewel of the rainbow...*

According to my dictionary, a jewel was "an ornament, a cut precious stone geometric in nature, or something regarded with deep affection." The *el* suffix came from either the Latin or Anglo-Saxon translation, added to turn verbs into nouns. So the root verb was Jew— obviously not the religious term. I scanned the pages for a different meaning and found an old term for Jew. "An over extension for trickery, or to go to great lengths to conceal something." *That fits*, I thought with satisfaction.

Next was the rainbow, sunlight reflecting upon raindrops to generate a spectrum of colored light. But this was too vague. The terms spectrum and light, however, could be the key. I had witnessed my first rainbow at the bottom of a waterfall while out walking with my grandfather. I had asked how it could be possible for such beauty to form. He had smiled and said, "The rainbow is a reminder from the Great Spirit, it shows us the way back home." That statement suddenly made sense to me now, but the wheels turning in my mind began to open up a Pandora's Box.

Long ago I had learned that humanity was no longer operating on the full spectrum. We fell from grace, and became separated from the knowledge of truth, for the truth of our true nature resided within as all-knowing children through the full spectrum of light once received from the father. These divine radiations were seven in number, covering the full spectrum of creation through manifestation. The other frequencies had been jammed. Why, I wondered, but the only thing I could come up with was that we got to big for our britches.

Feeling confident in my insights, I moved on. *It won't be found in external creations...*

So the jewel of the rainbow was attained from within. Chakra therapy taught that seven key glands of the endocrine system had colors associated with them that matched their individual centers, or chakra. I had taken a chakra therapy workshop where I learned to cleanse these centers of the negative energy that built up there. The negative energy could eventually cause problems with organs near those centers. The instructor said that where the mind goes, the body will follow, and where the body is, the mind will re-experience any suppressed emotions held in bondage during cleansing. These glands are like sponges soaking up spent feelings that bear matching vibrations and develop into energy cesspools. Chakra cleansing was long and hard and caused everything from indigestion to crying and fits of rage as everyone in the room relived their worst moments, expelling the unwanted energy with them. I myself got the runs for three days.

I started brainstorming on the connections. The inner rainbow was in me—in my body. The pineal gland had been compared to a crystal that received as well as sent vibrations, sort of like the old radio transmitters. Crystals were also known as jewels—and putting these two facts together had me quite excited. The pineal gland not only controls hormone and enzyme activity, but also could assist one's growth through the barriers of consciousness.

I could here Tiny's shrill voice now in my head, "The *image-nations elixir of life is emotion.*"

The heart must be the strongest emotional center, so heartfelt love must have a vibration strong enough to create a field of resonance. Once directed and reflected through mind, the field of resonance would be synchronized with the divine radiations of the Father.

So I'm dealing with a mental construct—and most likely a geometrical shape that is filled with love and intent, I thought with a firm nod of my head. And its vibratory frequency is capable of breaking through the presently jammed frequencies of creation and manifestation, enabling us the potential for truth and understanding and ultimately transcendence into the full spectrum of being.

The rest of the riddle, *"and cannot be pondered as duties demand, but search for it not and it will find thee in time, for there is none quite like the one at hand"* seemed pretty straight forward: they didn't want this secret interfering with the project, and that after this time sensitive transitions was over, I might find the time to journey further with this information. With confidence in my solution, I crawled into bed.

I arrived at the main office for the space program the next morning. Clarice, who had replaced Sergy as director after his death, had her eyes focused on the research papers in front of her as she scratched her head with a pencil. I knocked lightly on the open door. She smiled and lowered her glasses.

"I was hoping you would be arriving soon. We can use all the extra help we can get," she said.

"I'm here for training, not a labor position," I told her, unable to keep the alarm from my face.

"Wherever there's training, you will find labor, for they are one and the same!" Clarice said.

I laughed and said, "You wouldn't say that if you'd ever spent time working in the sanitation field."

"On the contrary, physical life is one big sanitation field!" she quipped.

We both laughed. It was good to see that Clarice had not lost her sense of humor with her heavy workload.

"How can I get started?" I asked.

"It's not as much a how as a where. You see, the space program is composed of smaller independent programs, and you need to learn about all of them. Involve yourself in everything from the construction of the rocket boosters, to shuttle revisions, to the astrophysics and engineering department. I am going to put you in the physics lab first, since this is where it all begins." Clarice handed me a room designation. "Board the transport south and get off at platform E. Report to assistant director, Ben Weinberg.

After I introduced myself to Weinberg, a balding man with half-inch thick glasses, he looked me up and down. "I know who you are, Mr. Olikai, but my question is how much do you know about astrophysics? I don't have time for tutoring!"

Coughing in surprise, I managed, "I'm familiar with the process but a bit rusty on the fundamentals."

Without a word, he wandered to the bookshelf and grabbed a thick volume. Handing it to me, he ordered, "Read this in full before returning." And then he walked away.

I spent three days reading that book, and then I spent three weeks in that lab listening to theories and equations, one upon another. The space program workers were all trying to find the optimal launch date. The important parameter was timing it such that the launch would not be affected by the intense electromagnetic field of the encroaching black hole.

The first obstacle was reaching the speed that could take the ship the distance to the black hole's ergosphere, estimated at ten and one half billion miles. (It made it easiest for me to follow the convoluted forces when I envisioned the ergosphere as the rim of a giant toilet that was constantly flushing). Once there, the ship's work was done; gravity would pull it the rest of the distance, constantly increasing its velocity to warp speed.

The current working theory was to generate additional thrust using Jupiter's magnetic pull as a sling to catapult the ship out of the solar system, a technique used in the Apollo 13 space mission that almost went to the moon. There were plenty more obstacles to tackle. The second: the asteroid belt that also circled the far reaches of Mars. We pondered a closer proximity to the sun, but just one bad solar flare—plentiful, thanks to the black hole—could cook the onboard computer through electromagnetic radiation. . Space junk, the millions of satellites and other pieces of equipment that were in continuous orbit around our planet, provided a third obstacle—more of an interplanetary obstacle course, actually.

Our biggest problem seemed to be Einstein's theory of relativity. We needed to reach the speed of light to travel the distance, but, since we were dealing with matter, we were light years away from solving the riddle, and I think Weinberg knew it!

One evening I pondered the hopeless efforts of the program from my pod. Current technology did not solve the problem in any way shape or form, and if we were going to overcome our obstacles, we needed to radically change our direction. Hoping for an inspirational thought, I meditated for two hours — nothing. The next morning I awoke with a great idea; I would ask Tiny to help us find the answer. Surely he would be willing to help. I threw on clothes and scurried to the old school building.

The old building looked dark and deserted. The front door was unlocked, and the hall was filled with dirt and papers lying about as if it had not been used for many years. I guessed that since I was one of the last newcomers to Tolemac, there was no need for the process anymore. I walked down the long hall where Tiny's class had once been held. Still there was no doorway, just a pale block wall in dire need of paint. Walking away in utter disappointment, I passed a door with a large padlock. *Wait*, I thought as a memory was tweaked. *This door led to the machine room before, right?* I could remember the old guy that looked like a janitor. He had been in our classroom and in the room of the machine; surely he would know how to get in touch with Tiny. I went to the records building to find out what I could about this mysterious janitor, thinking over Abigail's description of Tiny, how he had life without the physical handicaps.

I could not believe that it never had occurred to me before—that old man was Tiny's accomplice. The records indicated that the janitor during those years was Alfred Kingsley. Further investigation revealed that Mr. Kingsley died over ten years ago from natural causes. *Could it be possible that the secrets of the machines use and construction died with him?*

I was sure he must have had assistance from a director with influence to get the materials and with the scientific knowledge to put the materials to use. But both the original director and assistant director—Sergy in fact—had passed. But no project that big existed without records. I headed back to Clarice's office to get some answers.

After I explained what I was looking for, Clarice looked at me oddly and asked, "Why would you want to bother with that old machine? All Tolemac's humble beginnings aren't in any of the mainframe computers, and the system they used to file information back then is anybody's guess."

All the same, she pointed me to a back room full of filing cabinets, where I spent hours searching. I tried every possible technical term I could think of. I began to suspect that Tiny had influenced Sergy's brain as well such that, unbeknownst to Sergy, he worked like a programmed robot. I began to lose hope and, rubbing my head, slouched back against a file cabinet.

I had no intention of rummaging through all fifty file cabinets, stuffed haphazardly with everything from acorns to zebras. Instead, I relaxed my mind and thought about the machine's purpose and how it might work.

I figured that the only way that Tiny could alter the material world with his mental impressions was for matter to become more liquid by way of some sort of electron alteration. Tiny's machine could have somehow loosened up these electron groupings with some sort of polar discharge, but with what medium?

I poured through the science and chemistry that I had taken as a young man—especially the particle science. Particle waves, I had been taught, were responsible for much of the electron behavior. Electromagnetic radiation, the energy waves produced by the oscillation or acceleration of an electric charge, had both electric and magnetic properties. This sort of radiation can be arranged in a spectrum that extends in waves of varying frequencies; the higher the frequency, the greater the electron energy.

Little Albert said that the energy of the quantum is proportional to the frequency, and so the energy of the electron depends on the frequency. Then there is breaking radiation, how radiation emitted from electrons slow down in matter. So particles travel faster than condensed matter, which would make them easier to influence with external energy or mind energy. The vehicle must then be a spectrum of high-frequency vibration caused by some sort of electromagnetic radiation, a strong enough dose to alter space and time itself.

"That's it!" I exclaimed. This must be how Tiny was able to cause those wonderful illusions like the floors and walls falling away and all of us flying through the air in our desks when the machine was in operation. How ingenious!

Now I applied my insight to a directed search of the file cabinets, using topics like particle waves, radiation, and light spectrums. Still had no luck though. Finally I tried resonators. Sure enough the first file under that heading was full of mathematical equations and schematics written by Sergy himself, pertaining to Tiny's machine. I couldn't contain my excitement and jumped up and down in childish glee.

I skimmed the file. Near the end my high hopes vanished. The words "plutonium requirement" were emblazoned on the page. My heart sank! The machine ran on the most hazardous, rare substance on the face of the earth. No wonder it sat behind locked doors gathering dust.

I'd come too far to give up. Hoping that it might run off any fuel remaining, I got the key to open the door from the public works office and opened the padlock. There it was, a huge cylindrical metal tube that looked a lot like a huge clarinet, which made me snicker at the coincidence. After all, clarinets also produce a high frequency vibration.

A radiation suit hung on the wall. I slipped it on just in case of a meltdown of some sort. I began looking the machine over and found the rear compartment that had a sign warning for radiation.

I unlatched the compartment access and slid the door sideways. A small light blinked on. A small container that resembled an upside-down stainless steel coffee cup lay in a large dish of the same shiny metal sat idle in the small compartment, it looked amazingly simplistic. There were two buttons outside the access panel. I closed the door and pushed the first one and the cup and saucer began to descend into another compartment that was quickly covered by another sliding door. The machine whined loudly, and I jumped back. The machine suddenly stopped, and the small electronic readout above the door began flashing a low fuel warning. It was no use. Tiny could not be brought back without a lethal dose of radiation.

I went back to Clarice's office to put the file back in place and bumped into her.

"Did you find what you were looking for, Meno?" she asked. I nodded. "Yes, but I can't start the machine without plutonium."

"PLUTONIUM!" Clarice cried out in shock, as if I were a walking isotope. "That machine runs on plutonium? What exactly does this machine do?"

"It makes dreams come true, or better yet it's an illusionist's dream. If you had ever been to one of Tiny's classes, you would know exactly what I mean."

"Those classes were for new arrivals; I was born and raised here!"

As I explained all I new about what the machine could do giving her my best but limited description on how it altered matter. Clarice sat in silent awe, with her little mouth puckered in anticipation. Her eyebrows shot skyward as a sudden burst of inspiration swept across her face. "Meno, do you realize the implications of what you just said?"

"Of course I do. Why else would I be searching for a way to run it?"

"No, Meno," she said in a hushed tone, "this is not about seeing Tiny. This is more about being Tiny."

Now I was the one looking like someone stole my train called thought. "What do you mean, 'become a Tiny?' How can anyone become a Tiny?" But as soon as the words came out of my mouth, I realized that what she said made perfect sense. Soon I shared the devious smile that was upon her pursed lips.

We giggled like little kids, as if laughing out loud might draw too much attention to our newfound secret. After a few false starts, Clarice went on to explain, "You see, Meno, the only reason Tiny was able to manipulate the matter within that area was because he—and no one else there—was aware that he could. If this altered state of matter is indeed suggestible, all one has to do is have absolute faith and direction within their mental landscape to change the very surroundings to whatever their desire is for that experience. Once you break concentration, you return to the natural, condensed state of matter that is framed within the picture of your mind from your beliefs and expectations."

"Wow," I said, "that's very interesting, but without the plutonium it's useless!"

"We still have some in the lab that we use for experimentation. It will take more than that if we can use it for your trip out, but we can at least experiment with the machine's potential now."

I squinted in confusion. *Did I miss something?* I asked myself. "What do you mean by 'the trip out'? Was the machine coming with me on our maiden voyage?"

"Meno, you still don't see the big picture, do you? This machine, if my assumptions are correct, will solve all our problems with space and time travel. Electromagnetic waves need no material to travel through the vacuum of interplanetary space. They travel as any radio or wave of light does once inertia sets the course. This is only the beginning. There is also an advantage of traveling through a worm hole as a wave, as opposed to as a mass of matter, which is more susceptible to destruction by the incredible gravitational fields."

Once again, I was reminded of Clarice's brilliance. I asked, "Does this mean that I don't have to go to anymore of those fun sessions in the astrophysics lab?"

Clarice smiled. "Well, we will still need to get you out of earth's atmosphere, so why don't you report to the propulsion lab until I get some testing underway with our new toy."

That was music to my ears. The following two years, I worked alongside more brilliant minds. We figured out how to produce the liquid hydrogen and oxygen needed for the booster rockets and also retrofitted an old Titan rocket, transported from an old missile silo in sections years ago using the hydrogen balloon. Soon I joined the crew working on a fuel cell to act as the shuttle's power source. We took the design from a successful research institution that had managed to create the long-sought-after fusion reactor, just before the industrial collapse. The fuel cell ran off of water: it created hydrogen, then recycled water from the steam. The energy came from hydrogen plasma within a magnetic field.

Clarice just assigned me to a new team, working with the resonator. They had brought the machine into the canopy of old used galvanized steel roofing, erected as a place to work on the shuttle and its various parts. The modifications had already made the machine more powerful and lighter. They even had designed a place in the shuttle's cargo area to mount the machine.

The assistant director was Max, a tall, blonde, young man who did not care for shoes and seemed very excited about the device, unless of course his bulging eyes were an inherited trait. Max eagerly shook my hand, which simultaneously shook my entire body. His eagerness was a bit contagious.

"Do you want to take a trip?" Max asked.

"Sure, where to?"

"Anywhere you like!"

"Oh!" I exclaimed. "Maybe I will start with something simple, like my pod."

"Perfect. Just sit in the chair directly in front of the machine and imagine yourself in the comfort of your pod for as long as you can hold the image in focus."

I relaxed and re-created the environment in my mind, which was not as easy as one would think with all the noise in the work area, especially the whine of the resonator. Finally, I found myself sitting in the center of my pod. I sprung out of my chair is if it carried a thousand volts. My expression of surprise and bewilderment must have been marked—I was shocked back in to the hangar by the laughter of Max and the few others. They obviously knew the feeling well from earlier experiments. I composed myself, and when max stooped laughing, tried it again. Once again I concentrated on my pod. In no longer than the time it takes to focus, I was once again in my pod. This was fascinating. I was looking at the cup, half full, sitting on the table in the exact place I had set it before leaving. I reached for the cup, and my hand went right through it. This once again shocked me back into the hangar. And once again my startled look made the crew burst out laughing.

"Wow!" I said, "This is incredible. Everything in my pod was exactly how I remembered it to be!"

Max turned off the machine. "That's because you created the image of the pod from your memory, which is a bit more detail-oriented than the rest of ours, by the way, what were you reaching for?"

"A cup that I left on the table this morning," I replied. The crew all fell silent with their mouths open. Max finally broke the quiet.

"You really do have a photographic mind. That's even more incredible. With practice, you may be able to drink from that cup!"

"Could you also see my pod?" I asked.

"We would need to be in front of the machine," Max answered, "in order to be influenced by it."

"If the machine only changes what's in front of it, how are we going to get the machine and what's behind it to travel with the rest of the ship?"

"We are still working on that and are in the process of building a reflection device that will cover the entire ship, but you needn't worry about that. What you need to concentrate on is your ability to stay focused for a prolonged period."

"How long a period are we talking about here?" I asked.

"As long as humanly possible," Max replied. "You see, the particle-to-wave transformation will still need to be manipulated by your thought. No matter what your thought is, the longer you can hold it for, the faster you will travel and the further you will go.

"For example, if you were to hold concentration for one hour, traveling at the speed of light which is approximately 186,000 miles per second, you would travel roughly one million miles. If you could hold that concentration for twenty-four hours, you could travel about twenty-seven million miles. Not a bad distance for a day's work, eh?"

"But what if I needed to eat or relieve myself?"

"Your thoughts will only achieve so much. There will be times that you will need to slow down the ship in order to take care of any personal needs on board and with time you may be capable of doing both, traveling at the speed of light and your domestic agenda. The shuttle will not be traveling the speed of light for the entire trip, and you can only use the resonator when you are out of the gravitational pull of our solar system. Once outside our solar system, you can cruise along at the speed of light for as long as you like, provided you don't stop while traveling through the wormhole."

I practiced with the resonator almost every day for two years. I could reside in the image-nation for a record eighteen hours. The fantasy world that I had created was every bit as real as any other part of my waking life, with the exception that I had complete control over every aspect. I could even sit down to a nine course meal and be served by waiters who jumped to fulfill my every whim. I would savor every bite of the delicious ensemble that lay before me.

In the image-nation, I no longer felt that I was being controlled by external realities beyond my power. I could carry on in-depth conversations with wonderful characters that shared the same exact interests as I and dress them in the most ridiculous outfits imaginable. Sometimes we would be sitting next to a grand waterfall as we dined. Sometimes I had them eat branches from trees with their feet for my amusement. The more I lived in the image-nation, the more comfortable I felt there than anywhere else. In time, I no longer needed the resonator to travel deep into the image-nation. All I needed to do was close my eyes and relax and the hours would fly by. The characters gave me advice and even educated me about concepts that I was sure I had not studied before. *Was this a part of myself that I was unaware of, or were these characters now separate entities?*

During the waking hours I would sometimes forget that I was no longer in the image-nation and unusual things would happen. I had once been thinking of a shower and for a few moments I had found myself in the shower; the cold water shocked me into a neutral state of mind and I found myself once again standing in my pod, soaking wet.

Another time when I was soaking in the enrichment baths, I opened my eyes to find myself momentarily riding a horse with the guard, just as I had been daydreaming about. The scene was so startling that I began to stand and yell, scaring the hell out of everyone there. The following day a psychotherapist from the clinic was knocking at my door asking me a lot of strange questions and ordering me home for a few days, claiming that I was overworked.

Was I losing my grip on reality? Or was reality finally being revealed for what reality truly was? As time progressed, such things began to happen more often, like thinking of brushing my teeth only to find a toothbrush in one hand, or getting thirsty only to find a cup of water in my hand spilling all over the place.

Tiny and Abigail both had talked about how our reality was all Gods mind, about how we create what we are and a great deal of what we see like some sort of high powered movie projector through our root beliefs, assumptions, and expectations. Could this be the answer to what was happening to me, was I able to change the reality of nature through faith?

When Abigail said that the transitionals were removing any obstacles that could interfere with the transition into the new dimension in space and time, how else could they do this other than through their very belief and expectation in their own abilities to achieve it? And I was sure that if Tiny could achieve all that he did achieve without the benefit of a body, he did it all with mind and only mind, over the very matter he was able to control. I knew through my research into physics and quantum theory that it had always been assumed that the true nature of reality was influenced by consciousness, but who's. The quantum belief that in the beginning there was the quantum mind—a first cause, independent and non-local—that created space, time, energy, and matter.

There is the belief that light is the fabric of creation, wavelengths of radiant energy permeating all of creation. Then there is the universal law of expressive energy that states that changing the frequency of energy changes the patterns through which the energy is expressed. If all this were all true, than we as subscribers of mind are indeed constantly and perhaps collectively weaving space, time, and matter as we go, within mind, but I was sure that we had help from powerful outside sources that somehow energized the environment for us so that we could experience the physical spectrum. This would also mean that Abigail's theories on love and emotion were right, since love translates into a vibratory frequency, or particle and wave. Perhaps this is the secret behind the quantum leap. "That's it!" This is why Tiny emphasized over and over the necessity of following one's heart's desire. It would automatically have the power of emotional energy to create with!

I began to wonder if I really needed a resonator at all. Perhaps I could create the new dimension out of mind, using light as the vehicle. But this possibility felt a bit premature. Besides, how would the children get to the new destination?

Within a few years, I was training to pilot the shuttle. Since I could not actually fly the shuttle due to the ongoing work on it. A great deal of training was done by watching old flight training films and mocking flight in a make-shift simulator that had no movement other than my own but was somehow rigged to a computer monitor that told me when something was wrong. Luckily, piloting the shuttle would only be necessary if the onboard computer failed, so I wasn't too worried.

When I finished pilot training, the departure date was less than a couple of years away. I still found it hard to grasp that I would be leaving all I had known and loved behind. It was disheartening, and the pain caused me to withdraw at times. I began to meditate a great deal to try and gain control of myself; for at times I thought I was coming unglued. I quickly realized that leaving Tolemac would indeed be the hardest test that I could ever undertake and that nothing scientific or otherwise could prepare me for that.

21
TESHA'S GIFT

I tried in vain to sleep, but the wind was howling with some of the strongest gusts I had ever felt while in a bed. I hoped that it was just another mountain valley windstorm, but I knew better. These winds would slowly escalate to rip apart anything that stood in their path, and not even Tolemac could outlive them.

The week prior, for nearly an hour we had been bombarded with hail the size of grape-fruits, crashing through the greenhouses and playing havoc with the mostly glass pyramid covering the Center. I stopped by the greenhouse Tesha worked in to make sure she made it through the terrorizing pummeling. Tesha looked at the damaged plants in a state of shock, her long gray hair neatly braided down her back. She swung in my direction as she heard my approach.

"Meno, oh thank God! My hero has once again come to my rescue!"

We hugged, and she gave me a smile. Her once strong features had softened with time, but she still had my heart wrapped around her little finger.

"What are you doing here?" she asked, with a look of surprise and concern.

"I just wanted to make sure you hadn't been turned into crushed ice," I said as I stepped back to get a good look at her.

"No, I survived, but my greenhouse will need some serious fixing!"

We both stared at the large chunk of ice that glimmered in the mud of a hemp shrub. I looked up to make sure no more missiles were falling, but only shattered glazing remained. We spoke for a while, and she had much to say about her grandson Aries, who had just turned two. She cared deeply for her family and loved being a grandmother. The chat wasn't long enough, however. She had to hurry home to her wheelchair-bound husband, now suffering from a debilitating disease.

I only had a few weeks left to enjoy the people in the place I called home, so I cherished every waking moment as never before. I tried to visit as many as I could before the tie was severed.

They had begun the selection process of the children who were to take the long journey with me. It was a terribly hard thing, and many mothers vowed to take their chances with the Earth's changes rather than separate from their children. Other children were not healthy enough for the long journey, and age was a constant problem. Many of the mothers of five- and six-year-olds wanted to send their children, but the maximum age was only four. The preferred age was two, because of their small size and weight and which meant less consumption and waste, but all children under the age of one were denied.

Young children would carry little memory of their home, and muscular rehabilitation after the prolonged period in the sleep cylinders would be less severe than with a larger, more developed children. In the end, twenty-four children were selected to board for take off. I was responsible for their well being from then on. This weighed heavy on my mind, but in a strange way I kind of looked forward to it, never having a family of my own. I just hoped that I was up to the challenge.

Most of my training was completed, but I still made my daily visits to the various offices and departments to avoid any last minute surprises. The launch pad for the shuttle and its booster rocket was anything but elaborate, but it was an imposing site from anywhere in Tolemac. The platform was a large concrete hole in the ground positioned next to the old observation deck, which had been cut open at the top to steady the nose of the shuttle. They figured the rest of the platform could possibly keel over from the intense heat during lift off so they extended a steel webbed arm to the nose of the shuttle that would retract just before launching.

The shuttle looked much larger now, with its nose pointed towards the heavens; it was named Aquarius 1. Painted in red letters across the body. It was an intimidating sight that left me a bit spellbound.

The people of Tolemac, well aware of their fate, were constantly in a state of mental preparation for the great transition. They tried maintaining the status quo by continuing a life full of love and laughter. I couldn't find a single soul weeping or cowering. The great teachings and philosophies of Tolemac had been readying them for this all their lives. They were now above material loss, and it showed in the way everyone carried on.

I went by the guardhouse the following morning. Few men were left in uniform, and fewer horses in the stalls. I asked the man cleaning the stalls if Unkar was about. He smiled and said that Unkar was staying at the old soldier fort down the road, so I saddled up a pony and rode down. When I reached the fort, an old stick-built cabin with half the shingles missing, I was greeted by a slouching old man who walked with a cane. He looked up at me and raised his hand in gesture.

"My God, Unkar!" I hardly recognized him. The years had taken their toll, but I could still see fire burning in those eyes. I got down and embraced him. He invited me in, where he poured me, with a trembling hand, a cup of homemade liquor. We sat in silence for a moment. Eventually, he said;

"It's good to see you, my boy. I hear they're sending you on a permanent vacation. Who would'a thunk it? The snot-nosed kid I found on Bear Lake with his head in the sand would one day fly a rocket to hell and back!"

I held back a laugh, saying instead, "Yeah, that was some time, huh?"

"You know, Meno, I lost a lot of good men over the years, but none of them—including myself—could ever hold a candle to you. I knew you were different the first moment I saw you, with those wild wolf eyes and even wilder hair. None of us knew what to make of you back then. And that time you got a warning from an owl… Well, if that wasn't the darnedest thing I ever heard, but it saved our necks that's for sure. Except for Michael and Rudy, but that's all water under the bridge now."

I spent the rest of the day listening to the old Mongol's tall tales of fearless battles on the high plains. The old guy still had spunk and spirit; I'll say that much for him. I parted that evening fearing that, if I stayed longer, he would pass out from all the excitement.

A bit light-headed from the sauce Unkar kept insisting I drink, I rode back to the guardhouse and took in the views of the aspen covered hillsides. A red-tailed hawk circled high overhead, spying for prey. I wondered if any of it would survive. What a waste that such beauty could be destroyed, but I knew that it was all nature and that this was nature's way. The great purification. How long it would last was anybody's guess—one thousand, perhaps one million years, if time existed at all.

The next day I paid a visit to Abigail at the sub-center. She was reclined in a chair and looking up at the fish swimming by the skylight as filtered sunlight peeked through to the bottom of the center's overhead pond. She did not bother to get up, but just asked in a faint voice, "Who's there?"

"It's me, Meno." I said softly.

Abigail turned her head slightly at the sound of my voice. She was alone now. All the transitionals of the Star Delegation had passed over the years, and she now awaited a similar fate. I grabbed her hand and held it tightly to my chest as I looked into her eyes.

"How's my favorite girl today?" I asked under my breath.

She stared deeply into my eyes for a moment before she replied, "It's hard to leave, isn't it my dear?"

"Terribly," I replied.

"I know your heart's breaking Meno I can see it in your eyes. You have that displaced look of a transitional, for it's who you truly are now."

I could no longer control myself. The tears came like rain, and I wailed as she pulled my head to her chest.

"It's alright; everything is going according to plan except those little things called emotions. You must understand that the Father has great plans for all of us, and will see to it that all of Tolemac's inhabitants are taken care of. They will finally be able to go home and will no longer be kept in the regressed darkness of their fallen planet." She said in a hushed manner.

"The destination of your journey is not so much a question of where or when, but more along the lines of why. The Adam body has been limited since the fall of man, but all that will change with the cleansing, restoring your abilities through the newly adopted vibratory light. You will see what I mean when you get where you are going, for it's all prearranged."

Abigail bent forward and grabbed a small carved wooden box from the table and said;

"I want you to take this with you; the sacred sapphire no longer serves us here and belongs with you in the new world."

I pulled it out of the box and looked closely at it for the first time, it was shaped like a star tetrahedron with a Hebrew letter etched upon each of the faces spelling the name of God.

"What should I do with it?" I asked her.

"Just keep it as a souvenir, for where your going its power will not be needed."

The day before the launch Clarice drilled me in and out of the shuttle. We went over every aspect of the ship and its components, functions, and capabilities as well as a thousand possible problems and their remedies and alternate remedies. If there was anything that was not covered, it was irrelevant or infinitesimal because I'm sure I could have filled an encyclopedic volume with all the information on the shuttle and interplanetary space. The onboard computer was the real brain behind the flight. All I had to do was periodically check monitors. My main concerns were the propulsion speed, cabin pressure, and the chemical composition of the gaseous embryonic fluid that kept the children in limbo within their glass containers.

That evening there was a massive celebration at the center. Music filled the air, and people danced and ate from elaborate buffets created by the chefs. Several people, including Clarice, made lengthy speeches. They asked me to say a few words, but all I managed to squeak out was, "I'll miss you all terribly," before being overrun with emotion. I must have hugged over a hundred people and shook twice as many hands as I made my way out that night.

Late that night we got our first wake-up call in the form of an earthquake. Not a major one, but everyone was deeply concerned—especially since we were not over a fault line. It felt like Godzilla was jack hammering the entire village. After that, I was wide awake. *It's just as well*, I thought. *I couldn't sleep anyway.*

I remembered my geology instructor years ago talking about a large, potentially explosive caldera under Yellowstone that could blow anytime. He called it a giant ready to give birth—capable of a catastrophe larger than any seen since the dinosaurs' demise. Perhaps those tremors were somehow related.

The morning before take off was finally here—The end of the line. My hands trembled as I grabbed for a cup tea, but even that was hard to choke down. For the trip, I packed a bag of clothes and anything else that could be of aid, including my grandfather's bow and fishing rod and a good skinning knife. Even though the shuttle's cargo area was loaded with about ten years of condensed and dehydrated foodstuffs, along with enough plant seeds to establish another Tolemac, I still felt that I needed the tools for basic survival.

I wasn't sure what the new dimension would resemble but hoped it could at least support life. Clarice had said that the odds were greatly in favor of a return trip to a time in our distant past, just how distant she didn't know. She was basing her assumption on the fact that there was probably more past than future, but it was just a hypothesis. I took a long shower, knowing that it would be my last, and then headed over to the pod to say goodbye to my foster parents.

Yoshi greeted me at the door followed by Kam. They tried to maintain their composure on my account, but I could see the pain in Mother's eyes the moment I opened the door, as well as feel it in the tightness of her grip when we hugged. I was only too fortunate to have had them as parents. I sat with them for a while and spoke with Kam as Mother made more tea. Afterward she brought out a gift for me. I unwrapped it to find a framed photo of all of us together in the central park when I was still very young. I remembered the day it was taken. It was the first day we all began to bond as a family, the day our hearts became one. I had once again begun to shake and sob. We all hugged and wept.

As I walked down the stairwell leading to the transport, I began to have second thoughts about leaving. I felt like I was abandoning those I cared most deeply about during their time of need. Although my legs kept going, they weakened with every step. I thought about visiting Tesha one last time before lift off, but I didn't want an emotional scene in front of her invalid husband. I pushed the button for the tower instead and boarded the transport. I stepped out of the lower stairwell to the base of the tower I was stunned by the loud roar that engulfed me; a guard grabbed my bags and yelled over the roar that I should go through the side door to the front procession.

Over a hundred people stood by to see me off with ten times that along the perimeter, some of my co-workers and closest friends were waiting for me in a double line that looped around the base of the tower to the front entrance and then continued inside to the elevator. I shook and slapped at hands, hugged and kissed the many people that I had become well acquainted with, finally making it inside the building.

Unkar stood in his dress uniform among the few remaining guard at the end of the line. He smiled and said;

"I thought you might be able to use this."

From behind his back, he pulled the old samurai sword I had found in Harold Wiggans' closet.

"Please give this to the next samurai. I can see no need for it here," he said.

"It will be an honor my old friend." I said trying to get my arms around his still larger than life hulk.

I could see Tesha next to the door of the elevator. *I wondered how long she had been waiting there to get such a spot in line.* Tesha pushed the button to the elevator as I approached her. She looked at my eyes, then was distracted for a moment by what hung from my neck.

"The owl, you're wearing the owl," she whispered as we embraced.

"Well, someone has to watch over me while I'm gone to make sure I don't get skunked," I teased.

Tesha smiled, but before she could speak, the elevator door slid open with a ring. I took one step toward the door, but she put out her hand.

"Wait, Meno, there is something I need to tell you before you go!" The look in Tesha's eye's told me that this was serious. "Please understand that I don't want to hurt you or complicate your life anymore than it already is, but I feel you must know!"

Tears welled up in her eyes. "Gina is our daughter, Meno!"

I was unable to move. I couldn't absorb what I just heard. "Tesha, that's impossible because we never—"

"It was done by artificial insemination from the sperm you gave the lab had for DNA testing," she quickly interjected.

"We were going to approach you to ask you to do this, but we found that you were already on file. The directors decided it was best for everyone if it was kept secret."

"But what about your—"

"He's sterile, Meno. It was the only way I could conceive, and aside from my husband, there was no one else I would rather conceive with than you."

My God, all this time Gina was mine and I didn't even know. I just looked down and shook my head in disbelief. "Tesha, how could you?"

"There's more," she said. "Gina's son Aries is onboard the ship—our grandson Meno!"

I was speechless. *I have a grandson onboard my ship?* I quickly hugged Tesha and kissed her hard.

"Thank you, oh God, thank you for such a wonderful gift!" We hugged and wept together as the others all clapped and cheered.

Finally, I reluctantly let her go and boarded the elevator, but when I saw Gina a few rows back, I stopped the door from closing. She knew—I could see it written across her face. I ran out and hugged her as she began to cry hysterically.

"Oh Meno, Meno, please take care of my baby Aries!" She cried.

"I kissed her gently on the cheek and said, "I will protect him with my life." Crossing my arms over my chest in guard fashion.

I made it up that elevator but held the door closed until I could regain my strength and composure. As the door slid open, the last entourage began to clap and I could hear the onboard computer counting down the minutes before takeoff. Clarice and her crew of overworked staff cheered. I embraced them all, including the bare-footed Max, whose crying brought tears to my eyes that I didn't think I had left. They suited me up. At the end of the line, I finally reached Abigail; cool as a cucumber as usual.

"What's the matter, my precious?" she asked.

"Love, only love!" I replied through trembling lips. I wiped my eyes while feeling extremely frail and emotionally exhausted.

Abigail gazed compassionately at me and said, "Indeed, my love…indeed!"

I buckled in and checked the monitors. The time clock on the instrument panel began flashing 7-7-7, logging the month, day and hour of departure. I was an emotional wreck. Doubt and fear twisted my stomach into a giant knot, but the shuttle countdown continued regardless. Twenty seconds. Fifteen. Ten. The shuttle began to rumble and shake, but I knew the boosters had not begun to ignite. *My God, we were having another earthquake!* Five seconds. The rumbling got stronger, whipping the ship like a tree in a windstorm. I began to wonder if we were going to make it off the ground. Three. Two. One. I heard the booster ignite and the tethers release, then I saw a plume of vapor that obscured the sun.

I began to feel the force of lift off as the wobbling subsided. The sky changed back to bright blue, and the negative G-forces pushed down on my body like a medieval winepress. I wasn't sure if I had reached the seven miles per second necessary speed for leaving the atmosphere, but I was sure I couldn't bear much more. Then I felt the heat searing the nose of the ship from the ionosphere. Finally, the pressure began to subside.

After a while I went over a brief systems check and peered through the portal to Earth. Part of North America was partially obscured from the sun by a thick dark cloud. *Perhaps it's just a dust storm?* I thought, but in my heart I knew. *How ironic, it was as if it all was waiting for me to leave before it began.* But irony had nothing to do with it. I waved back at my humbled home and said, "Goodbye, my love." I doubled over against the wall of the shuttle, shaking and shuttering, as my heart went numb from all the pain of their suffering. I wailed with anger, "WHY! WHY! WHY!"

My anger soon turned into fatigue and I drifted off to sleep and was quickly awaken by the old familiar sound of Tiny's giggling. "He-he-hee!"

When I awoke, I was no longer onboard the shuttle, but rather sitting on a sea of blackness that got brighter with each passing second. I immediately recognized the room of the old school. I was sitting in the same old seat when Tiny materialized before my very eyes, wearing the exact same frock coat and silly hat as before.

"Meno, my boy, my wingless little cherub, weep no more. Your loved ones are with me now and will never again suffer the hardships of three-dimensional space and time. Look!"

With a sweep of his arm, I could see them all, gathered at Tolemac's Center in a large circle, cloaked in light, laughing and loving, and carrying on as if nothing had happened, but the lighting was different, as if it came from a different star, one far brighter with a whitish light that seemed to illuminate them. Tesha and Gina were there with Tesha's husband, who was no longer confined to a wheelchair, and with Tesha's grandfather. Unkar could be seen hugging a large number of guards—guards who had passed on year's prior, including Volsung.

I recognized Lance as he made his way over to Tesha, then gestured for her hand in dance. They began to waltz across the floor as if on air. There was another face there that I was trying to place that seemed to be getting a lot of attention. I had only seen him in a picture but now recognized him as Tolemac's founder— John Olandis. They all turned in my direction to applaud and wave. Once again I wept, but this time the aching in my heart was gone as tears of joy flowed like rain.

"Thank you, Tiny. Thank you so much!" I completed the last word only to find myself once again in the shuttle and wondering if it all was just another one of Tiny's games. But I no longer cared, for I now was able to let go.

Looking over the children's capsules; I tried to make out their tiny faces through the vapor. Baby Aries lay there, totally innocent and unencumbered by all that had transpired. They were the reason for the journey, and between him and the others there was the promise for a better tomorrow. I was just a messenger.

I settled back into the cockpit and buckled in, the journey would be long, but I had nothing but time now, as if time even existed. I stared out into the deep recesses in space and saw a million miles of illuminated celestial seas and hoped the new world would be a more hospitable one, but soon realized that hope had nothing to do with it.

THE END

EPILOGUE

The children all stared out into the vast sky in awe of such a tale. My grandson Aries looked up at me with his bright eyes and asked; "What was it like out there in the stars?"

"Lonely, son, very lonely, but I always had my friends from the image-nation to keep me company."

Over the years we built structures out of sun dried bricks and cultivated our fertile fields with grain and a variety of vegetables. The children grew stronger than I could have imagined. My best guess was some strange increase in the magnetic field of the planet was contributing to it.

We had stripped the shuttle of every piece of usable material we could find, and the captain's chairs were still quite comfortable sitting against my wall. We even used the glass for dehydration chambers for fruits and meats, and the metal hull made great solar concentrators for heating water and food alike.

We crudely armed ourselves and only went out during the day and in groups due to the constant threat of large wild animals that roamed freely. The large cats were the biggest threat—at least a third larger than the cats I had known at Tolemac, and just as sneaky. Plenty of other predators, like snakes and river alligators, were also much larger than normal. But the mastodons were by far the largest things we had seen and would startle easily when they inadvertently wandered into one of our fields. The Indigenous peoples of the area became friendly over time and taught us methods to combat the beasts that became troublesome.

One standing guard with a bow or spear watched over the others as we worked in the fields. The monkeys that lived in the giant towering trees would usually howl whenever there was trouble afoot, giving us a natural early warning system.

The once dead sea was once again full of a multitude of life, and the coral was a paradise of unsurpassed beauty. But we couldn't stray too far out because of the enormous sharks that were constantly feeding. The fishing was as easy as building rock reefs to trap a variety of specimens that wandered to close to shore in search of small minnows and plankton.

I taught the children much of what I had learned from the now legendary Tolemac: all the great teachings, philosophies, and of course, the power of the image-nation. Life was free and easy, and the children soon had children of their own who mingled and played with the native children. The red-skinned native inhabitants soon accepted us and we began trading with them; typically they traded animal hides for our grain. I learned some of their language over the years, which was a crude form of Basque, but most communication was done with a hand sign language that I was still trying to become fluent with.

I had finally earned enough respect to bee invited to the large stone circular dwelling of the locals, to meet their elders, which turned out to be an extraordinary event. We sat down on elaborately carved logs and feasted on fowl. Although these people lived in a primitive manner, they were not at all ignorant of their world and lived like one large family, sharing everything with anyone.

In general, the natives were large boned with tall, strong sinuous bodies, well defined noses, and high cheekbones. The one thing that definitely set them apart from us was their thumb location. It was higher up on their elongated hands.

The chief elder summoned his staff by opening his hand and closing his eyes. It materialized at will.

He looked at me with a superior smile, as if to show me up with his grand ability of magic. Just to prove that I was his equal, I held out my hands, which soon held the ancient samurai sword, still in its jeweled scabbard. The chief's wide-eyed response was child-like as he looked over the sword in amazement. I pulled the blade out slightly and told him not to touch its razor sharp edge before handing it to him as a gift. The old chief sat speechless as he fondled the cold, shiny steel. He pulled the blade out and swooped it in the air, then downward. He accidentally struck his staff, which split cleanly in two. The old chief grabbed at his staff in disbelief that such a cut could be made with so little effort. Before I could voice my objection, he slid his finger over the blade, then pulled his finger back in a frenzied response.

The old chief gazed at his bleeding finger, then back at me, and began to howl with laughter, quickly followed by the entire camp. We feasted some more, and he told me the story of his people and the great land they called Atlanda. That afternoon we traveled on foot accompanied by many of his followers to see what he called the House of the Great Spirit. We traveled to the summit of the outlying hill. I stopped dead in my tracks and my jaw dropped by what my eyes beheld: there in the vast open plain stood a colossal pyramid, ten times the size of the one that had been in Tolemac, gleaming like a polished stone, with a multi-prism apex shooting intense beams of light like a brilliant star.

At last I knew I was home.

Printed in the United States
84515LV00007B/9/A